THE LAST GUN

OTHER FIVE STAR WESTERN TITLES BY LAURAN PAINE:

Tears of the Heart (1995); *Lockwood* (1996); *The White Bird* (1997); *The Grand Ones of San Ildefonso* (1997); *Cache Cañon* (1998); *The Killer Gun* (1998); *The Mustangers* (1999); *The Running Iron* (2000); *The Dark Trail* (2001); *Guns in the Desert* (2002); *Gathering Storm* (2003); *Night of the Comancheros* (2003); *Rain Valley* (2004); *Guns in Oregon* (2004); *Holding the Ace Card* (2005); *Feud on the Mesa* (2005); *Gunman* (2006); *The Plains of Laramie* (2006); *Halfmoon Ranch* (2007); *Man from Durango* (2007); *The Quiet Gun* (2008); *Patterson* (2008); *Hurd's Crossing* (2008); *Rangers of El Paso* (2009); *Sheriff of Hangtown* (2009); *Gunman's Moon* (2009); *Promise of Revenge* (2010); *Kansas Kid* (2010); *Guns of Thunder* (2010); *Iron Marshal* (2011); *Prairie Town* (2011)

THE LAST GUN

A WESTERN DUO

LAURAN PAINE

FIVE STAR
A part of Gale, Cengage Learning

Detroit • New York • San Francisco • New Haven, Conn • Waterville, Maine • London

GALE
CENGAGE Learning™

LIBRARY OF CONGRESS CATALOGING-IN-PUBLICATION DATA

Paine, Lauran.
    The last gun : a western duo / by Lauran Paine. — 1st ed.
    p. cm.
    "A Five Star Western."
    ISBN-13: 978-1-4328-2522-5 (hardcover)
    ISBN-10: 1-4328-2522-4 (hardcover)
    1. Sheriffs—Fiction. I. Paine, Lauran. Ghost meadow. II. Title.
    PS3566.A34L37 2011
    813'.54—dc23   2011031261

First Edition. First Printing: November 2011.
Published in 2011 in conjunction with Golden West Literary Agency.

Printed in the United States of America
1 2 3 4 5 6 7 15 14 13 12 11

CONTENTS

GHOST MEADOW 7

THE LAST GUN 125

★ ★ ★ ★ ★

GHOST MEADOW

★ ★ ★ ★ ★

I

He was the color of summer dust and had black eyes with hair to match, and, although it was customary among his kind to wear braids, John Morning Gun, who had spent two-thirds of his life among whites, reflected his inner ambiguity by wearing his hair fairly short, except for a thick length in back that he did not braid, but instead wore straight, with an animal vertebra holding it tightly in place. Morning Gun was tall and spare. He was also quick, observant, and given to long silences. In the *rancherías* he was known as a white Indian, and around Fort Laramie, where he was employed as a government hunter, he was known as "different," which was interpreted in half a dozen ways depending upon who used the term in connection with Morning Gun, and the degree of their prejudice, of which there was enough to go around.

He sat on the little shaded porch of the adjutant's hutment waiting for the conference inside to end, and during that time he watched troops cuffing mounts, hauling armloads of laundry to the wash house, and sweating in the midday summer heat while forking a load of timothy hay off a four-wheeled rack into the hay barn.

Inside the palisade, Fort Laramie was an insular world. Outside, particularly over at the town, not only were the people different, but the way they lived also was; civilians had little discipline. John Morning Gun knew about discipline. After the death of his mother—four days after he had been born—his father had loaded her body onto a horse, packed his possessions, and rode into the mountains never to return. The missionaries at their little log compound had taken in John. Now, thirty years later, he knew about discipline, first from the missionaries, then from his first and only employer, so far anyway, the U.S. Army.

Morning Gun was not a full-blood. In fact, it had not been his father who had been Indian, but his mother. His father had been one of those ubiquitous French-Canadian *voyageurs* who looked Indian, were not Indian, and acted more Indian than full-bloods acted. His dead wife, the Crow woman, had been called Snow Blossom. But in coloring Morning Gun looked full-blood. Most people assumed that he was, and because he did not discuss his personal background, or anything else personal, no one refuted the allegation that he was a full-blood.

Morning Gun's value to the Army lay not entirely in his ability as a hunter, tracker, horse wrangler, or non-drinking scout. It was in his ability to speak English with almost no accent, and in fact speak it more grammatically than nearly all the enlisted personnel at the fort, and many of the officers. Morning Gun's mother had been a Crow. Crows were for some obscure reason disliked and held in contempt by all their neighbors, including the Northern Cheyennes and the Sioux. But if a man was tall as the Sioux, shrewd and observant like the Cheyennes, and dressed in the motley manner of settlement tomahawks, and spoke very little Crow, or Cheyenne, or Sioux for that matter, and was fluent in English, did not wear a Crow roach or Sioux braids, then the tribesman who could not classify him properly simply said he was either a settlement Indian or an Army Indian. Even his name gave no clue, and, anyway, on the paymaster's records that was also incorrect.

He had been born shortly before noon on a bitterly cold February day thirty years earlier, in his father's hide tent that had been pitched as close to the fort's log walls as the Army would permit. It was common for Indians to name children for whatever first impressed their mothers after giving birth. It was also commonplace back in those days for the opening of the fort's log gates to be accompanied by the firing of a cannon.

It was always assumed that cannon shot had been what had induced John's mother to give him his name. If anyone had bothered to look into the matter, they would have discovered that morning guns were fired as the big log gates were opened, usually about 6:00 in the morning, and John Morning Gun had not made his appearance in the world until after 11:00. The gun his mother had heard had been fired in honor of a trooper who had died a day or so earlier, and who had been buried that close to midday. It had not been the morning gun, it had been a mourning gun. If having his name arbitrarily altered had not bothered General Ulysses S. Grant, why should it bother John Morning Gun? It didn't. As nearly as those who knew John best could discern, very few things bothered Morning Gun. Not even the expressions of contempt he encountered occasionally among the soldiers. Or, if that and other things bothered him, it never showed.

He was, as Sergeant Flannery said, a dependable, decent Indian. Sergeant Michael Flannery was not only ham-fisted, red-faced, orange-haired, and pugnacious, given to drinking too much once he got started, but he was also big, raw-boned, and most important of all he had been in charge of latrine details around the fort for three years. No trooper argued with Mike Flannery unless he enjoyed such things as digging in hardpan, emptying slop buckets every day, and flies. If one of the periodic epidemics of dysentery arrived, the latrine detail worked through days of unimaginable horror.

Morning Gun had another friend. His name was Lieutenant Albert Winthrop. He had been posted to the fort directly after

11

graduation from the U.S. Military Academy on the Hudson River. Lieutenant Winthrop knew nothing about Indians. He knew even less about the West. His father had been successively a governor back East and a senator. Albert Winthrop had grown up remarkably free of prejudice, except against Democrats. He had been in Wyoming Territory thirteen months, and was reluctantly, sadly forming a prejudice. Not against Indians or the preponderantly treacherous civilians in his area, but against the Army. He had grown up with stars in his eyes. Thirteen months in Wyoming had been the greatest disillusionment of his life. But Lieutenant Winthrop was young, seven years younger than Morning Gun, and had such a fresh, clear, unmarred complexion that he looked much younger. It was unlikely, as demoralizing as this disillusionment was, that before the end of his life he would not encounter others just as demoralizing. But right now, as he and Sergeant Flannery stated their case before the post commander and his adjutant, Lieutenant Winthrop could read the adverse decision on the face of the two superior officers even before the seated captain leaned forward on the desk and said quietly: "To my knowledge, Lieutenant, this has not happened before. That it has happened during my tour as commanding officer requires that I take the proper steps to correct it . . . Lieutenant, I know that you and Sergeant Flannery have faith in Morning Gun. So have I. But the word of one Indian against the word of almost a dozen other people who saw those cattle being cut out and driven toward the mountains by Indians. . . ." The officer leaned back in his chair. "Lieutenant, what did you expect an Indian to say? I want you and Sergeant Flannery to take a detail and look for those cattle. I don't want you to take Morning Gun as scout and tracker. Take. . . ." The captain turned toward his tall, blank-faced adjutant. "What's his name, George?"

"Pierre Burdette. They call him Pete, sir."

"That's your answer, Lieutenant. Take Burdette. And, Lieutenant, be very careful. You know by now it's not just the Indians, don't you?"

"Yes, sir."

The captain said: "Dismissed!"

The outside orderly, at his table in the small outer room, raised his eyes only after the sergeant and lieutenant had passed through to the yonder porch. Sunlight bounced back toward the orderly's open front door. He squinted and leaned to hear the lieutenant mutter something, and to watch the tall Indian arise to follow the other two men down across the parade ground in the direction of the horse area. When the tall adjutant strolled from his inner office into the orderly room, and looked down, the enlisted man gently wagged his head, then turned back to his paperwork.

Flannery perched his strong, lean body upon an empty wooden horseshoe keg and watched the boyish-looking officer. Morning Gun leaned nearby in impassive silence. He had been on the post a long time; he could have told the young officer it would be useless, maybe even damaging, for him to brace the captain. Winthrop looked older and tired as he stood in the shadow of a wash-rack overhang gazing out across the mustering area. He did not repeat what the captain had said about the Indian but simply said: "You're to stay on the post, John. The sergeant and I are to take a detail and go after them."

At Morning Gun's steady gaze toward the officer, Flannery added the rest of it: "And take Pete Burdette."

Now Morning Gun's gaze moved from Winthrop to Michael Flannery. He said nothing.

Flannery addressed the lieutenant. "He'll lie when the truth will fit better, Lieutenant. I've been on patrols and scouts with him many times. And there's something else."

Winthrop turned slightly to face the sergeant.

13

"Pete and that drover who brought in the beef allotment pee through the same knothole."

Winthrop's brows dropped a notch as he gazed at the older man. He thought he understood but was not quite sure he did.

Flannery spoke more plainly: "Burdette and that drover drink together in town. I've seen Pete ride out to the drover's camp night after night."

The officer was still faintly scowling at the sergeant. Flannery shot a mildly exasperated glance at Morning Gun, then stood up off the little keg. "Lieutenant, I know this is a hell of a thing to tell you. The captain was wrong. This ain't the first time cattle have disappeared from out there at the holding ground. Not only since he's been here, but before he came out here, too."

Lieutenant Winthrop's stare hardened on the sergeant. He had become disillusioned with the Army, but for some reason he did not like to hear a non-commissioned officer make the kind of statement Flannery had just made. He said: "Make up the detail. We'll leave first thing in the morning."

Flannery reddened a little and nodded his head, then turned to watch the officer walk out into the sunlight on his way to his quarters. Behind him Morning Gun said: "You scared him. What you said sounded like it wasn't just Indians or thieves who got away with those cattle."

Flannery made a gesture of futility with his arms and sank back down upon the little wooden keg. "The trouble is, John, a man could get real old on this post waiting for someone to come out here who don't get scairt. Jesus! I know what I'm talking about. Do you expect they got corruption like this back in Washington?"

Morning Gun grinned in the shadows of the overhang. "President Grant's brother stole allotment beef and re-sold it. Remember the scandal?"

Flannery sounded doleful when he replied: "They never should have taught you to read, John."

Morning Gun's grin lingered. "Indians haven't believed you people are gods for hundreds of years. Mike, some of those cattle that've been siphoned off in the dark didn't end up in white stew pots. Indians've stolen their share."

Flannery shrugged that off. "That's not the point I wanted to make. But you've got to be careful what you say to officers. I wanted to tell him that the drovers who deliver the herds up here ain't the real thieves. That captain said no cattle had been stole until he showed up to take command. You know what that means, John? It means that someone who is supposed to keep the tallies and the books, and make sure the drovers get paid according to the number of cattle they're to deliver on a government contract are certifying that all the cattle have been delivered, and he's got to know damned well that they haven't all been turned over to us. What happened this time was simply that the fellers who drove off the cattle took too many and were too careless about how they did it. That's all it means. Hell, every herd that comes up here is shy the full number. You know that as well as I do, John. As well as someone else has to, by God, because he lies in the papers he makes out approving payment for the drover."

Morning Gun said: "Who?"

Flannery arose irritably and looked out across the compound. "I'm just a non-com. I don't know anything. I'm not supposed to know anything."

II

The result of the post adjutant's inquiries had indicated that the beef thieves had driven the cattle almost due west from Laramie, then southward where the land opened up into a wide, long trough of land down toward Colorado. The boundary between

Wyoming and Colorado was not very far down in that direction. As the detachment rode through a blustery, alternately
warm and cold springtime day, Lieutenant Winthrop, wrapped
in his campaign coat and with his hat pulled down, gazed off on
his right toward the mountains. They had eyewitness sightings,
and some old, unreliable tracks to indicate the thieves had gone
southward. Albert Winthrop may have lacked experience with
Indian raiders, but over the last thirteen months he had learned
a lot from listening. Now he gazed dead ahead where the thick,
short man on the big-rumped, seal-brown horse was plodding
along, his incongruous small-brimmed city hat sticking up above
the moth-eaten massiveness of an old knee-length buffalo coat.
Burdette had been around a long time. Longer than any of
them, not just in years but in Wyoming Territory.

He was following those unidentifiable tracks as though he
were certain they had been made by the missing cattle. What
nagged at Lieutenant Winthrop were the stories he had heard
about Indians avoiding areas like this which had roads travers-
ing them. With stolen cattle—any cattle at all for that matter—
Indians would not pass openly in country like this. He told
himself the tracks would turn westerly soon; the thieves would
leave open country for the mountains. But when the detail of
twelve men stopped in the lee of a sandstone shelter to rest the
animals and Burdette came back where the officer was standing, smiling to show three gold teeth, with his little dark eyes
fixed upon Winthrop, he gestured with a mittened hand and
said: "They had a hell of a start on us. But I expect if we was to
push right along, we might be able to come onto something.
Cattle can't be drove hard, like horses can, Lieutenant."

Winthrop gazed at the shorter, older, and darker man. "You
think they continued southward?"

Burdette's smile broadened. "I expect so. Unless we find that
they turned off downcountry somewhere."

"This is open country, Mister Burdette."

The scout understood Winthrop's implication. "Well, sir, if they come down through here in the night . . . which I'd have done in their boots just exactly because it is open country, they wouldn't lose no cattle, would they, like they'd sure as hell do if they taken them into the hills?"

Winthrop did not press this conversation. He watched the troopers at work on their meager rations, and eventually strolled over where Sergeant Flannery was examining one of the hoofs of his horse. He said: "Anything wrong?"

Flannery straightened up, wiping his hands. "You mean with my horse, sir?"

Winthrop stood gazing at the raw-boned man with the green eyes. "What else would I mean?"

Flannery's bold gaze crinkled with sardonic humor. "You might mean, sir, that we're never going to find those cattle."

"Why, Sergeant?"

"Because there's lots of cattle down through this slot. There's ranchers on both sides of the stage road, and they got free-ranging cattle all around through here, and we're not following fresh tracks. Most of all, Lieutenant, we're not following barefoot horses."

Winthrop shoved cold hands deeper into his coat pockets and let his gaze drift back where Pete Burdette and some enlisted men were talking.

Sergeant Flannery watched the officer for a moment, then spoke again. "Being an officer gives a man a chance to speak his mind, Lieutenant."

Winthrop showed irritation. "What you'd like to say is that someone on the post besides the drover helped someone steal the cattle, isn't that it?"

Michael Flannery's smile faded as he returned the officer's troubled gaze. "Lieutenant, there's a lot I'd like to say. I've been out here a long time. Right now, what I'd like to say is that Pete Burdette is getting our tails froze off for nothing. We're not going to find those cattle, and we're not going to find Indians driving them. I thought you believed what John said when we went out to the holding ground day before yesterday. Hell, Lieutenant, you stood up to the captain about that. It wasn't Indians."

Lieutenant Winthrop gazed moodily southward. He had not only stated his belief, based upon Morning Gun's judgment, that Indians had not stolen the cattle, but he could have added something to it right now. He did not like Pete Burdette, or trust the man. Instead of mentioning these things, he brought his gaze back to the raw-boned Irishman. "The problem as I see it, Sergeant, is whether or not Burdette is taking us on a wild-goose chase. Each day that passes we're losing more chances of ever finding those cattle."

Flannery agreed instantly. "Yes, sir, an' that's what I meant a minute ago. Burdette's doin' this on purpose."

Winthrop's gaze hardened a little. "Pete Burdette . . . ?"

Flannery did not falter. "Why not, Lieutenant? Him and most of those drovers are as close as peas in a pod."

Winthrop looked over where the man in the old buffalo coat was swinging his arms in the cold, still talking with the enlisted men. "You can't just guess about things like this, Sergeant."

Flannery's wide, thin mouth pulled up at the corners. "Lieutenant, if they'd've let us bring John along, we maybe would be riding in a different direction."

For a while Winthrop stood in silent thought, then, as he was turning away, he said: "But they didn't. . . . I agree with you about one thing. Morning Gun would be more helpful than Burdette is."

Flannery watched the officer go to his horse, catch the tracker's eye, and jerk his head. When they were astride again, still heading southward, Flannery delved inside his coat for a plug, tore off a corner, pouched the cud, returned the plug to an inner pocket, then leaned and lustily expectorated. Afterward he rode along, studying the man out in front in the old buffalo coat.

The wind increased. They were passing down through a broad slot with mountains on both sides. Any ground-hugging wind in this kind of country was compressed between mountains and with only one funnel to flow through, of necessity had to become prolonged and fierce. If there could be a saving grace to something like this, it had to be that both horses and men had their backs to the wind. But wind in the Laramie plains country was endowed with a capacity for cutting through the thickest clothing. It was not the cold that increased Sergeant Flannery's irritability, as much as it was his solid conviction that they were making this long, forced ride with no prospect of accomplishing anything, and they still had to ride back, *facing* the damned wind when they turned northward.

Two hours later, when Burdette led them aside into a spit of pine and fir trees that served as a windbreak, Flannery got down with the others, and sprang his knees a few times to get some of the cold-induced stiffness out. When a bull-necked, leathery-faced trooper spoke from nearby, saying unprintable things about springtime in Wyoming, Flannery nodded absently while watching the lieutenant and the tracker in conversation up ahead. He spat, rubbed his hands together, then tucked each one under an armpit. His irritability had progressed through indignation to anger. Burdette was making a monkey out of the lieutenant, which, as a non-commissioned officer, Flannery normally would not have objected to, except that this particular officer did not go around with a damned ramrod up his back. Also, what Sergeant Flannery considered as Burdette's under-handed duplicity was responsible for the suffering among the detail, which included himself.

Flannery had been a soldier for a long time. He had seen things that angered him, but after so many years, while he never learned to accept stupidity, dishonesty, and pomposity with grace, he had just about become fatalistic about it. Then Winthrop had come along, and what that damned tracker was doing right now amounted to the deliberate discrediting of a green officer, who happened to possess the virtues Sergeant Flannery had once had, and still had but not in the same degree as the lieutenant had. He knew from watching Winthrop that disillusionment was setting in. He also knew from years of experience with other officers as fresh and idealistic as Winthrop was, that when it got bad enough, they either quit the Army, or they turned to whiskey.

Flannery swung his arms and saw the tracker and the lieutenant break off their discussion and head for their animals. Flannery turned and growled at the detail, and, as he, too, swung across the McClellan and evened up the reins, he watched Burdette from narrowed eyes. They would not be able to get back to the post today, and, although they were equipped to spend the night out, it was not going to be a pleasant bivouac.

Unpleasant overnight camps were nothing new to Sergeant Flannery. Since being posted to Wyoming Territory he had rarely survived any other kind, and normally, on patrol or reconnaissance in the past, he had accepted the discomfort with soldierly fatalism, but this time he knew as well as he knew his name that the lieutenant, and all of them for that matter, were being made fools of, and that made a difference as he plodded along, watching Burdette with his green eyes in slits. Sleeping like cocoons on half-frozen ground was bad enough, doing it because the scout was being crafty made it worse. But Flannery kept his anger inside. When they eventually arrived down where there were more trees to break the bitter wind and swung off to make

camp, Flannery got as busy as the other enlisted men organiz-
ing the camp. When Lieutenant Winthrop came over where the
men had a whip-sawing fire going and hunkered down near the
sergeant, Flannery deliberately smiled as he said: "How much
farther south does he aim to go?"

Winthrop gathered his coat close and leaned toward heat
when he replied: "No farther. We'll turn back in the morning."

"No more tracks to follow, Lieutenant?"

"He didn't say that. He said they've been making better time
and widening the gap, and, unless we're prepared to spend two
weeks in the field, we'd better just go back."

Flannery turned toward the fire and held out both palms. His
smile was gone; there was a high flush in his face, and he had
no more to say.

The lieutenant went after his blanket roll. One of the squatting enlisted men waited until Winthrop was beyond hearing,
then said: "That's what the Army is all about. Ride out, ride
back, get in line to wait, freeze your tail off . . . or damn' near
die of thirst in summertime . . . and put in the time until your
enlistment is up."

That bull-necked man with the leathery face pushed closer to
the blaze. "What did you think it was, bein' a hero?"

The discussion lagged for want of other participants. Flannery looked for Burdette. He had his own little fire in a secluded
area with trees on three sides. He was cooking something, was
smoking a little pipe, and on the ground in that thick old coat
with patches of hair worn off put Flannery in mind of an old
bear with mange.

A tall, gaunt soldier, following the sergeant's stare, said: "You
fellers remember Sergeant Evinrude? He was invalided out with
a ruined back about six years ago. One time him and me was in
Laramie having a few drinks, and he told me something about
Pete Burdette, said Burdette used to trap and pot-hunt for the

settlements back in the early days. Said he lived with the Indians for some years, and got into trouble once when the Army found a bunch of their horses in some Indian camp where Pete was living."

Flannery had never heard this tale, although he had heard others about their scout. "How did he get out of it?"

"Evinrude said he swore up an' down the Indians had stole them horses and that he hadn't known a danged thing about it." The tall, lean man shook his head. "The patrol fetched back some of the Indians, and Burdette taken off for higher into the mountains and didn't come back for several years."

A soldier waited, then said: "That's all?"

The gaunt man nodded his head.

Flannery finally had enough heat penetrating his clothing to relax his muscles. He saw Burdette arise from his cooking fire and head back through the trees. For a while Flannery remained in place, then he casually arose and walked out into the settling cold and blustery darkness. No one paid much attention.

There was a little moon that cast almost no light, and a million stars that cast slightly more light, but among the trees visibility was about as it would have been if there had been no stars, so Flannery had to pick his way carefully. He particularly did not want to make a lot of noise.

When he passed Pete Burdette's little untended fire, he did so well to the north so he would not be outlined by it. Back where the men were sitting, someone suddenly laughed loudly; evidently the heat was relaxing everyone a little. Flannery halted until the noise of laughter ended, then listened. But the wind made many different kinds of sound as it beat through tree limbs and against the congealing earth, so he continued his scout relying almost entirely upon his eyes.

He found Burdette by accident, as the shorter and thicker man came forth from a thorn-pin thicket and struck a match to rekindle his little pipe. Wind whipped the flame out almost immediately but not before Burdette had sucked twice, fast, to get the shag burning again. Flannery waited beside a tree until Burdette started past in the direction of his camp, then stepped out to block the scout's progress.

Burdette recoiled, his right hand dipping to brush back the coat. Flannery's teeth flashed in the gloom. Burdette recognized him and let go with smoke and profanity at the same time. "You liked to scairt the hell out of me!" he exclaimed.

Flannery stepped a little closer, still smiling.

III

They were a mismatched pair, like a horse in harness with a burro. Flannery was tall and lean, Burdette was shorter, thick and solid. The bear-skin coat made him look much thicker. Flannery was a career non-commissioned soldier who was unaccustomed to tact—unless he was speaking to an officer. Scouts and Army hunters were not in the officer category. In fact, on most posts they weren't considered even to be in the class of private soldiers. Flannery said: "Pete, those are old tracks we been following."

Burdette removed his little pipe, spat, plugged the pipe back between his teeth, and steadily eyed the sergeant. "Whose fault is that?" he eventually asked.

Flannery was not to be diverted. He said: "This whole country down here's got cattle through it. And there ain't been any barefoot horse tracks."

Burdette did as he had done before, he stared at the larger man and sucked on his pipe before eventually speaking. "I'm the scout, Flannery, you ain't. Indians don't have to ride barefoot horses. I've seen 'em riding shod horses and so have you." Burdette cocked his head a little. "What are you gettin' at . . . and, remember, the lieutenant's goin' to hear about this?"

Flannery's deep-down indignation rose up a notch. "Is that supposed to scare me, Pete?"

"No. It's supposed to make you think before you get to runnin' off at the mouth. Sergeant, we never been friends, and that's all right with me. But you want to be a mite careful."

Flannery considered the older man. When he spoke, his voice was tinged with irony. "You're goin' to tell me you got the captain's ear. I figured you'd be too smart to threaten me."

"I ain't threatenin' no one, Sergeant. I know how many times you been in fights and all. I know your reputation. I don't want no trouble with you if I can avoid it."

Flannery bobbed his head. "Good. Then tell me straight out why you brought us down here when you know damned well those stolen cattle didn't go south at all?"

Again the scout puffed and eyed Flannery with his head to one side. "They didn't go south? Then which direction did they go in?"

Flannery did not know so he said: "Not south. So what you're goin' to tell me right here and now is why you been tellin' the lieutenant we're following their marks?"

Burdette removed the pipe and knocked out the dottle on the palm of a gloved hand. He was pensive when he eventually looked up again. "Flannery, you are tryin' to make trouble. I know how you do this, I been on the post as long as you have. You keep this up, and when we get back to the fort I'm goin' to the captain. We *are* followin' their tracks!"

"You're lying, Pete. We both know it and I want to know why you're lying."

Burdette stowed his little pipe somewhere inside the old coat, and afterward pushed back the coat on both sides with his hands on his hips. He showed no fear at all of the taller and younger man. He carried one of the late-model Colt six-shooters, a better, more advanced sidearm than the Army had issued to its non-coms and officers.

"Sergeant, the officer believes me. That's what matters. Not what some non-commissioned lifer believes. Sergeant, you make trouble right now and I'll shoot you."

Flannery had his sidearm, but made no move toward it. He instead smiled at the older man, ignoring the threat. "It wasn't Indians, Pete. You know that it wasn't. And they didn't come down through here. If you want to report me when we get back, you go right ahead."

Burdette picked out just one of those statements. "Wasn't Indians, then who was it?"

"White men."

"You're crazy, Flannery."

"White men this time and other times, too. You and the drovers know that. Pete, I've watched you take details out like this over the years, an' you never brought back no cattle nor no cattle thieves."

Flannery let it lie between them without putting it into words, confident that Burdette knew exactly what he was implying.

Burdette understood. He said: "Flannery, you'd better have something more than Irish blarney to back that up. You called me a liar, and now you're sayin' I'm helpin rustle cattle."

The taller man looked down. They were no more than ten feet apart, much too close for the scout to get his gun out before Flannery rushed him. "Who was it this time, Pete?" he asked quietly.

Burdette's weathered, tan face looked much darker in the night; if there was red in it, that was not noticeable, but the expression was readable. He was coldly furious and calculatingly silent. For a long time he returned the sergeant's stare before speaking again. "I'll give you a warnin'," he said. "Don't stick your nose where it's got no business."

Flannery was not intimidated. "That's no warning, Pete.

That's admittin' something. You want to tell me who stole those cattle now? You're not goin' to get a chance to use that gun before I beat your damned brains out, if you don't."

A sharp, angry voice cut in from behind Flannery. "Sergeant! What the hell do you think you're doing?"

Lieutenant Winthrop walked stiffly around in front of Flannery, his eyes narrowed in anger, his shoulders squared and both gloved hands fisted at his side. They exchanged a wintry long look before the officer ordered Flannery to return to the bivouac for enlisted men.

Flannery stood his ground for a moment, then wheeled and stamped back the way he had come through the trees.

Lieutenant Winthrop faced Pete Burdette, still furious. If the scout expected some ameliorating words, he must have been surprised when the officer spoke to him. "What did you mean that he shouldn't stick his nose where it didn't belong?"

Burdette shifted his feet a little before answering. "I meant that he ain't the scout, I am. And I know my trade better'n any damned soldier knows it. That's what I meant, Lieutenant. I'm a civilian, I don't have to take no crap from any soldier."

Winthrop regarded the scout for a moment before speaking again. "It didn't sound to me like that's what you meant."

"Well, Lieutenant, I can't help what it sounded like to you. That's exactly what I meant. He's mad because we been ridin' in bad weather for so long. Hell, I don't make the weather. And I been on plenty of scouts before where we come back empty-handed, and that ain't been my fault, either."

Winthrop turned and walked back through the trees, leaving Pete Burdette to stand out there a long time, looking after Winthrop, his expression gradually turning crafty and hostile. When he eventually got back to his little fire, he had to go hunt up more dry twigs because there was nothing left but red embers.

The wind died sometime in the night, which was somewhat

of a blessing, but when wind died on a cold night, the temperature plummeted, so shortly before dawn, when Sergeant Flannery routed out the detail, there was frozen earth underfoot, a condition that inevitably soured dispositions and sharpened the talent men had for profanity.

They struck camp in haste because the lieutenant wanted to reach the post before evening. Two miles on their way northward they encountered some packers coming in from the westerly mountains with a string of sixteen handsome big Missouri mules. While the lieutenant rode over to talk with the packers, Flannery and the other enlisted man squatted where thin sunshine fell across their backs. Burdette, as usual, did not go over among the soldiers, but hunkered by himself on the lee side of his horse, even though there was no wind blowing.

Two more hours northward, with Sergeant Flannery maintaining at least some semblance of military order by riding a couple of yards ahead of the detail, Lieutenant Albert Winthrop looked back and curtly beckoned. Flannery obediently gigged his mount. He had been looking at the lieutenant's back since they'd struck camp, wondering whether he'd got all the disciplining he was going to get last night, or whether the lieutenant would make formal charges when they got back to the post. An argument was hardly enough to warrant a complaint and disciplinary action, but a man could never be sure with officers, especially with one like Winthrop who was going through a bad time of disillusionment and frustration.

When he got up beside the officer, Winthrop faced him and said: "Don't do anything like that again."

Flannery nodded. The officer's remonstrance hadn't sounded even annoyed, and his attitude was not as it should have been when he was scolding an enlisted man.

"Those packers were returning empty from the mines in the westerly mountains."

27

Flannery nodded about that, also. Those packers didn't have any connection with him bracing Burdette, as far as Flannery could see.

Winthrop loosened his coat because as the day advanced the heat increased. It was turning out to be one of those magnificent springtime days with wildflowers along the way, a few drifting thin high clouds, and a brilliant sun.

"Those packers," Winthrop said quietly, looking past Burdette who was about half a mile ahead, "have been over quite a bit of country. Northward for a couple of weeks, then down through the mountains on our left. They didn't see any Indian camps, Sergeant."

Flannery's suspicion stirred but he still said nothing because quite clearly Lieutenant Winthrop had more to say.

Winthrop turned his head slowly. "Up north and according to the packers about fifty miles through the mountains at a series of gold diggings, while they were trading up there, some stockmen arrived in the meadows with a band of cattle."

Flannery fished inside his coat for the plug of tobacco and worried off a cud. He spat, eyed the lieutenant with sardonic green eyes, and straightened up in the saddle. "Ours," he said. "Except that the packers didn't know that."

"And I didn't tell them, Sergeant, and you're not going to mention this to anyone."

As though the admonition was not only uncalled for, but irritating, Flannery scowled at his officer and did not deign to offer assurance. Instead he said: "The brand . . . ?"

"The same, Sergeant. The previous owner's brand and his road brand."

"Indians?"

"Of course not, Sergeant."

Flannery spat aside again, eyes puckered in faint amusement. This was the same man who yesterday got his back up when

Flannery had reiterated what Morning Gun had said about the rustlers not having been Indians. Flannery took a sideswipe of his own, but he was careful in the way he did it. "And here we are, down where those stolen cattle never come."

Winthrop reddened a little and slouched along a short distance in silence before saying: "I've been thinking, Sergeant. We're going to keep this between us, and, when we get back to the post, I'm going to get Morning Gun to ask for leave, then go up into that northwesterly country and find at least one of the hides off those cattle the miners butchered, and fetch it back to the post."

"With the brand on it."

"Naturally," replied the officer, watching Burdette up ahead. The scout had finally shed his mangy old riding coat and was riding, twisted from the waist, while he tied the coat behind his cantle. "Sergeant, stay away from Burdette."

Flannery was perfectly agreeable. "Yes, sir. That suits me fine. Suppose he goes and complains to his friend, the adjutant, that I called him a liar?"

"I'll handle that," stated Winthrop with full confidence that he would be able to. "By any chance do you know the drover who brought in that last herd of cattle?"

"No, sir. I know a few of them, but not that one."

"Too bad," muttered the lieutenant.

Flannery knew what the lieutenant had in mind, but as far as he knew there was no one on the post, except Pete Burdette, who knew the stockman. His thoughts reverted to the packers. "Did you get the names of those traders?"

Winthrop had. "Yes. They make up their packs of trading goods down around Fort Collins in Colorado, but they trade up through the gold diggings of southern and western Wyoming. They'll be back through in a couple of months. I got an address down in Fort Collins where they can be reached." As the officer

29

finished speaking, he gazed at Flannery. "They also gave me some other names."

Flannery smiled a little. "Descriptions would most likely be better, Lieutenant. Rustlers change names oftener you an' me change shirts."

"I have their descriptions, too," stated Winthrop, looking ahead again. "But what they couldn't provide me with was anything about someone around the post who helped those men steal the cattle, so I didn't ask. But I need to know that."

Flannery nodded his head. "They wouldn't have known, if they just bumped into the rustlers. Anyway, if you hadn't gone and got your hackles up last night, I'd have got that information out of Pete."

Winthrop slowly wagged his head. "If you had, you'd have spilled the beans, Flannery. If Burdette is part of it, which I don't know is the case, but if he is, and you'd kicked the wadding out of him to get answers, what do you think he'd do the minute he got back to Laramie?"

Flannery avoided an incriminating, and embarrassing, answer by saying: "I'd kind of like to make that ride into the mountains with John. This is the most beautiful time of the year for. . . ."

"You are going to stay on the post, Sergeant. Morning Gun can make it better without you along, and I've got something in mind."

Flannery rode along in silence for a long time, feeling much better than he had felt yesterday. He could even smile at Burdette's back half a mile up ahead.

IV

They made it before the evening meal, but without enough time left to do much more than care for their animals, and afterward, when Lieutenant Winthrop presented himself to the adjutant's hutment to report, he was told by the orderly that the captain and adjutant had ridden down to the town and would not be back until only God knew when. It was the same steady-eyed, stone-faced orderly who had seen Winthrop and Flannery storm out of the adjutant's office after their meeting with the captain, and this time, as he watched Lieutenant Winthrop depart, his lips pulled back in a humorless smile.

Flannery was out back leaning on a corral, chewing and talking to John Morning Gun when the lieutenant made a round that took him back there. The other two stopped talking when he came up, which irritated him, but he simply hooked a boot over the lowest rail and told Morning Gun what he wanted him to do in the morning—ask for leave for a week or two, find one of those hides with a brand on it, and bring it back.

John Morning Gun thought about that for a while before agreeing. Then he walked away, leaving the sergeant and lieutenant alone. For Morning Gun the decision had not been difficult; the reason he was slow to assent was because his mind was full of the things Flannery had told him about their ride southward. He had been convinced from their first brief little cursory scout after the cattle had been stolen that the thieves had not been Indians. Until the detail had returned, though, he had gloomily considered anyone's chances of proving it just about impossible, because something he had noticed at other times seemed to be working. The willingness of the Army to believe reservation jumpers were at the bottom of everything bad that happened.

After he walked away, Sergeant Flannery mused aloud to the lieutenant: "Suppose they won't let him go?"

Winthrop answered shortly. "He's a civilian. They can't prevent it."

"They can fire him off the post."

"They won't do that," stated the lieutenant.

Flannery shrugged. He would know tomorrow whether they

could prevent it or not; meanwhile he had something else on his mind. "I saw Pete come out of the adjutant's hut a while ago."

Lieutenant Winthrop said nothing. He was watching the horses in the corral. They had been fed and were lipping up the few remaining stalks they could find.

Flannery decided to risk the lieutenant's anger and said: "The adjutant's orderly, Corporal Krause, sat in there for more'n an hour with Burdette."

Still the officer watched the horse, his face reflecting somber thoughts while he remained silent.

Flannery's patience was slipping a little. "Lieutenant, I can talk to Krause."

Finally Winthrop spoke. "Like you were going to do with Burdette? Sergeant, you'll end up in the stockade, and, if anyone in uniform is involved, your action will simply let them know you suspect something. Just be patient. I know it's hard, but it'll be worse if we start accusing people with nothing to go on. We'll do nothing until Morning Gun returns."

Flannery, too, faced ahead to watch the horses. In his mind there was a question. *Suppose Morning Gun returns without a hide?* But he said nothing.

Lieutenant Winthrop strolled away, heading for the officers' hutments, and Flannery got a fresh chew of molasses-cured tobacco in his cheek and wandered over to the latrine area to make sure the detail was at work. It was; at least the men were busy when Flannery arrived, so he headed toward the barracks.

That leather-faced, bull-necked trooper who had been with the detail was sitting out front, whittling in very poor light. He snapped his Barlow closed and pocketed it as the sergeant walked up. With his eyes on Flannery he said: "Mike, there's something *underhanded* going on, isn't there?"

Flannery looked down, then turned to expectorate before answering. "Otto, you been soldierin' as long as I have, so you

reach and shook his head. "Why in hell do we always have to get one like you when they send the replacements?" He moved like a crab, to one side, then farther around until the big recruit had to shift position, which was what Otto expected. While the recruit was shuffling his feet, Otto went in low.

Anderson's thick arms came up, hands clubbed for battle. Flannery swore at Otto: "Damn it, keep out of this!"

Neither Burck nor any of the other men seemed to have heard. Otto straightened up to draw a strike. When it came, Otto went inside it and hit Anderson first in the middle, then over the heart, and finally, as the big man's arms were dropping, squarely in the face. Anderson's body wilted, his eyes were glazed. Otto straightened up, took the measurement, and dropped the larger man with one not particularly powerful blow alongside the head.

There was not a sound in the barracks. Sergeant Flannery blew out a big, noisy breath, and leaned to raise the table. Otto Burck turned toward the wide-eyed troopers and smiled. "It don't go no farther than this room." Then he went back to his bunk and Sergeant Flannery, red in the face, went over and stood, looking down.

A man across from Burck's bunk who had watched the entire affair lying flat out with both hands under his head said: "He saved your bacon, Mike." Several other of the old hands muttered agreement and Otto smiled up at Flannery, then looked around for the button and thread he been working on when the ruckus started.

Flannery turned on his heel, red as a beet, and walked back out into the chilly night. He was still out there when Burck came forth and, leaning on the nearest hitch rack, said: "You could have done it maybe better'n I did, Mike. What that farm lad needed to learn was that this ain't back East, and on a post the old hands outnumber the greenhorns."

Flannery turned. "It wasn't your affair, Otto."

Burck gazed with narrowed eyes around the large, dusty parade ground. "I know. It seemed to me, him and the other replacements had to learn they're a minority. That's all I wanted to get across to them. I didn't mean to step on your toes."

Flannery's indignation faded a little. After a moment he stepped closer to the porch and leaned there, shaking his head. "That son-of-a-bitch is as strong as a bear."

Otto chuckled. "Yeah. While you was out with the detail, I been watchin' him. He's been talkin' like that since he arrived. It was goin' to happen, Mike, whether you came back in time or not."

"I guess so. Well . . . all right. You most likely made a believer out of him."

"Mike, about this underhanded business that's goin' on. . . ."

"Go to bed," stated Flannery shortly, and went back inside, leaving Burck leaning out there, shaking his head.

The barracks was quiet when Flannery entered. The old hands were bedding down as though nothing had happened. The replacements were also bedding down, but probably for a different reason; they had something to think about. Private Anderson was in his blankets, his face to the wall. Flannery stopped briefly to watch him, then went on his way. He was tired, the day had begun early even by Army standards, the ride had been long, and most of all he had felt bitter about a number of things for several days.

The bugler trumpeted new life into the post in the predawn, and by the time daily details had been read off at first muster, Sergeant Flannery learned from one of the stable men that Morning Gun had left the post during the night. Later, when he was standing nearby watching Anderson and the other new men taking over the previous latrine detail, Otto passed by saying: "Lieutenant Winthrop wants to see you at the corrals."

Flannery went down there expecting to be told what he already knew, that John Morning Gun was gone. He was only partly correct. The lieutenant did indeed inform him of this fact, then he also said: "Adjutant Fessler is going to brace you. Burdette complained."

Flannery eyed the officer. "Just brace me?"

Winthrop nodded. "This time. Next time he's going to have you reduced in rank. He would have tried it this time but Burdette told him I witnessed your near attack on him. I told the adjutant Burdette was making a mountain out of a molehill, that we were all tired and discouraged." Winthrop gazed around the horse area where men were working without noticeable enthusiasm or haste. "Stay away from Pete."

Flannery agreed. "Yes, sir. Thanks for scotchin' it. The adjutant don't like me. He'll put this into his little black book."

Lieutenant Winthrop said: "Do you like him, Mike?"

Flannery smiled broadly. "No, sir, now that you mention it, I sure don't."

"Then keep your big mouth closed when he bawls you out," stated the younger man, and walked away.

Flannery laughed to himself and watched Lieutenant Winthrop cross in the direction of the mess hall.

Later, when the adjutant's pale-eyed, thin-lipped orderly came looking for Flannery, and told him that by order of the post adjutant he was to return to the adjutant's office with him, Flannery was prepared. The adjutant was a large, handsome man who appeared as the ideal of what newsmen and others thought a frontier Army officer should be. And he worked at maintaining that image. He also worked at cultivating the post commander's confidence and friendship. Also, it was true that he did not like Sergeant Flannery. Whatever his reasons, he kept them to himself, but when his orderly, Corporal Krause, ap-

peared stiffly in the office doorway to announce that Flannery
was waiting, Lieutenant Fessler nodded, stood up to smooth his
uniform. When Flannery entered and the orderly closed the
door behind him, Lieutenant Fessler clasped both hands behind
his back and stood like a large, blue statue, gazing steadily at
the equally as tall but less handsome and elegant non-
commissioned officer.

He finally spoke. "I have a complaint against your conduct
while on patrol with Lieutenant Winthrop's detail."

Flannery was at attention, looking straight back. "Yes, sir!"

"You threatened Mister Burdette."

"Well . . . yes, sir!"

The adjutant frowned. "Did you or did you not threaten him,
Sergeant?" Before Flannery could reply, the large officer un-
clasped his hands and leaned with them atop the desk, his eyes
wide and angry. "You don't say you're going to beat someone's
brains out unless you are threatening them, Flannery."

"Yes, sir . . . I threatened him."

The lieutenant continued to lean on the desk and glare. He
straightened up slowly, and considered some papers atop his
desk before speaking again, and now his voice reflected strong
reluctance. "This has been a warning, Sergeant. You've made
trouble at other times. This will be your final warning. If you
come up before me one more time, you'll be reduced to private
rank."

"Yes, sir."

They looked steadily at each other for several seconds, then
the adjutant made a curt gesture of dismissal, and turned his
back. "That's all. Dismissed!"

Flannery was careful to close the door after himself with
care. His eyes met the gaze of Corporal Krause. The orderly
had a hint of a very faint smile down around his lips.

For a moment Flannery stood near the orderly desk, looking

down, then he abruptly left the building, went down off the little porch, and halted fifty feet out in the sunshine to look back before he continued on his way.

V

They had a patrol to ride the fourth day after the disappearance of Morning Gun, with the adjutant along. Because his commission was oldest he was technically the officer commanding, but because Lieutenant Winthrop was by the post commander's orders in charge of the patrol, Lieutenant Fessler rode along as an observer. There were several designations to fit this kind of situation. The adjutant invoked none of them; he was a discreet man when discretion was required. As he rode with Albert Winthrop, he was pleasant. Not quite unbending, but pleasant.

Lieutenant Winthrop, on the other hand, was reticent. He allowed himself to be drawn out only on general matters, such as the weather, the purpose of the patrol, and eventually, as their discussion continued, his thoughts about an Army career. He told George Fessler that when his last two years were served he would leave the Army. The adjutant grew thoughtful after that, not commenting until they had a noon halt beside a cold-water creek that was literally hidden by willow thickets that ran north and south as far as the men could see. Then, while lying in the sunshine and shade, Lieutenant Fessler made a suggestion.

"You can request a transfer, Albert. You can put in for something east of the Missouri where there is civilized life and better accommodations."

Winthrop ate and watched a high, stem-winding, red-tailed hawk cover more of the pale sky each time he widened his sweeps.

"The captain would approve a transfer for you," stated the handsome adjutant. "One thing that can be said in favor of Captain Brewster is that he understands things like this. He's transferred a number of officers since I've been out here."

Winthrop turned narrowed eyes. "You like it out here, George?"

Fessler was brushing dead grass off his tunic when he replied: "After four years I'm accustomed to it. I wouldn't say I like it, but then I don't quite dislike it, either."

Winthrop searched the sky for the hawk, but its widening circles had carried it beyond sight from the ground by the creek. Winthrop changed the subject. "How did Flannery take being reprimanded?"

Fessler stopped brushing off grass. He did not answer the question directly. "Flannery is one of those wise old lifers. He has been in trouble of one kind of another ever since I've been here. He's been up before me before. It's infuriating to have one of those lifers stand at attention looking you straight in the eye, sneering at you without showing anything on their faces. Flannery isn't the only one, but he's the worst." Anger had prodded George Fessler further than he would ordinarily have gone, so when he paused and saw Winthrop pluck a grass stalk and chew on it while looking stonily dead ahead, Fessler backtracked a little. "I know he backed you on that story about white men having run off the cattle. I know you take him on details and patrols with you."

Winthrop took the grass from his lips and squinted at it. "He's experienced, George, I'm not."

Fessler accepted that as an oblique apology for Winthrop's taking the sergeant with him, and felt better. He said: "That damned Indian left the post almost a week ago."

Winthrop continued to gaze at the stalk of grass in his hand. "You mean Morning Gun?"

"Yes. Without permission."

Winthrop dropped the grass and turned toward Fessler. "What permission? He's a civilian."

"But he's in the employ of the Army, Albert. He can't just get on his horse and ride off." Lieutenant Fessler paused, then threw up his arms. "Indians!" he exclaimed, getting to his feet. "No sense of order, no sense of time. . . ."

Winthrop arose smiling bleakly.

They got the detail astride and struck out again. For a long while Winthrop rode with a closed face, silent and thoughtful. But eventually he turned toward Fessler and said: "George, there aren't any Indian *rancherías* any more. If Indians stole the cattle, where would they take them?"

Fessler scowled at the ears of his horse. "How does anyone know why Indians do things? I've been on this post and others like it for nearly eleven years. It's always the same with Indians. They sit down and listen to whatever we say, and they ride off, leaving you wondering if they understood, if they agreed or not. How would I know what they did with those cattle, except that you can bet your spurs that they ate them."

Winthrop dropped the subject of Indians. He had not realized until now that the post adjutant despised Indians. It surprised him only because he had not encountered this attitude in Fessler before, but he had encountered it many times in other places, among other men.

They had a vast expanse of prairie in front of them when they turned back. Sergeant Flannery had not once got close to the officers. He only met Lieutenant Winthrop's eyes once; that was when the detail came about to head back to the fort, and nothing passed between them by word of mouth or by glance.

Flannery chewed his tobacco and watched the officers up ahead. When Otto Burck came up and said—"It's not too bad with summer on the land."—Flannery looked at him and offered a wooden nod in agreement, then continued to watch the officers.

They reached the post in late afternoon. The officers handed

41

their reins to enlisted men, then strode slowly in the direction of the adjutant's little log building. Flannery went with the others to care for the animals. He helped care for the two spare horses, then went out front to watch the adjutant's hutment, and, when Lieutenant Winthrop eventually emerged, he managed to strike out on an intercepting course. They met not far from the dining hall. Lieutenant Winthrop turned and soberly said: "Go meet him, Mike."

Flannery nodded his head. "I thought that was why you turned back early."

Winthrop sighed. "If he's got a hide, don't let him ride in with it. And when you fetch him back, wait until after dark, otherwise Burdette's going to see the pair of you."

Flannery was agreeable to that. "Then what?"

"Keep him down by the corrals. I'll come down as soon as I can."

"Lieutenant?"

"What."

"Do you know why the adjutant thought it might be a good idea for you to transfer out?"

Winthrop considered the lanky man. "You've got good hearing, Sergeant. Sure I know. At least I can guess why. And because you hate him, you think he's involved with the cattle thefts."

Flannery gently shook his head. "No. Not because I don't like him. I think his damned orderly's up to his neck in it, too."

Winthrop said: "Go catch Morning Gun before he decides to ride fast to get here before supper."

Flannery watched the officer walk away, and turned to head back the way he had come. He had no idea who else in the detail might have seen the distant horseman about the time Winthrop ordered the detail to turn about. He was sure that he and the lieutenant were not the only ones, but at least the others had no reason to attach any great significance to a lone horseman approaching from the direction of the northwesterly mountains. He mounted his animal behind the corrals and left the post by avoiding a direct course across the parade ground. It helped that everyone was cleaning up for mess call. The sentry at the gate looked curious, but Flannery dropped the man a roguish wink as though he were on a whiskey run to the town, and the sentry winked back.

Evening was slow arriving, which was a harbinger of summer's longer days, shorter nights, and warmer weather. Flannery, who had a fresh cud to compensate for the meal he was missing, boosted his horse over into a lope and only glanced back once, when he made a wide sweep of the entire area, searching for the rider he and Lieutenant Winthrop had recognized earlier. Just for a moment he thought he had a glimpse of another horseman northwest from the direction of the fort, but when he looked again, there was no such sign.

Between Flannery and the post there was considerable rolling land. There were also thick stands of creek willows. He kept the horse loping until he could discern the oncoming horseman again. He seemed in no hurry. It worried Flannery for a mile or so that the rider might not be who he thought it was. But any time horsemen ride with other horsemen over the years, they can recognize them by the way they sit a saddle even at considerable distances. It was Morning Gun. Flannery swept down into a deep swale and breasted the far ridge, then halted. Morning Gun was dead ahead about a mile and a half, and he had seen, and recognized, the raw-boned sergeant. Morning Gun changed course slightly so that they would meet atop the rim. Flannery sighed and swung to the ground to wait.

Dusk was coming. Far out, and also far back, it was no longer possible to make out movement. Flannery squatted, eyeing the oncoming rider. He was not sure in the poor light, but he thought Morning Gun had something behind his saddle.

He was right. When the tall Indian arrived and swung to the ground before greeting Flannery, he began freeing the saddle thongs on both sides of the rear skirt. Flannery led his horse close. When Morning Gun let the bundle drop, Flannery caught the smell and wrinkled his nose as the Indian turned, and smiled.

"I only brought back one half," he told Flannery. "The half with the marks on it. It was a big hide, more than a horse wanted to carry, along with a saddle and a rider." Morning Gun knelt and unrolled the hide.

Flannery leaned in the settling early dusk, read the brands, and straightened up. "We got plenty of time," he informed the Indian. "Winthrop don't want you on the post until after dark. That's a stinkin' hide, John."

Morning Gun looked down. "It wasn't fresh when I dug it up." He looked at Flannery again. "I found four of them buried in the same place." He fished inside his coat and brought forth a soiled scrap of brown paper. "Names," he told Flannery, handing over the paper. "Miners. They bought eleven head. The rustlers took the rest of the cattle on among the other diggings."

Flannery held the paper up close to read the names, then pocketed it and moved back a short distance. Green hides had an aroma all their own, particularly when they'd been disinterred and carried on horseback under a hot sun for a few days.

Morning Gun delved in a saddle pocket for jerky. He offered Sergeant Flannery several curled, lint-encrusted sticks, and Flannery shook his head. He was hungry, at least he had been, but right now he had no appetite at all. Morning Gun began chewing jerky. Once, he stopped chewing long enough to say: "White men, Mike."

Flannery told him about the detail Burdette had led southward. Morning Gun chewed and listened, then made a grunt of scorn. "He's not that green, Mike. Pete's good at readin' sign." Morning Gun spat out some gristle his teeth could not make a dent in. "A miner told me those fellers told him they'd bought the cattle from a trail drover who was headin' to Montana with a big drive."

"He tell the miner anything else?"

"Just talk."

Flannery glanced at the descending night, then down at the rotting green hide. "By the time we get back it'll be dark enough."

Morning Gun was starting to kneel when the gunshot blew the stillness apart. He heard and felt the bullet pass him. He heard it strike flesh with a solid sound, and dropped flat.

Sergeant Flannery went down in a heap, arms wind-milling wildly for seconds under the impact.

Morning Gun lunged to grab and hold tightly to the reins of his startled, panicky horse. He managed to keep the animal with him but Sergeant Flannery's animal broke away clean and ran in terror back the way he had come.

Morning Gun twisted to look back in the direction that gunshot had come from, but could see nothing. He lay still, gripping one rawhide rein until he distantly heard a horse running, then he got to his feet and led the horse along as he went over where Mike Flannery was lying.

VI

Flannery was alive but there was not much hope. If he had been closer to the post and the surgeon had been at hand, he might have made it. At least that was Morning Gun's opinion as he knelt. Flannery's eyes were so dark they seemed almost black. His face was rigid in an expression of shock, of disbelief. He did not seem to realize Morning Gun was with him, even when John leaned to ease open the soggy shirt, then made a little hissing sound as his breath went out.

Morning Gun leaned down and spoke. "Mike? I'm afraid to move you. I'll go to the post for help."

The stiffness gradually departed and Flannery turned his head to meet the Indian's black gaze. "I thought . . . back a mile or so I thought I saw someone. Tell the lieutenant it looked like. . . ."

Morning Gun reached for Flannery's hand and held it gently. He remained in that position, holding the hand, for several minutes, then gently placed the hand at Flannery's side and stood up. There was not a sound; the sky was sending forth pale, pewter light. He went to his horse to swing up, and, after gazing a moment at the green hide, he rolled it, retied it behind the cantle, then swung up.

He rode slowly for a mile, then changed direction just in case that bushwhacker was still around, and rode directly to the post, coming in from the southwest, down near the palisaded wall of the horse area. He left his animal tied outside, scaled the wall, landed lightly in the darkness, and stood a long time studying the little squares of orange lamp glow that showed from most of the hutments. It was his intention to approach Lieutenant Winthrop's quarters. He had no idea that the lieutenant had been fretting down among the corrals for more than an hour, until he started forward, and was seen by a stationary shape, which moved with a fluid motion to intercept Morning Gun near the mule sheds.

Morning Gun stopped stone still as the silhouette came closer, then softly asked him: "Where's the sergeant?"

Morning Gun answered shortly and evenly: "Dead. Where we met, someone was out there. I think maybe they meant to shoot me, but I was leaning forward. The bullet hit Mike slanting upward from the guts. It was like butcherin' pigs. Blood everywhere."

Lieutenant Winthrop seemed to stagger. Morning Gun watched him for a moment, then spoke again. "We got to get him away from out there. Animals will smell the blood." Then he also said: "I got a hide with the brands on it, and I talked to some miners who bought the beef. It was white men."

Winthrop seemed not to be listening. Finally he said: "I'll get a horse. Meet me out a ways from the post gate."

Morning Gun waited until the officer was gone, then returned to the wall and scaled it. His horse was tired and hungry. If there had been a way to get a fresh animal and let this one rest, he would have done it. There was no way. He met the lieutenant, did not wait for him to get close, but turned doggedly in the direction of the dead man.

The moon was high before they got there. Winthrop stepped down and stood like granite, gazing at the dead non-commissioned officer. For him, the fury that had come in the wake of his shock and surprise had to wait. Flannery's killing created a distinct, large problem. For one thing, Flannery was not supposed to be out here. For another thing, if it was learned on the post that he had been shot to death by a bushwhacker, the entire command would be boiling mad. Finally, if one of the other scouts from the post came out here with a detail, they would find the tracks of another rider, someone Flannery had met out here. That, more than anything else, would put the fat into the fire.

Morning Gun was squatting near his horse, chewing jerky and waiting. When the officer finally spoke, Morning Gun stood up.

"We can't take him to the fort. He can be missin' for a day or two, which will cause trouble, but he can't be dead from a bullet. That will cause an investigation and all hell will bust loose."

Morning Gun spat out a piece of jerky he could not swallow. "You go back," he told the officer. "You're supposed to be on the post. I'll take Mike back into the trees and lash him up there the way the Indians used to do. Lieutenant, what about this hide with the brands on it?"

"When you reach the post, hide it somewhere."

"It smells bad."

"Cover it. Hide it and cover it. Morning Gun, they're going to ask you where you've been."

The tall Indian caught hold of his reins. He was not very concerned about that. "I went to visit some people I know in the mountains. Old friends. That's all." Leading his horse over beside the corpse, Morning Gun was gazing solemnly downward when he spoke again. "Who killed him?"

Albert Winthrop said nothing. He helped the Indian get the body across the seat of Morning Gun's saddle, then stepped away as the Indian began making the body fast.

While his back was to the officer, the Indian asked the same question a second time. "Who killed him?"

Winthrop was not watching because it made him ill to see Flannery's head hanging down like that. "I don't know. You saw no one?"

"I heard a horse running, afterward. His horse run off, too, back toward the post."

Winthrop swore. He would have to find that horse and somehow get him into the post. That might not be too difficult. He hoped it would not be. But something else occurred to him. Had anyone seen Flannery ride out? He would bet a lot of money someone had because it was not possible to leave the post on horseback without at the very least encountering a sentry.

He went to his horse, caught the reins, and stood in thought until the Indian turned, watched him for a moment, then said: "Now it's all goin' to come out."

Winthrop had been thinking the same thing. "Yes. Be careful

what you say when they ask you where you've been. If they ask you about Flannery, you've been off the post a week, you haven't seen him."

Morning Gun gravely inclined his head, still studying the lieutenant. "The adjutant's orderly will bawl me out. What about you?"

Winthrop turned toward the Indian. "I don't honestly know, but one thing is damned clear, Morning Gun. Whatever we do from here on must be done quickly. I wish now I'd walked away when Flannery was going to whip Pete Burdette on that scout southward."

Morning Gun's expression did not change. "I think it had to be him, too."

Winthrop had no intention of going into that, so he felt the girth and turned his horse once before swinging up over the McClellan. "We'll meet tomorrow. I'll hunt you up when I think it's safe. Morning Gun, be careful."

Winthrop had the cold in his face on the ride back, without being aware of it. The sentry at the gate was stamping his feet and blowing on his hands when the lieutenant rode through and responded to the sentry's salute. Dawn was only a couple of hours away.

There was no one in the horse area to care for Winthrop's horse, for which he was thankful because he did not want diversions while he worked and thought, then went over to his quarters to get warm, but not to bed down. He remembered the pinched, leathery face of the sentry at the gate; he had been a friend of Mike Flannery. There would be others like that, mostly among the old hands. Winthrop dug out his cached bottle of single malt whiskey, sat near the little iron stove, and sipped. He was not a drinking man, but tonight he had a need for warmth inside as well as outside.

He thought he probably had one day, at the very most two

days, to unravel the affair of the stolen cattle. He was almost certain he knew who had trailed Flannery, then shot him. He thought he knew why that had happened, too, but how to prove it was something altogether different from guessing about it. And there was the fact of the sergeant's absence from the post. Winthrop took another couple of sips and re-hid the bottle, then cocked his chair against the log wall, and closed his eyes. He was not asleep when a light knock rattled across the hut-ment's door, but the sound startled him, and for a moment he continued to lean there, gazing across the little hot room. The second time knuckles rattled the door, Winthrop arose, ran bent fingers through his hair, and went to the door.

The sentry who had passed him through an hour or so earlier was standing out there, bundled against the cold. He looked steadily at the lieutenant and neither nodded nor spoke. Winthrop opened the door wider and jerked his head.

Heat hit Otto Burck like a wall. He blinked, then reached to loosen his coat as he turned to watch the officer close the door. Winthrop gazed enquiringly at the enlisted man but Burck said nothing until his coat was open and he had shoved back his hat.

"Sergeant Flannery rode out last night and hasn't come back," stated Burck.

Winthrop walked toward a little table as he said: "I'm not the officer of the post tonight, Private Burck."

The bull-necked man acted as though he had not heard that. "Then you rode out and come back a little while ago."

Winthrop stood studying the powerfully built friend of Mike Flannery. He pointed to a chair and Burck ignored the offer to remain standing. "Lieutenant, something is wrong," he said, never taking his eyes off Winthrop's face. "I know there is. I asked Mike about it, and he got mad. You're his friend. I sure don't want him to get into trouble by leavin' the post without permission. There'll be muster in a couple of hours and, if

Mike's not back for that . . . him and Lieutenant Fessler don't like each other. Mike's rank come to him the hard way, Lieutenant."

The uneven way Otto Burck made his statements reflected his worried concern. Lieutenant Winthrop sat down at the little table, hands clasped atop it, and gazed a long time at the older and heavier man. "Who else left the post tonight?" he asked, watching Burck's face closely.

"No one that I know of, but I only come on duty after you and Mike rode out. Before that a big recruit named Anderson was on the gate. He told me you two had rode out. He said that was all that left the fort."

Winthrop frowned with concentration. "Anderson . . . ?"

"Big farm boy," stated Burck. "He came in two weeks ago with the replacements. Started out bein' a troublemaker."

Winthrop gave up trying to recall a trooper named Anderson and said: "You were Sergeant Flannery's friend. I've seen the two of you. . . ."

"*Were*, Lieutenant? What do you mean I *was* his friend?" growled Otto Burck.

The lieutenant gazed at Burck without answering for a while, then arose and paced closer to the stove. Over there, he absently reached to close the damper halfway. He was sweating. "Private, maybe someone else rode out before you went on gate duty."

"No, sir. Anderson said there was no one went out or come in." Burck's face was closed down in a harsh expression. "Lieutenant, I still am Mike Flannery's friend. Why did you say I was his friend?"

Winthrop had made his decision. He said: "Sergeant Flannery was ambushed and killed tonight, Private."

Burck took his eyes slowly off the officer and looked around for the chair. He sat down and with both scarred, big hands hanging between his knees looked steadily at the officer. "Who killed him?" he asked quietly. "Why?"

Winthrop returned to the table. Instead of answering Burck's question, he asked one of his own. "How about the civilians, Private?"

Burck was still too stunned to pick up an implication so he said: "What civilians? You mean did a civilian ride out through the gate tonight?"

"Yes."

Burck's blue eyes were narrowing upon the lieutenant. "I told you, twice now, only you 'n' Mike rode out." Then he paused before also saying: "Not while I was out there. I'll ask Anderson again, but he said no one but you two rode out. What civilian, Lieutenant?"

He knew Private Burck by reputation, and gently shook his head. He did not need Burck to go to Burdette's camp and do to him what he had arrived just in time to prevent Flannery from doing a couple of weeks ago. He side-stepped a direct answer. "That's what I want to know."

Burck sat a moment with beads of sweat forming on his weathered countenance, then got heavily to his feet. "I'll find out," he said, and approached the door as Winthrop gave him a warning.

"Don't say anything about the things we've been talkin' about, Private. Above all, don't mention that Mike is dead. And don't. . . ."

Otto Burck's big fist wrapped around the latch as though he meant to tear it loose and he glared at the officer when he interrupted to say: "You better tell me what's wrong, Lieutenant."

It was not the menace in Burck's face and his attitude that made Lieutenant Winthrop point to the chair Burck had just vacated; it was his desperate need for an ally. "Sit down," he said, and this time he waited for Private Burck to obey, then Lieutenant Winthrop began at the beginning and talked for a solid half hour.

When he was finished, the bugler calling the post to life was the only sound for a long time in the little log house. Finally Burck arose and returned to the door. From over there he said: "All right. I'll find out if anyone else rode out last night . . . an' I know who you mean . . . Pete Burdette. I'll find that out, too."

Winthrop stood up tiredly. "Not with your fists, or you'll spoil everything."

Burck stood looking at the other man a moment, then pulled open the door and disappeared out into the cold, gray predawn light.

VII

Tiredness made men forget—tiredness and shock and pain. Lieutenant Winthrop had forgotten to look for Sergeant Flannery's horse, and, by the time he remembered, muster had been called and Sergeant Flannery had been put on report for being missing and off the post. But all things did not happen for the worse; although the mount sergeant reported a horse missing, the one assigned to Sergeant Flannery, no one went looking for the animal, and a kind fate helped by not having the horse wandering around outside the fort. In fact, that particular horse was never found. Not by the Army, anyway.

Lieutenant Fessler made a point of encountering Lieutenant Winthrop after the orders for the day had been posted. They met over near the enlisted men's barracks where Fessler had seen Winthrop talking quietly with an enlisted man the adjutant recognized as Private Burck. The adjutant, who was a fastidious man, something that must have caused him frequent moments of agony during his tour of duty at Fort Laramie, eyed Winthrop with mild disapproval and said—"Dull razor, Albert?"—and, when Winthrop nodded without speaking, the adjutant spoke again. "You know how I feel about Sergeant Flannery, but being Absent Without Leave isn't like him. Unless of course he'd been drinking. The Irish are like the Indians, they can't handle their liquor."

Winthrop gazed steadily at the larger man and said: "It happens to the best of them, George. General Grant was Absent Without Leave."

Fessler pondered that, decided it could not be true, and said so.

Winthrop smiled. "He was sent to a post called Fort Jones, out in California, and never reported."

Fessler never argued with anyone who disputed him when there was a ring of truth to their words, so he changed the subject. "What in the devil do you suppose got into Flannery? This time it will mean the loss of his stripes."

Winthrop was watching two men walking together from the barracks nearby in the direction of the corrals. One was Otto Burck, the other one was a massive, stolid-moving man whose uniform was still very blue. He answered the adjutant in an absent manner, and started to move away. "I guess time will tell."

Fessler watched Winthrop for a moment, then turned as his orderly beckoned from over in front of the adjutant's office.

Winthrop reached the mount area moments after Burck and the big replacement got down there. He saw them over near the mule sheds and, as he approached, he heard Burck say: "I didn't call you a liar, Anderson. I simply said that someone else did ride out last night, while you were on the gate."

The large man did not look angry, just very large and capable. "It's the same thing," he retorted. "An' in front of those other fellers."

Lieutenant Winthrop walked up, looking from one man to the other. The mule sheds were where these affairs were normally settled because they were out of sight of most of the other buildings inside the walls. "What is this about?" he demanded sharply. The big man looked dispassionately back and shrugged mighty shoulders. Winthrop ignored Burck. "If you have energy to spare," he told the big recruit, "there are work details to help you get it out of your system."

The big man finally spoke in a faintly sullen tone. "Burck said someone besides you 'n' the sergeant rode out last night while I was on guard duty at the gate. No one did, and that's the same as callin' me a liar, Lieutenant."

Winthrop glanced at Otto Burck, who had told him not more than a half hour ago that a third rider had indeed left the post by the front gate: Pete Burdette. Otto gazed back with no expression.

Winthrop faced the big man. "You are Anderson?"

"Yes, sir."

"Sergeant Flannery rode out."

"Yes, sir."

"Then I rode out."

"Yes, sir."

"And a civilian rode out between the time Flannery left and the time I rode out."

Anderson hung fire, then said: "No, sir. I never left my post and no one rode out except you 'n' Sergeant Flannery."

Lieutenant Winthrop smiled at the big man. "You didn't leave your post, not even to pee, Anderson?"

"Well, yes, but that only took maybe five minutes."

Winthrop continued to smile at the large man. "If someone wanted to leave by the gate without being challenged, he'd wait. That's what happened. While you went over behind the wash house to pee, a man led his horse out, closed the gate after himself, and, when you returned, he was gone."

Private Anderson gazed a long time at Lieutenant Winthrop. He had learned several things about Fort Laramie over the past couple of weeks, and self-restraint was one of them. He finally caved in. "If you say so, Lieutenant, but I sure never saw no one, nor heard no one, and no one come through the gate before I went off duty."

Winthrop nodded about that. "And there is a regulation about fighting, even down here, Private Anderson. Violation means ten days' bread and water."

"Yes, sir. We wasn't fightin'."

"And you're not going to, are you?"

"No, sir."

Winthrop jerked his head. The large man saluted and shuffled back the way he had come. Otto Burck wagged his head and told Winthrop about the earlier fight they'd had, then he said: "But I think I maybe misjudged him a little. He's still green and troublesome, but I think there's hope."

Winthrop ignored that. "Where is Morning Gun?"

"Out back in the sun. He wouldn't even go over and eat."

"Did he tell you where he's been?"

"No, sir. We're friends and all, but only when he wants to be."

"Are you sure about what you told me an hour ago?"

Burck nodded his head. "The horse had rolled and it wasn't so easy to make out whether he'd been rode or not. But he had. The dirt from rollin' was sticking to the sweaty place where the saddle had sat." Burck's blue eyes did not blink. "Maybe a horse could work up a sweat without bein' rode, but a saddle blanket can't. Burdette's was still wet with horse sweat."

Burck stood eyeing the officer for a moment or two, then made an observation. "He's goin' out this mornin' and I'd like permission to shag after him."

Winthrop's interest quickened. "How do you know he's going out?"

"From over at the shoein' shed I watched him right after

he'd eaten. He got busy around his camp, brushed the horse, carried the saddle out back, and tied a ridin' coat behind the cantle."

Winthrop was tempted to turn, but from the mule sheds he would not have been able to see over where the civilian scouts and hunters had their own little private *ranchería*.

"Lieutenant . . . ?"

Winthrop only knew that Otto Burck was a lifer, a seasoned man on patrol and details. He did not want Burck to get caught shadowing Pete Burdette, so he said: "No. I'll get Morning Gun to do it."

Burck protested. "He's dead on his feet, and besides that you can smell him from two hundred feet away. Lieutenant, I've done more of this kind of skulkin' than you know about. I've been in the Army since the Indian skirmishes."

"He'll kill you, Burck."

"Not if he don't see nor hear me he won't, and even then it won't be like bushwhacking someone in the dark. I'll lift his hair if he tries it. Only he won't know I'm within miles of him."

Winthrop sighed. "All right. I've just detailed you to ride out and look the loose saddle stock over Burck, be back before *Retreat*."

Winthrop left the oaken enlisted man standing in shed shade and went in search of Morning Gun. He found him, not quite by smell as Burck had suggested might be possible, but by snoring. Morning Gun was slumped against a hay shock back where he could have been located only by accident, sound asleep. Flies were walking over him with eager anticipation. When Winthrop shook Morning Gun awake, the flies fled in all directions.

The Indian rubbed his eyes and said: "He's hid in some trees. But we can't leave him there very long. It's hot today."

Winthrop sank to one knee. "Where is the hide?"

Morning Gun pointed toward a pile where there were even

more flies, and where wheelbarrow tracks led from the stalls out back to the pile. "Under there. It can't add much to that smell. But we can't leave it there very long, either." Morning Gun picked hay off his stained and soiled clothing. As the officer explained to him that Flannery's friend, Otto Burck, was now involved with them, Morning Gun said nothing, but when Winthrop had finished the Indian looked up. "What about the adjutant?"

Winthrop slowly smiled. "Go up there as you are and report in."

Morning Gun considered that for a moment before getting to his feet, also smiling. As he walked away, the horde of flies flew busily in his wake.

Winthrop got a horse and rode beyond the walls to look for the horse he fervently hoped he would not find. He made a very wide ride in all directions before returning with the heat beginning to make things, including people, wilt. As he was putting up the horse, Corporal Krause appeared to say that the adjutant wished to see him.

He had found no trace of Flannery's animal, which helped his mood. By the time he reached Lieutenant Fessler's office, except for sweat that made him itch a little, he felt better than he had felt since viewing the dead body of Sergeant Flannery. There was one small window in the rear wall of the adjutant's office. It and the door to the outer office were wide open. When Winthrop appeared, Lieutenant Fessler was standing by the window. He turned, nodded, and without moving from the window he said: "The damned Indian just reported in. My God . . . can you smell it? I swear he hasn't touched a bar of soap all year."

Winthrop was sympathetic. "When people live out of doors all the time, I guess it doesn't bother them. Where has he been?"

"In the mountains, something about visiting friends and sick relatives. I didn't know he had living relatives. Somewhere I was told he was raised by missionaries and was an orphan."

Winthrop let that pass. "That's all he had to say?"

"Yes," stated the adjutant from over beside the wide-open window. "I think I convinced him that, whether he thinks so or not, he is under orders just like everyone else on this post."

Winthrop nodded about that. "And gave him hell."

Fessler waved a limp hand. "No. I just wanted to set him straight about a thing we call responsibility, then get him the hell out of here. It's going to take days to air this place out."

As he finished speaking, the adjutant eyed his desk but made no effort to leave the window. Instead, he gestured. "There are the papers you can sign for your transfer. I spoke to Captain Brewster. He said he'd prefer that you stayed, but if you're mind's made up . . . sign them and leave them with Corporal Krause whenever you have the time. Albert, if you take that damned Indian out on a detail, you'd better find a creek."

Winthrop picked up the papers and walked out. He did not stop at the orderly's table to sign them. In fact, he did not even look at Corporal Krause. He went to the officers' wash rack to bathe, then he changed his clothing, and the last thing he did was drop the papers from Fessler's desk into the little wooden box he used for kindling wood and fire-starting paper.

He did not know the northwesterly mountains. In his thirteen months on the post he had only once even come close to them. That had been when he had ridden out with the entire command, under Captain Brewster, for one of the Army's infrequent showing-of-the-colors formations. They had gone to the edge of the foothills, and because there was nothing over there that was likely to be impressed by their numbers and weaponry except perhaps some shy elk, they had turned back.

Now, he went over to the rear porch of the small post hospital and leaned in the shade, looking toward those distant, blueburred heights. He had a hide from the stolen cattle, with the incriminating marks on it; he had a dead non-commissioned officer almost certainly shot from ambush by someone who knew Flannery had suspected the thieves had not been Indians, and who also had reason to fear what Flannery might say on the post; he had the word of Morning Gun that there were more of those cattle up in the mountains, along with a number of miners who had bought the cattle in good faith from men they could very probably identify on sight. Most of all, he could not put off forcing this affair to a head very much longer. Sergeant Flannery deserved an honorable military funeral, and, as Morning Gun had said, the weather was warm. It was very likely going to remain that way, and perhaps get even warmer.

He needed a detail to do what he had in mind. That posed no problem. The post commander was a firm believer in uniformed details making a show of patrolling the area. What he knew he would not get without explaining why he needed it was the post commander's permission to be gone with a detail for a week, and perhaps even longer, and there was no way he could give his reasons without also offering the proof he did not have. Nor was he convinced that if he told his story to the post commander, and got permission to make his reconnaissance in force, that when he returned the people he suspected were involved with the cattle-stealing ring would not have fled. The alternative to doing this correctly was to do it in violation of the Army's regulations. Winthrop leaned on the railing of the little porch along the back of the post dispensary and pondered the probable results of what he was going to do. He was not going to make the Army his career. On the other hand as long as he was in uniform, he was subject to Army disciplinary action, and most probably a dishonorable discharge after serving his time as a prisoner in the stockade. He did not want to remain in uniform, but neither did he want a dishonorable discharge.

A solid set of footsteps on the porch caused him to straighten up from solemn consideration of the far mountains and turn. Private Burck nodded and walked on up, his blouse dark with sweat, his thin-lipped, wide mouth curled in an expression of harsh satisfaction.

VIII

As a lifer, Otto Burck knew when it was, and when it was not, permissible to dispense with the Army's rigid codes of conduct for enlisted men toward officers. This was one of those times when it was permissible, so, as he leaned upon the railing a few feet from Lieutenant Winthrop, and he said: "He went in a beeline to the drover's camp. I'd say the drover and his two cowboys are fixin' to strike camp. They were loadin' a wagon when Burdette arrived. Him and the drover went out a ways to talk. Burdette's been usin' his hands to talk with ever since I've known him, and, while I couldn't get anywhere nearly close enough to hear what he said, he gestured toward the mountains, toward the fort, then he talked like a Dutch uncle for a long time without usin' his hands at all. When he was finished, the drover brought over a bottle and they sat on the ground for the rest of their palaver. There was one other thing. That drover and his riders haven't been at their camp for about a week, maybe longer." Burck's blue eyes fixed themselves upon Lieutenant Winthrop. "They was in the mountains."

Winthrop met the steady gaze. "How do you know that?"

"Because one of them cowboys workin' at loadin' their wagon called over to the other cowboy who was near their cookin' ring to fetch a little sack of rocks he'd got from a miner."

Winthrop leaned on the railing, again studying the hazy mountains. "Anything else?"

"Not much. I let Burdette head back and lay in the bushes for a half hour more. The drover went over to the wagon, and directly him and his riders busted out laughin' about something. Then I got back to my horse and returned. You said to be here before *Retreat.*"

Lieutenant Winthrop leaned in silence for a long time, then turned his head. "I'm going into the mountains," he told the other man. "Without getting permission from Captain Brewster." He waited for Burck's reaction, and, when the trooper simply leaned there saying nothing, Winthrop added a little more. "I thought about taking a detail. The trouble with that is Burdette will see us leave, and maybe so will that drover. I could get around that by leaving after nightfall."

Burck finally spoke. "You couldn't do it, Lieutenant. Details don't ride out after nightfall except for emergencies."

Winthrop smiled at Otto Burck. "You are right, Private. The only thing left, then, is not to take a regular detail, to take Morning Gun and maybe one or two others."

Burck continued to look at the officer. "I guess you know what you're saying, Lieutenant . . . court martial at the very least."

Winthrop nodded his head. "I'm not going to make a career out of the Army, but, even if I was, Sergeant Flannery deserves better than he's going to get from the Army unless I do something about it. Either way, I'm going to be in trouble."

Burck sighed. "You know how long I been in the Army, Lieutenant? Since you was in knee pants. You know how many times I been as high as sergeant, and been busted back to a private trooper? More times than you got fingers on your hands." Burck paused to expectorate lustily beyond the little shaded porch. "It was goin' to happen the same way with Mike because he couldn't shake off being an idealist. He thought everyone, but especially officers, should be downright honest. I know better. By the time Mike would have known what I know, he'd have been busted back a lot of times, too. But you're right.

He was an honest man and deserves a hell of a lot better than the Army's going to give him. Tell you what, Lieutenant. You and me and Rourke could leave in the dark and be two-thirds of the way to those mountains by sunup."

Winthrop knew Private Rourke the same way he knew dozens of enlisted men, by name and by sight, and that was all. Rourke was a wide-shouldered sinewy man with very dark hair and eyes. Lieutenant Winthrop did not know it, but Patrick Rourke was the lanky enlisted man who had not even stirred off his bunk during that savage barracks brawl a few days earlier. What Winthrop did know about Rourke was that he was a dry, shrewd, taciturn, very experienced lifer who was in Otto Burck's category.

Winthrop said: "I'm not even sure you ought to go with me. Rourke doesn't even have your excuse . . . friendship with Flannery. And you mentioned it . . . court martial. Rourke would have to be foolish to get involved in this."

Burck said: "Maybe he won't want to. You said you'd need a couple of men. I'll go, and I'll leave it up to Pat whether he wants to go as well. And, for your information, he was a friend of Flannery. A good friend. All right if I tell him Mike is dead and how he got killed?"

Winthrop nodded unenthusiastically. He was having some early feelings of guilt. "You stand to lose more than you can gain, Burck. How much longer before you are discharged and pensioned?"

"A little shy of two years," replied Burck, straightening up. "Hell, Lieutenant, if I go to the stockade for two years, I can do that much time standin' on my head." He grinned. "I'll go talk to Rourke."

Winthrop said: "Are you on the gate tonight?"

"No, sir, but Pat Rourke is." That amused Otto Burck, so, as he moved away, he was grinning.

The lieutenant crossed to the site where the civilian scouts and hunters had their particular area. It was orderly because the post commander required that, but it was nowhere nearly as orderly as it could have been, and that was no accident. The civilians could be paid off, but that was the worst that could happen, and they knew it. Also, this was the way they showed both independence, and veiled scorn for the Army, mostly for officers.

Burdette was not there, but his pair of saddle horses were, which suggested to Lieutenant Winthrop that Burdette had not left the post. He made a dour guess that Burdette was probably over at the adjutant's office. He and Corporal Krause were friends. Otherwise, there was a squawman named McGuire who could have been a Mexican but who was probably black Irish. There was also a lanky Tennessean named Taylor, who claimed to be a relative of a former President, Zachary Taylor. Winthrop had been out with both McGuire and Taylor, and of the two he preferred the Tennessean who, despite his insistence on a relationship that was doubtful and a slow, languid way of moving and thinking, was a very good man on a scout.

Taylor was sitting in shade doing absolutely nothing. He had watched Lieutenant Winthrop cross the grinder and was ready to smile when the officer walked up to his ramada where horse equipment, even cooking and camp utensils, were scattered in something less than the variety of order Captain Brewster required. The lanky man languidly touched the brim of his old hat and smiled as the lieutenant stepped into ramada shade. He said: "The sergeant ain't come back yet. There's sure a lot of talk going on about that."

Winthrop settled on a rickety bench, shaking his head. "No sign of him yet. There's always talk. I've never seen an Army post where there wasn't talk."

The Tennessean grinned and bobbed his head about that. It

was gospel truth, and that was a fact. "Burdette said him and Mike come near to lockin' horns a couple weeks back when they was out on a detail with you."

Winthrop was not going to feed that story, so that Taylor could feed his own gossip mill. "Mike's always getting someone mad at him," he replied, and leaned back in pleasant shade, gazing away toward the blurry mountains. "Morning Gun came back."

Taylor already knew that. "So I heard."

"Said he was visiting relatives and friends up in the mountains."

Taylor's languid smile lingered but his pale eyes turned shrewd. "Naw, Lieutenant. There ain't been no Indians in them mountains since old Red Cloud led 'em north."

Winthrop leaned comfortably, still peering northwesterly from narrowed eyes. "They could slip back. They've been doing that for years. Maybe just a few, to hunt and make meat."

Taylor's smile remained, but was fading now. "Naw," he said again. "There's too many miners and little raggedy-ass settlements up in there now." Taylor paused, then resumed speaking as he warmed to his subject. "I ain't been up there in about a year, but all the good valleys been staked out and settled. Indians would starve up there. Them miners been killin' off the game until there's hardly anything left. They'd do the same to Indians, if they found any up there."

"Any large settlements?" asked Winthrop in a casual manner.

"A couple, Lieutenant. You never been back in there?"

"No. Just once got to the foothills with a detachment, then we turned back."

Taylor fished inside a torn, not very clean shirt pocket and withdrew a limp brown plug that he offered. "Chew?"

Winthrop declined.

As he used a wicked-looking boot knife to carve off a cud,

the Tennessean said: "There's a settlement called Beeville. It's got the best meadow. Maybe twenty miners work the diggings in the mountains around there. They got a few married men at Beeville, with woman and kids. Then there's a place called Boston. It's about ten miles as the crow flies north of Beeville. The country around Boston is rugged."

"Is there a meadow at Boston?"

"Well, not much of a one, and it's got rocky soil. They say there's been more pay dirt taken out around Boston than any other place up there. Then there's the individual diggings. They're up darn' near every creekbed throughout those mountains, and sometimes those men'll step out from behind a tree and aim a rifle at you." Taylor chuckled. "They're almighty leery of strangers. I was told to be careful of them loners. I run across some of them. Lieutenant, I don't think they're scairt someone is goin' to jump their claim. I think most of 'em are as crazy as a pet 'coon from livin' alone in them mountains for so long."

Winthrop declined a drink from an earthen jug the Tennessean kept in the shade beneath his bench, and wandered back in the direction of the corrals. When he found Morning Gun, the Indian had bathed and changed his clothes. He had even dunked his old hat in a trough and had it sitting atop a post to dry out.

Winthrop sat down to ask Morning Gun about Private Rourke. As always, Morning Gun thought over his answer before offering it. "He came here from Fort Abraham Lincoln. He was a sergeant over there, it was told by Corporal Krause. He came here with no stripes on his sleeve."

"Is he a good man?" Winthrop asked.

Morning Gun pondered that for about ten seconds before answering. "Yes. He's an old hand. He don't waste time and he isn't mean. He don't even say very much, but I've been out with him. Yes, he's a good man." The black eyes slewed around. "Why?"

"Because Burck wants to bring him along when you and Burck and I ride out tonight."

"Where to?"

"Beeville first. Is that where you got the hide?"

"No. I got it north of Beeville on a rocky meadow called Boston. Tonight?"

"Yes. You said we can't keep that hide much longer, and you said Flannery can't be left in his tree much longer."

Morning Gun leaned on a mule-shed wall, gazing at the ground. "Rourke would be worth taking along. And Burck." The black eyes rose to Winthrop's face. "Without leave, Lieutenant?"

"Yes."

"They'll shoot you."

"No they won't. I'm not deserting, just going Absent Without Leave. But they don't even shoot deserters in peacetime."

For a long time Morning Gun studied the lieutenant's profile, then he said: "What time tonight?"

"Midnight."

"You want to bring back the cattle, and, if we can find them, the white men who stole them?"

"Yes. And on our way back Flannery's body," replied Winthrop, turning slowly to return the Indian's gaze. "And anyone we can find up there who'll ride back with us as witnesses against the rustlers. And when we come back, I want to be able to point at that damned drover and anyone else who was involved in the rustling . . . and in Flannery's killing."

Morning Gun dropped his gaze to the ground again. "That's a lot," he murmured. "They don't like Indians up there, and maybe soldiers, too. How do we get out the gate?"

"Rourke has guard duty at the gate. We'll lead a horse along for him." Winthrop studied the Indian's solemn face, then also said: "I'd like you along because you know that country and you know where the cattle were sold off and butchered, but even if we fetch back all we are going up there for, Captain Brewster isn't going to congratulate us. He's a book soldier."

Captain Brewster did not trouble Morning Gun particularly. The worst the captain could do to a civilian scout was fire him off the post. He wagged his head gently. He had to go along for one particular reason. He was the only one who knew where Sergeant Flannery had been hidden in a tree. He said: "I'll be down here when you're ready."

Winthrop showed a wintry smile. "I don't want to get you into trouble any more than I want to get Burck and Rourke into trouble."

Morning Gun almost smiled at that statement. "We're all going to be in trouble. Good thing people can't be crucified any more." He was thinking of the stories with illustrations he had seen during his maturing years at the missionary school. He raised his head so that Winthrop could see the faint smile on his dark face. "I've been arguin' with myself for a year now about whether to stay where I get fed three times a day, and they feed a horse for me, and pay me in silver money each month, or whether to try to be a blanket Indian. I've never been one. Maybe I can't be one. They don't teach you how to live like an Indian at missionary schools. They tell you how unsanitary and bad it was to be like that. But I'd like to try, once, anyway. Maybe when they fire me from here, I'll go up north and make the attempt. Maybe what we're goin' up there to do will have made the decision for me. I'll be down here when you come, Lieutenant."

Winthrop arose, dusted his britches, and sauntered back in the direction of his little log hut. At least Morning Gun had something he wanted to do after the sky fell; Albert Winthrop had nothing. He hadn't even thought about what would come after the sky fell. He just told himself he was going to be responsible for the other three—and that he must be crazy to do what he was committed to.

IX

Private Patrick Rourke was either a fatalist, or an individual without nerves. At any rate he was on the gate with his rifle, wearing his Army-issue coat and making his sweep of the post, back and forth at intervals, when the last light went out around the compound. He halted, leaned aside the rifle, dug beneath a layer of clothing for his tobacco plug, and picked off as much lint as he could see in the moonlight, then bit off a cud and cheeked it. If anyone had been watching, they would have assumed Private Rourke was bored, but he was unique in that respect; he never appeared tightly wound. He spat, stood a moment gazing down in the direction of the horse area, then picked up the weapon and walked back across the big, barred log gate. Upon the opposite side, he spat, studied the heavens, which had been showing increasing moonlight over the past week, then he glanced in the direction of the barracks.

A couple of horses squealed down among the corrals; otherwise, the post seemed dead to the world. There had been a time when the overhead catwalk was manned twenty-four hours a day, but it hadn't been since Rourke had been on the post, and in fact for much longer than that. The fort's importance as an outpost of the nation—of civilization for that matter—had reached its peak more than a decade earlier. Since then it had been sliding toward oblivion. In another ten or fifteen years the Army would probably withdraw the soldiers and let the place deteriorate as so many other forts had done, eventually picked to pieces by scavengers who needed doorjambs, windowsills, hinge and gate hardware, and eventually the old logs for fire-wood.

But tonight the fort was quiet and serene by moonlight, Private Rourke its guardian, until his relief arrived in theory an hour after midnight, except that Rourke and Burck had arranged for another sentry to take over when Rourke rode away. The other sentry was another of the old lifers on the post, and, while being importuned to replace Rourke, had listened, had agreed, then had gazed at the other two with a look of mild reproof; he thought they were going down to the town and get drunk.

Rourke leaned, chewed, and watched for movement down in the mount area. When he eventually saw it, he spat, sighed, hoisted the rifle, and made another march across to the far side of the gate, then grounded the gun to watch as three shadows leading four horses came up from behind the barracks into clear view over by the post dispensary, coming directly toward him. He had a solemn expression as he watched. A man did not absolutely have to be a fool to do this, but it certainly was one of the qualifications.

Burck came first, nodded, and without speaking handed Rourke the reins to a saddled animal. Morning Gun and the lieutenant were already opening the gate. As Rourke and Burck watched, the sentry said: "Hammer will be along in a few minutes. He'll put the bar back up. I wouldn't be surprised if he was over yonder, watching from the shadows."

Rourke started forward in response to Morning Gun's gesture. "If he is, he isn't goin' to believe this . . . an officer goin' out with us."

They did not make a sound, and once outside Burck pushed the big gate closed before mounting and walking his horse in the wake of the others.

Lieutenant Winthrop wanted to be as close to the foothills as possible before first light. He was not especially concerned about someone up in the mountains seeing them—three men in uniform and an Indian—he just did not want anyone from the fort to be able to see them. Of course, if it came down to it, Captain Brewster could put Burdette, or one of the other scouts on their trail. Ordinarily he would not do that, Winthrop told himself. He'd swear and fume and get red in the face, then get busy with the paperwork that would start the wheels of a court martial turning. Captain Brewster rarely rode out any more. Lieutenant Fessler would, if ordered to lead a detachment after the 'deserters,' but George Fessler was not and never had been someone who willingly traded his office, coffee, and stove warmth for riding out.

Lieutenant Winthrop pushed right along. Morning Gun rode with him and said nothing until they had been out several hours, then he simply reined down to a walk. The soldiers could do as they wished.

They, too, slacked off. It was possible to make out mountains dead ahead by then anyway. They would not quite reach the foothills by dawn, but they would be so far away that no one would be able to see them from the fort, not even with Captain Brewster's brass spyglass from the catwalk. There was almost no conversation. They knew where they were going, and why. Beyond that, each of them had his private thoughts to live with.

Patrick Rourke's thoughts had to do with the stunning shock he had felt when Burck had explained about the murder of Sergeant Flannery, where the bushwhacking had occurred, and Burck's personal conviction about why it had happened. Rourke, like the majority of the enlisted men, did not care much for the civilian pot-hunters and scouts. He especially did not care for Burdette; his reasons for this dislike were private, and they were strong even before Otto Burck had mentioned that he thought Burdette was probably the skulking son-of-a-bitch who had shot Mike Flannery.

As for the others, they, too, were dwelling within themselves. For the lieutenant and the pair of enlisted men, the end result of what they were doing was in their view immutable, so thinking about it did no good. Winthrop thought about what was ahead, and he was grim in his resolve. Morning Gun alone among the four men viewed what might lie ahead not as the culmination of something, but the beginning. He removed gloves to blow on his hands and turned toward the lieutenant to say: "We got to angle more northerly if you want to go direct to Boston."

"We're closer to Beeville. We ought to go up there first, then head for Boston if there's nothing at Beeville."

Morning Gun tugged the gloves back on and rode with slack reins watching the foothills march down to meet them. Beyond were the rough, forested slopes leading to higher elevations. He had a vague idea that his mother may have lived up here at some time, but because the people at the missionary school either did not know about that, or would not give him the satisfaction of their information, if they had known, Morning Gun could only speculate. As they entered the rolling lower country, he mentioned his idea to Albert Winthrop, then added something to it. "Most people don't know what it's like not to know anything about your family, your father and mother. It's a bad feelin', Lieutenant, a kind of empty feelin'. Nothin' to hold to or build on."

Winthrop rode in silence for a while, gazing at the Indian, then he made a prescient comment that surprised Morning Gun. "Worse for an Indian. Whatever they had before got destroyed, and that left them hanging between two worlds without really belonging to either."

Morning Gun gazed at the lieutenant, nodded, and rode ahead to begin leading because he was the only one of them who knew which trails to take. Sometimes a person found real depth of understanding where he didn't expect to find it.

They rode against their cantles as the land tipped upward. Morning Gun never looked back or to either side after he cut across a pair of wagon ruts that appeared among the trees from the northeast. This was the winding, bumpy road used by the people up at Beeville on their infrequent trips down out of there. It was a long ride up, and they had covered more miles than horsemen ordinarily covered unless they were in a hurry by the time the sun was climbing across a flawless sky.

It was cool, fragrant, and shadowy in the timber. The farther they traveled, the fewer stumps they encountered. Townspeople and settlers did not go this high to cut winter wood, nor did the people of Beeville have to come down this far because they had thousands of acres of timber around their big meadow. When Morning Gun breasted a gravelly flat ridge where nothing grew but some wind-warped rock pines, he halted, looking dead ahead. The others ranged around him, also looking down across a big grassy meadow where tendrils of breakfast fire smoke hung softly above a number of log houses. To Albert Winthrop, who had never seen one of these hidden mountain settlements before, it was picturesque and peaceful. There were horses and mules grazing on the meadow, along with a few milk cows. There was a narrow, deep, brawling white-water creek running on a kind of dog-leg course from over where most of the houses were, down across the meadow. He sat a long time in silence, and eventually said: "You can *feel* it, no need to own a clock, no need to worry about what someone is doing in Washington, no need to fight or worry."

Otto Burck nodded his head without speaking. Patrick Rourke, who had seen these hidden places before, and who had come from Manhattan Island back East, spat, lifted his rein hand, and was ready to ride on down there. He was untouched.

Morning Gun took the ruts down off the ridge. They sashayed back and forth, which was the way people driving wagons preferred to climb up mountains or go down them; it was easier on the livestock.

Morning Gun looked back halfway down and said: "You better do the talkin', Lieutenant. They most likely haven't had a soldier patrol up here in a long time, and they're goin' to figure that's what we are." He let that sink in, then said something he had told Winthrop yesterday: "They don't like Indians. No one in these mountains does."

Otto Burck spat aside before replying to that. "I'd guess they got their reasons, John. Trouble with hide-bound folks who live to themselves in places like this is that they don't know a hell of a lot about how things are now . . . not like they was ten, fifteen years ago."

Morning Gun faced forward, said no more, and led them on along the wagon road, down the slopes, and around the switch-backs until they came up through a thinned stand of trees to the edge of the meadow. Lieutenant Winthrop thought the meadow had to be no less than three, maybe four hundred acres in size. It was many times larger than it had to be for the number of animals grazing on it. He could guess the reason for that. Up here where snow came early, piled high, and remained until late, anyone owning grazing animals had to put up hay to see them through. Not everyone was equipped to grow hay, and even fewer people liked doing it.

They saw a stocky man out with some horses turn and watch their approach. The stocky man suddenly turned and walked very briskly in the direction of the irregularly spaced log houses. Rourke said—"The fat's in the fire, gents."—and smiled to himself because that stocky man would have run if he hadn't been conscious that the riders behind him would see him do it.

The cabins were all on one side of the meadow—the north

side, which was where the winter sun held longest. There were several geranium beds among the log houses. Winthrop guessed that those would be the residences that housed women. But even the unadorned log houses had a clean, sturdy look. There were several little log barns. Those would have been built by the settlement dwellers who owned the livestock out on the meadow.

Otto Burck looked at the lieutenant with a dry smile. "Rip van Winkle would feel right at home here, eh, Lieutenant?"

Winthrop nodded, and watched men come forth in response to the information disseminated by the breathless, stocky man. A few women came to stand in open doorways, also soberly watching three men in blue uniforms being led by a tall Indian across their meadow. One thing was clear enough; Morning Gun had probably been correct in guessing those watching people had not been visited by an Army patrol in a long while. In fact, the closer Lieutenant Winthrop got to them, the more it seemed that they had not had any strangers up in here in a while, or, if they had, visitors were so rare that everyone turned out to watch them ride up.

He had his scabbarded carbine—Army issue with a trap door and a hammer twice as large as was necessary—and his holstered sidearm. His companions also had sidearms and carbines. Morning Gun was the only one of them who had a lever-action Winchester. As they neared the dusty, grassless place where those miners were standing, Lieutenant Winthrop urged his horse out ahead and raised his right hand. One or two of the miners returned his salute, but most of them simply stood like statues until Winthrop reined up and gave his name and rank, and pulled off his gloves, waiting to be invited to dismount. A large, brawny man with a chestnut beard and a great mass of unshorn hair of the same color made a little gesture. "Get down, gents. If you're of a mind to stay a spell, there's corrals out back. My name is Amos Bonnifield . . . from Kentucky."

They dismounted, and several of the men turned impassive, weathered faces toward John Morning Gun, who seemed not to notice this. Amos Bonnifield pointed in the direction of the corrals, then began to lead the way. The other men, six in number, were joined by a seventh man, younger than the others, and trooped in Bonnifield's wake like downy ducklings following a mother duck. Lieutenant Winthrop saw Rourke and Burck exchange a look from the corner of his eye.

Out back, when they were off-saddling to turn their horses into a large peeled-pole corral, Amos Bonnifield waited until Lieutenant Winthrop had turned his horse loose, then leaned on the corral beside the officer, gazing from perpetually squinted eyes at the horses as they got down to roll forth and back in hot dust to get the itch out of their backs. He said—"We don't get soldiers up here very often, Mister Winthrop."—then he made a sardonic smile. "Last time I saw a lot of soldiers was about the time of Appomattox." The sardonic smile lingered and the squinted, steel-blue eyes rested upon Winthrop's face. "I wasn't wearin' blue, Lieutenant."

Winthrop smiled back. "That was a long time ago, Mister Bonnifield. I had two uncles who didn't wear blue, either . . . but my father did."

With the ice broken—comfortably, Albert Winthrop hoped—he said: "I'm looking for some cattle and the men who drove them up through here a while back."

"How long ago, Lieutenant?"

"About three, four weeks back, Mister Bonnifield. Mostly, I would like to find the men who drove them."

Bonnifield's narrowed eyes did not move. "When I saw you ridin' across the meadow, I figured it might be something like this." Bonnifield straightened up off the corral poles and turned. "You gents most likely wouldn't object to some cold buttermilk." Again Winthrop saw Rourke and Burck exchange a look, but this time the look was easy to decipher. Rourke and Burck were not dedicated buttermilk drinkers. They had been hoping the man with the chestnut beard might have mentioned something a little more fortifying for men who had been in the saddle since the middle of the previous night.

X

Amos Bonnifield led the way toward the front of a large log house, and called for someone named Kate to fetch a pitcher of buttermilk and cups, then he led the way to a large old wooden table beneath a cottonwood tree, and gestured for the men to be seated. Other settlement men lingered, some leaning, some at the big old table, and some content to squat on the ground in cottonwood shade. Morning Gun remained standing. Even after the buttermilk arrived and he was offered a cup, he did not approach the table.

Amos Bonnifield was one of those individuals whose style of life had little to do with the passage of time. He stoked and lighted a pipe, got up a fair head of smoke, then sipped his buttermilk before he said: "About those cattle, Lieutenant. We bought some steers and butchered them." Bonnifield's habitually squinted eyes were fixed on Albert Winthrop, and, when the officer asked what had become of the hides, Bonnifield gave a forthright reply. "We tanned 'em. Livin' as we do, Lieutenant, we make use of just about everything."

Winthrop smiled, mentioned how much he enjoyed the buttermilk, then said: "Could I see one of those tanned hides?"

Bonnifield nodded but made no move to leave the table. "You want to see the mark, is that it?"

"That's it," concurred the officer.

"Was those cattle stolen, Lieutenant?"

"Yes. From the Fort Laramie holding ground, Mister Bonnifield."

That younger man, the last one to join the others when the detail had arrived, got lazily to his feet and turned to walk without haste in the direction of the corrals behind the house they were all sitting in front of. Morning Gun's black gaze followed the younger man as Amos Bonnifield finally shoved up to his feet, saying he had one of the tanned hides and would fetch it.

During his absence a long-faced thin man with hound-dog eyes and a scraggly beard asked the lieutenant how he had known the drovers had brought the cattle to Beeville. Winthrop's answer was not quite the truth, but it could have been. "By tracking them," he said, and the thin man subsided. Around him in the shade the other settlement dwellers looked solemn and thoughtful.

When Bonnifield returned carrying a large cowhide that had been tanned with the hair off, and had a golden, supple texture to it, which meant that among the people of Beeville someone was probably a professional at tanning, the same woman who had brought the buttermilk was with him, and, although Albert Winthrop had glanced at her before, this time, when she helped Amos Bonnifield spread the hide on the table, he looked longer. She had the same chestnut-colored hair as Amos Bonnifield, and she was sturdy, muscular, with a golden tone to her skin. She raised startlingly blue eyes to meet the lieutenant's gaze, and slowly smiled. When he smiled back, she looked elsewhere.

Private Rourke leaned with a big hand and traced out the two brands, one a road brand, the other a rancher's mark, then he settled back on the bench in silence and slowly lifted his cup of buttermilk.

Bonnifield watched the soldiers' faces, and read in them what he thought he might see there. He straightened back with a sigh. "Right brand, Lieutenant?"

Winthrop nodded, raising his eyes from the hide to the big

bearded man. "I'm afraid so, Mister Bonnifield."

A raw-boned, graying man with a hooked nose and twinkling eyes said: "Well, Lieutenant, you're goin' to have to use a stomach pump to get your beef back."

There was a ripple of quiet laughter. Winthrop was smiling when he looked at the handsome girl. She was barely smiling, and was watching him. He shoved back his hat, then gave his head a rueful little wag. "It's not a few steers, gents. We'd like to get the cattle back, but maybe it's too late for that. What we'd like. . . ."

He was interrupted by sounds of battle behind the house. One man was swearing, ripping the words out. Everyone arose and faced around. Amos Bonnifield took long strides, heading in the direction of the scuffling sounds. Lieutenant Winthrop was directly behind him. Farther back, Patrick Rourke and Otto Burck were among the other men. The moment Bonnifield saw the struggling men on the ground near a saddle horse tied to the outside stringers of the corral, he roared like a bear and lumbered ahead. Albert Winthrop had one clear sighting before the big bearded man obscured the view. John Morning Gun was rolling atop that young man who had walked away some time earlier. Morning Gun had a brown fist cocked when Bonnifield caught his arm from behind and whirled him off the younger man.

Bonnifield was an individual of great strength, and right now his beard seemed to bristle. He was furious. The other settlement men ran over to assist the younger man to his feet, then one of them, a short, massive man, lowered his head like a bull and started toward Morning Gun. Otto Burck, who had the same build but was taller and larger, had no difficulty intervening. He caught the shorter man by the back and with a grunt heaved him sideways. The short man went down, dust flew; he rolled over and got up onto his knees, spitting dirt and glaring.

Albert Winthrop turned on the others. He made no move toward his holstered sidearm when he said: "That's enough! Settle down!" He turned toward John Morning Gun. "What happened?"

Morning Gun was dusting himself as he replied. "He come out here to saddle up right after you said the cattle was stolen. He was saddling a horse when I asked him what he was doing. He got mad." Morning Gun straightened around, eyeing the rumpled, battered young settlement man. "All I wanted to know was where he was going."

That bull-like short man was on his feet now. He glared and said: "You damned Indian, it's none of your business what folks do. For two cents I'd. . . ."

Otto Burck pointed a stiff finger at the shorter man. "You're not going to do anything, so shut up and simmer down."

Albert Winthrop was looking at the younger man. Morning Gun's implication was clear to all of them. He said: "Where were you going, mister?"

The younger man stepped back among his friends and turned defiant. "Anywhere I wanted to go, soldier, it ain't none of your damned business."

Lieutenant Winthrop glanced at Amos Bonnifield, and in a quiet voice he said: "I'd like to know."

Bonnifield, still red in the face, looked menacingly back at Winthrop, but no words came for a while, and, when they did, he spoke to the younger man. "Answer, Rufe. Where was you going?"

"Up to my claim is all," muttered the young man sullenly.

"Why didn't you say that?" Bonnifield asked, beginning to look more disgusted than angry.

The younger man's eyes blazed. "I don't have to tell no damned Indian anything."

John Morning Gun walked to a stone trough to sluice dirt off his face and hands; he had his back to the others and did not seem to care what was said behind him. Patrick Rourke went over there, took down the dipper hanging on a peg nearby, and dipped up some water. Quietly he said: "Where'd you think he was going, John?"

The tall Indian was using his shirt tail to dry off when he replied. "To pass the word around the mountains that there was soldiers up here lookin' for cattle thieves."

Rourke did not drink the water; he instead flung it away and replaced the dipper, then sat down casually upon the edge of the trough, gazing at the rumpled young man. He did not say a word.

Amos Bonnifield said nothing, either, but the look he put upon the younger man spoke for him. He turned on his heel to lead the way back around front. As he passed the younger man, he said: "You stay here. Unsaddle that horse, turn him in, and stay where I can see you." As he marched past he said: "Lieutenant. . . ." Winthrop went with the older man back to the big old table with the hide still atop it. The others remained out back, muttering among themselves.

Bonnifield sat down with a great sigh and said: "He helped them with the damned cattle when they was comin' up our road. He was at his mine when they went by. They paid him for helpin' them."

Winthrop remained standing, eyeing the older man and thinking. "Was he going to warn them, Mister Bonnifield?"

"Most likely, Mister Winthrop. Rufe's . . . well, aside from bein' under my feet all the time because he's courtin' my daughter, Rufe's had a little trouble up here now and then." Bonnifield raised squinted eyes. "He's been over to the Boston meadow for a few days. That's where your cattle are."

"Are the drovers with them, Mister Bonnifield?"

"I don't know. I didn't ask Rufe, he never volunteered

anything, and mostly we don't go over there very often, got plenty to do around our own settlement. I might as well tell you, Lieutenant, because I've seen the man a few times over the past ten years or so . . . I don't know his name but he's dark like one of those old French-Canadian trappers who was in this country a long time back. Wears an old scraggly bear-skin coat when it's cold."

Lieutenant Winthrop did not seem to be breathing when he said: "What about him, Mister Bonnifield? Was he with the cattle thieves?"

"He come through here on his way up to Boston meadow lookin' for them. Him and Rufe talked, then this dark feller rode north toward Boston. Lieutenant, I've seen him a couple of times down at Laramie, with soldiers. Maybe you know who I'm talking about."

Winthrop did not say whether he knew the man or not. He said: "If Rufe was going to ride up there, Mister Bonnifield, it would seem to me he knows the thieves are still up there. Does it seem like that to you?"

Bonnifield turned to watch the men straggling back in the direction of the big old table when he replied. "I'd say it's likely, Mister Winthrop."

The lieutenant leaned on the table speaking quietly and quickly, desiring to get something said before all the other men arrived. "Can you keep Rufe here while I ride up to the Boston settlement, Mister Bonnifield?"

The older man faced forward again and leaned powerful arms atop the table. "Yes. But for soldiers to go through these mountains without someone seeing them and carrying the word ahead ain't possible."

Rufe and Morning Gun were with the solemn, silent Beeville man who shuffled back into the shade, and got comfortable there in total silence. Rourke and Burck had cuds they were masticating as they resumed their former places at the table and did not look at anyone. They had thoughtful expressions. Although they were a long way from being greenhorns, they, like everyone else out there at the corrals, had heard enough to have formed suspicions. The atmosphere was strained now. It had never been unguarded, but now it was much more so as Lieutenant Winthrop rummaged for something to say that would be innocuous enough to dispel at least part of the tension.

He had an ally. The handsome big girl with the dark golden chestnut hair came to the doorway of the big cabin and said: "Father, it'll be on the table in five minutes." Then she looked directly at the lieutenant and extended an invitation to eat. He accepted for his detail, and with a decent excuse to leave the table arose and jerked his head. All three of his companions walked back to where that stone trough was to wash. Behind them, watching their departure from guarded faces, the settlement men were silent and grim-faced until that bull-like short man growled his thoughts.

"They never come into the mountains they aren't lookin' for trouble. There's no call for soldiers to be here anyway. All we did was buy some cattle and pay cash for 'em."

No one took up the short man's cause, so he walked stiffly toward a small log house, freshly re-chinked, that had a steep, peaked roof and some large old varmint traps draped from pegs on the front wall.

At the trough Lieutenant Winthrop told his companions what Bonnifield had told him when they had been alone at the table. Morning Gun, rubbing a sore place, spoke cryptically. "He most likely won't be the only one. I told you they don't like Indians in these settlements. I guess I should have told you they aren't happy toward the Army, either."

Patrick Rourke finished washing and shook off surplus water

before offering his thoughts. "John might be right, Lieutenant. Maybe that wasn't the only one who'd try to get up yonder and warn the thieves. I think the answer to that is for us to get up there first. Leave right now."

Otto Burck was thinking of something else. "The only person I know who wears a moth-eaten old bear-hide coat is Pete Burdette. Jesus! If he's in it with the others, he's been able to let them know everything that's been goin' on at the fort . . . like takin' you on a wild-goose chase, Lieutenant."

Winthrop had had the same thought back there in tree shade when he and Bonnifield had been talking. At first he had been shocked. Now, the shock was gone. He dried his face and hands, looked at the others, and groaned aloud. He had led them right into the middle of a genuine and dangerous mess.

Morning Gun, sitting relaxed upon the stone trough, said: "Leave your uniforms here, get some old clothes from these people. Then we leave here about dusk and get up to Boston meadow in the dark."

Winthrop, Burck, and Rourke turned slowly to gaze at the tall Indian. He ignored them to sit watching their saddle animals in the corral.

The handsome big girl with the large, robust figure appeared out back and called to them. Rourke and Burck stood transfixed; they had not noticed her before, but they certainly noticed her now. Winthrop smiled and nodded his head, then led his companions toward the house. The sun that was on its downward slide meant less in open country than it meant in timbered country where tree spires cut it off a couple of hours before it happened down where they had come from on the Laramie plains.

XI

The meal consisted of great amounts of heavy food, thick steaks, bowls of boiled potatoes, grainy home-made bread, and more buttermilk. While the men were eating little was said, only afterward, when they all trooped outside, which was customary because smoking or chewing in a house was not considered to be good manners. Out there, the lieutenant sent his three companions out back to look at their saddle stock, then he faced Amos Bonnifield. "I need your help," he told the large man. "We'd like to borrow some old clothes and leave our uniforms here."

Bonnifield did not look surprised. He stepped to the edge of the porch and perched upon the log railing as he regarded Albert Winthrop. Eventually he said: "All right." It was as simple as that, no question, no argument, no surprise. "I ain't sure it's going to disguise you, what with you fellers riding Army saddles and packin' Army weapons, but all right. You better not wait too long, though. I can keep any eye on Rufe, but I got no idea if someone else from here mightn't have the same idea."

Winthrop agreed. He left the big older man on his porch and went out back to get his companions. He returned to the house with them by the rear door. Bonnifield and his handsome daughter were laying out clothing. It looked large for the soldiers, but without a word they went into another room and changed. The clothing hung on Albert Winthrop, fit Morning Gun fairly well for length, but otherwise fit him like a cracker sack. Rourke rolled up cuffs and sleeves, but only Otto Burck did not have to do much. He looked at the others, then grinned from ear to ear.

When they returned to the parlor, Amos Bonnifield was not there, but his daughter was, and, whether she wanted to laugh at their appearance or not, she showed nothing in her face when she spoke to the lieutenant. "Does your scout know the way to Boston?"

Winthrop nodded his head.

She then switched her attention to John Morning Gun. "Don't take the open trail from here. Go west a mile or so, then parallel the trail."

John nodded stoically. It had not been his intention to use the marked trail, not after what had happened at the corrals, but he said nothing.

The handsome girl went as far as the back door with them, then stood aside as they trooped toward the corral to rig out their animals, all but Lieutenant Winthrop, who paused in the doorway, looking at her. "I'd like to thank your paw," he said.

She brushed that aside. "He's not here. Lieutenant, be forewarned, the men at Boston settlement aren't like us. If there's trouble, they'll all join in. I've heard it said there are fugitives from the law at Boston."

Winthrop smiled. "Thanks for the warning. With any luck we'll back tomorrow for our uniforms. We're obliged to you for your hospitality. Is your name Kate?"

She nodded, watching his face; he knew what her name was.

"Kate, when we come back. . . ."

"I'll have some cold buttermilk waiting," she told him, turned, and went back into the house.

All the way to the corral Lieutenant Winthrop faintly scowled. If she hadn't cut him off, it had certainly sounded as though she had.

His horse was already rigged out. John Morning Gun swung up and turned northward without speaking or glancing back. He did as the girl had suggested; he left the worn old dusty trail and went westerly through the trees, then, with an Indian's infallible sense of direction, he turned northward again. This ruse was still no guarantee of anything. Someone could have ridden away from Beeville while the soldiers had been eating. But, as the officer told himself, it was better to travel this way than to use the main trail, although it might make it a little difficult if there were ambushers up ahead.

They encountered no one and were kept occupied picking their way around mammoth old deadfalls that a horse could not jump over, as well as stands of trees so closely spaced they had to split up and meet beyond them, and, as they rode, the light down upon the forest floor began softly to fade.

Morning Gun stopped them once, handed his reins to Burck, took his carbine, did not say a word, and walked ahead through the timber. The others dismounted to wait, standing in silence to pick up any sound, leaning on their saddle guns. It was the first time since arriving in the mountains that they were aware of real peril. That scuffling back at Beeville had not been like this at all.

The forest was without a sound. Even the birds were silent, if they were overhead. Rourke and Burck exchanged a guess. "John didn't like the stillness," one said, and the other one confirmed this idea. "It's not natural this time of the evening."

They were both correct. Lieutenant Winthrop left off listening and turned to watch their horses. At first the animals simply stood patiently, but after about fifteen minutes they threw up their heads, little ears pointing in the direction Morning Gun had taken, and the lieutenant gestured for Rourke and Burck to seek cover. He did the same, then the three of them waited, hands on weapons.

Morning Gun reappeared soundlessly, Winchester in the crook of one arm. When the soldiers walked out, he waved a hand rearward. "Been a bear up there tearin' bark off the trees for grubs." He dropped the carbine into its saddle boot and without another word mounted and struck out again, but now he angled more to the west, his idea being simply not to have their saddle animals pass through an area where the rank smell of a bear lingered. Even so, the horses were nervous.

They passed down across a grassy glade, keeping to the ring of forest on its east side, and pushed on up to the opposite crest. Up there, Morning Gun abruptly halted and sat motionlessly until Otto said: "Cookin' fire." Then the scout nodded, and swung off once more, handing Burck his reins. As before he took the Winchester with him. But this time the shadows were firmly settled before he returned. He squatted beside the horse and said: "There's some cattle on the Boston meadow about a mile and a half ahead."

Otto had a question. "What about the smoke?"

Morning Gun, who had been about to mention that, held up one hand with four fingers and his thumb extended. "Five men at a camp up there." He lowered the hand and gazed steadily at the lieutenant. "Pretty dark, hard to make them out."

Winthrop also had a question. "Burdette?"

Morning Gun's reply was a little slow coming. "Maybe. Like I just said, it was hard to make out much more than that there's five of them loafing around the fire. They're cookin' sage hens, and they got a bottle." He paused, which was his custom. The others waited, their eyes on his face. Morning Gun looked steadily at the lieutenant. "I know one of them. It's that drover who brought the cattle up to the fort."

For a long moment no one commented, not until Morning Gun also said: "The other two are maybe his riders. I guess the others might be men from the Boston settlement. But those cattle are the same kind of stock that was delivered to the post."

Winthrop was standing at the head of his horse when he spoke. "How far?"

"Maybe a mile and a half, like I said, Lieutenant."

"How close can we get?"

Morning Gun was arising to his full height when he replied.

"They're out near the middle of the meadow by a creek. We can't get any closer than the trees on this side until after full dark. Even then, it's a long way to crawl."

Winthrop gestured. "Take us as close as you can," he said, and stepped up.

From this point on they rode in silent single file, like Indians, being careful about noise. The gloom was thickening. If there was to be a moon tonight, there was no sign of it down where they were riding. Only the smoke scent grew steadily stronger to indicate they were getting closer.

There was a thick, very massive low roll of mountainside to be crossed before they could see the meadow. Morning Gun did not take them up and over it; he instead went eastward until the slope tapered away, then he rode westerly again. The idea of crossing that unforested hill even at night had not appealed to him. He thought they were safe, but after what had occurred at the corral back yonder, he preferred being extremely careful.

Albert Winthrop thought about the man called Rufe, too, and something Bonnifield had said about there perhaps being others back at Beeville who might try to warn the cattle thieves. He had never been in action before. He had been trained for such a condition, but it was not the same. Certainly, under the present circumstances, it was not the same. This time, the Army was going to be outnumbered even if nothing serious happened. He glanced at Otto Burck, then at Patrick Rourke. They were riding with their heads up, eyes moving. Obviously they were not as green as he was at this kind of an affair. Winthrop's lips tightened a little. This was not an Army affair. In fact, if the Army knew where he was and what he was doing, quite possibly it would send a strong detachment after him, which meant that win or lose he had enemies in back as well as in front. If that wasn't enough, he now knew he and his companions were in an area where soldiers were not particularly admired. Finally, if what the handsome big girl with the beautiful hair had said was true, up ahead they were going to face people who were likely to be even more hostile than the settlers had been back at Beeville. He looked again at the pair of enlisted men. They were chewing, peering through the gathering late dusk, and now they had carbines balancing across their laps.

Morning Gun raised a hand, stepped down, and wordlessly went in search of a tree to tie his horse. The others followed his example. When they came forward, the Indian used his Winchester to point with. "To our right down where the trees end, you'll see their fire."

With that said, he struck out, and, because this was a forest with the usual clutter of rotting limbs, underbrush, and treacherous footing, he moved slowly, frequently looking back to watch the soldiers. If someone fell or was tripped by a root, it would not be heard out where that fire was, but he did not want it to happen. A sprained ankle or injured knee was nothing they needed at this point.

The fire burned like a red jewel out through the trees, visible a great distance. Upon the far side of it a fair distance, there were other lights, lamps showing through cabin windows. The smell of wood smoke was stronger when Morning Gun finally stopped, leaned upon a shaggy-barked old fir tree, and waited for his companions to finish their study and speak. It was a long wait. Lieutenant Winthrop wagged his head. There was only one way to reach that rustler camp: by crawling through the grass, which was tall enough to provide shelter at night, but during the daylight hours no such attempt would have succeeded.

"At least a mile," he observed.

Morning Gun said nothing.

Otto Burck spat and turned slightly to study the more distant log houses. "I don't mind wearin' out the knees of my britches," he said musingly, "but I'd hate to get about halfway and have some damned dogs start raising hell when we're too far from here to get back."

Morning Gun was realistic about that possibility. "Up in a place like this, dogs bark at something every night. Bears, lions, even skunks and raccoons." He paused, still watching the distant fire. "I don't think we can catch them without a fight." Winthrop turned to look at the Indian's profile. "If that's the drover and his riders," murmured Morning Gun, "we got to make a complete surprise, or there's going to be blood. I've seen those men at the holding ground. They're experienced. They've been up a lot of hard trails."

Burck jettisoned his cud and met Patrick Rourke's gaze. Burck made a tight little grin. "You're crazy to be up here," he said softly, and Rourke agreed with that while resuming his study of the distant fire. "You're dead right. You're crazy to be up here, too."

Lieutenant Winthrop had heard little of this exchange; he was speculating about how far across that open meadow they might be able to ride before they would have to start crawling. Patrick Rourke scotched the idea accidentally when he said: "We couldn't ride out there anyway. No place to tie the horses."

Morning Gun hoisted his carbine and looked impatiently at the officer. Lieutenant Winthrop said: "Walk. We won't have to start crawling for a ways yet."

Morning Gun obeyed, eyes fixed upon the fire. Winthrop was correct. Even though the moon was now rising, and it was fuller than it had been last night, there was one of those typical mountain shades of blackness that seemed not to be limited to the heavily forested uplands; it also spread an aura of sootiness part way across open meadows such as the one Morning Gun was crossing now, with the other men around him. They saw humps to their right, which were bedded cattle. Morning Gun led the way well away from that area so as not to arouse the animals, and they almost walked into another bed ground where cattle had caught either their sound or scent, and were staring, ready to spring up. Some of the animals arose before the danger of two-legged things being close really posed a threat.

Morning Gun waved an arm, then sank to the ground. The others followed his example. They remained flat and still for a long time before Morning Gun left his Winchester in the grass and started to snake-crawl. Lieutenant Winthrop scowled, but kept silent. They watched the Indian until the backgrounding humps of bedded cattle obscured him, then they simply waited. There was no hurry to reach the rustler camp anyway.

Morning Gun came crawling back after a while, and sat up. "Same brands," he told Lieutenant Winthrop, and gestured. "Maybe ten, fifteen head that I could see."

Winthrop acknowledged this with a dry comment. "Good thing we got here when we did . . . the figure missing as I heard it was thirty head."

As they arose to start forward, the bedded cattle sprang up, but they did not run, they stood poised to though, until even the smell of the two-legged creatures was faint.

XII

They halted when a distant bark of coarse laughter reached them. Lieutenant Winthrop thought they had covered more than half a mile, but in such light the only way he could arrive at any figure at all was by the nearness of the fire. He looked at his companions and Otto Burck grinned, then groaned and got down on all fours. The others said nothing. Now the lieutenant took the lead. He had to stop often, because, although this meadow looked smooth, it had small, sharp rocks all over the upper layer of soil. It was hard on hands and knees.

They had the fire as their beacon. The more distinct it became, the more encouraged they were, and the next blast of laughter sounded clearly. They halted eventually when the lieutenant thought they might be in rifle range. This time, he put into words what had been forming in his mind since the last halt. "When I signal," he told Burck and Rourke, "you two go west and come down upon them from out there. Morning Gun and I will keep going from the south." He started crawling again before the others could say anything. Finally it was possible to make out individual outlines. There probably had been five men at the rustler camp when Morning Gun had scouted it earlier, but now by the lieutenant's count there were seven men, and that made him halt again after only a few yards, and turn back to his companions. Patrick Rourke had made the same tally and shook his head at the officer. "Big odds," he said, "even if we surprise them."

That was true. It was also very possible that, if the rustlers had been drinking, that they would not yield even though they might be caught by surprise. Morning Gun sank low upon the chilly ground. "We wait," he announced. "Those other men must be from the cabins. Maybe out here to drink whiskey with the rustlers."

There was no alternative, unless they cared to take a long chance. Albert Winthrop sat flat down with his carbine in the grass, and examined his knees. One trouser leg was worn through and the other one would be worn through if they had to crawl much farther.

They got as comfortable as they could, with cold mountain air closing in upon the gravelly valley. The men at the fire were warm, recently fed, and had some whiskey. There was quite a contrast between the two groups. Rourke smacked his lips and Burck grinned. A drink of that whiskey would go a long way right now toward dispelling the cold. Lieutenant Winthrop sat gazing in the direction of the fire, but when he spoke, it was about something that had nothing to do with getting warm.

"I think Bonnifield's daughter doesn't like soldiers," he said.

Burck and Rourke exchanged a wide-eyed look. Morning Gun, who had been watching the camp, turned his head slowly. None of them spoke until the lieutenant spoke again. "There is a lot of that, but if it wasn't for the Army out here. . . ."

They waited for him to finish. Instead, he sat perfectly still with his head cocked. It was Morning Gun who said: "There is a rider comin' from behind us."

Burck twisted to look back. He had already decided who that would be. "Someone from Beeville. Likely the one they call Rufe. I hope to hell he didn't see our horses."

The distant rider was moving at a slow lope. If he had found their animals and had turned them loose to set the soldiers and their scout on foot, they were not in an enviable position. Otto did not think the oncoming rider had found their horses. He told them that without giving his reason for saying it. He was listening. When he spoke again, it was to make a suggestion. "We can't shoot him, and we sure as hell can't outrun him."

Lieutenant Winthrop looked toward the fire, then in the direction from which the rider was approaching. It seemed unreasonable to believe the horseman was not heading straight for the fire. If he were indeed from Beeville, abroad this late on a cold night and aiming toward the fire, it was very likely that he had left his settlement to get over here and warn the rustlers about an Army detail being in the area, asking questions about stolen beef. He arose, left his carbine in the grass, and walked back the way they had come to this spot. As he moved past the two enlisted men, he said: "Cover me. I'll meet him out yonder. If it is someone from Beeville, I'll try to get him before he recognizes me."

No one moved to go with him, or to speak, but all three men watched him walk out into the ghostly night. The only distraction was the whiskey-inspired noise over at the camp where someone pitched another couple of logs onto the fire, and sparks rose wildly for almost a hundred feet into the air. What made the interception possible was something Lieutenant Winthrop had not even thought about. He saw the rider, finally, saw that his course was straight for the fire, and moved across to intercept the man. He drew his Army issue revolver, held it slightly to the rear, and moved swiftly.

The horse saw Winthrop before the rider did. The horse would have shied but the rider had a strong hand on the reins and swore when the animal would have moved away from Winthrop. They were face to face at about fifty feet when the rider finally let up on berating his horse and looked toward the fire. What he saw was a man standing directly ahead of him, smiling in the star shine. The man raised his left hand and continued to smile as the horseman dropped to a walk and came right on up.

When they were close enough to each other to make out more than a ghostly shadow, the rider drew back to a halt, then leaned on his saddle horn, looking down at the smiling man wearing the outlandish, too large clothing. He did not recognize Lieutenant Winthrop in time. The naked six-gun rose slowly until it was pointing directly at the rider's middle chest.

The rider was flabbergasted and did not move. From the opposite direction came another burst of loud laughter. Evidently the cattle thieves and their guests from the settlement had made quite a dent in their whiskey supply.

Lieutenant Winthrop cocked his weapon and said: "Get down."

The rider swung to the earth and stood at the head of his horse, staring. He finally recognized Lieutenant Winthrop, but his mouth still hung slackly. What had completely fooled him had been Winthrop's attire, the one thing Winthrop had forgotten about until this moment when he saw gradual recognition spread over the man's face. He ignored the success of his capture, and why it had been so easily accomplished. He told the rider to disarm himself, and, after that order had been obeyed, Winthrop told the man to lead his horse and walk ahead. Winthrop did not have to tell him when to stop.

The moment he saw the other three men, each one aiming a cocked belt gun at him, the man stopped. Behind him the lieutenant dryly said: "I guess Amos Bonnifield didn't do a very good job keeping tabs on this son-of-a-bitch."

They told him where to sit, and Morning Gun took his horse and, without a word, stripped it and turned the animal loose, then stepped over the saddlery in the grass and put up his six-gun as he and the man who had attacked him back at Beeville looked at one another. Private Rourke holstered his weapon as the lieutenant moved closer to face the young man Bonnifield had called Rufe. Not a word was said. The captive appeared to sag against the ground; he seemed sure of his fate. Otto Burck walked behind the prisoner and swung his pistol barrel in a short chopping motion. Afterward he looked at Albert Winthrop and softly said: "That was too damned close. Did Bonnifield deliberately let him come over here?"

Winthrop turned from the slumped body, shaking his head. He did not believe Bonnifield would do such a thing, but he did not put it into words.

Over at the fire several men were on their feet now, completely oblivious to the grim affair that had transpired within their hearing. They were all talking loudly at the same time. Two of the men started walking away in the direction of the distant log houses. There were only two lighted windows over there now. As they strode away, one of the cattle rustlers called after them, and the other men at the fire laughed.

Morning Gun turned toward the lieutenant, waiting. Burck and Rourke were also waiting. Winthrop faced the distant campfire and, after a long moment, gestured for the two enlisted men to go around to the west. As they were moving away, Morning Gun leaned over the unconscious man, flung away his six-gun, and stepped over him. He and the lieutenant then went ahead a yard or two before dropping to the ground to crawl.

At the fire a man arose, complaining of the cold. His back was to the officer and the scout. He had a blanket around his upper body that he carried with him as far as a pile of saddlery carelessly flung down. Over there, he dropped the blanket, knelt, and worked with his back to the men watching from several yards southward in the grass. When he finally arose with a cry of satisfaction and turned back toward his friends at the fire, he was struggling into a moth-eaten old bear-skin coat.

Lieutenant Winthrop lifted out his Colt and held it as he started forward very slowly. Beside him a few feet on his left, John Morning Gun kept abreast. They were protected less by grass now, than by the blinding flames of the renewed fire, which was in the faces of the cattle thieves. The rustlers had lost all their earlier exuberance. They were tired men, as well as being half drunk. One spoke and the others ignored him until his voice lashed out in anger, then someone answered him.

"What difference does it make? Even if one of 'em was to figure he might make some money ridin' down there and tellin' the Army about us an' their god-damn' cattle, they wouldn't get up no detachment before we could see 'em comin' for ten miles." This same garrulous voice then posed a question. "Sam, what's the good of goin' back after the damned wagon anyway?"

The angry man had a strong Southern accent. Burck, Rourke, and Morning Gun recognized it instantly. Only Lieutenant Winthrop did not know the drover.

"I'll tell you why we're goin' back after the rig 'n' the team . . . because I'm not about to give them Yankee bastards nothin'. Not even one lousy blanket."

The voice was thick and slightly hoarse. The other rustlers

seemed unwilling to press this dispute and silence settled again. At this moment there was a solid sound a few yards to the west of the camp that even crackling wood did not obscure. The rustlers turned instantly, each one of them reaching for a weapon. Half drunk or not they were as deadly as rattlesnakes.

Lieutenant Winthrop swore in a harsh whisper and raised up onto his haunches, swinging his Colt to bear. Someone out there, either Burck or Rourke, had stumbled over something and had fallen heavily.

Morning Gun raised a hand lightly to the officer's arm. He was as motionless as stone, seemed to be holding his breath. Morning Gun was playing a hunch; he had seen how the outlaws had reacted, but did not expect shooting. There were animals out there, too.

It was a shrewd guess. The man with the pronounced Southern accent subsided with a scornful snort. "What's the matter with you? A damned cow is out there. You seen 'em when we was makin' camp, didn't you?"

His companions put up their weapons and looked into the fire, too humiliated to speak. The Southerner bore down on them. "Ain't nobody up here to bother us, for Christ's sake. If they'd been comin', they'd have done it a week or more back. Pete? You still scairt of this place? You hearin' things, too?"

Burdette's broad back, broader inside his old bear-skin coat, was hunched toward the fire. He did not reply.

The Southerner showered scorn on them. "You act like a bunch of damned redskins. Where is that bottle them boys brought out here?" Someone held a bottle aloft. The Southerner snatched for it. "You believe that crap about ghosts?" He paused long enough to swallow three times and put the bottle aside as he struggled to catch his breath. "Green whiskey," he panted. "Green as a damned gourd. Pete, that story you told us . . . look at them boys, they're scairt stiff. Ghosts, for Christ's sake, you idiots, there ain't no such a thing as ghosts. Pete, you made that story up, didn't you?"

Burdette did not move but he answered. "I didn't make it up. I could show you the grave."

The Southerner scoffed. "In the dark? Like hell you could."

"In the dark," stated Burdette. "That was a long time ago. There wasn't no settlement up here then. I told you . . . they didn't call it Boston Meadow then."

"Yeah," replied the Southerner, his voice thick with contempt and ridicule. "Yeah, Pete, you told us, they called it Ghost Meadow back in them days." The Southerner laughed and tossed the bottle over to Burdette. "Drink, Pete." He laughed again. "Didn't you never hear that ghosts won't have no truck with fellers who been drinking?"

Burdette tipped back his head, then passed the bottle to the man nearest him, on his left. He spat lustily into the glowing fire and looked at the Southerner. "I buried her not three hunnert yards from this very fire, along with her pots and all, then I got on my horse and never stopped again until I was in southern Canada. You want to know why I came back?"

The Southerner had his six-gun in his lap, wiping it when he answered. "Naw, I don't want to know why you come back. I just want to know that we can get back to the holdin' ground before sunup, hitch up the wagon, and get the hell out of this lousy cold country." He stopped wiping the gun and raised his face. Red firelight flickered across it. Morning Gun leaned to whisper. "That is the drover. Are you ready?"

Lieutenant Winthrop did not answer because one of the other men spoke first. "Hell, what are you talkin' about? We can't get back down to the fort before sunup. Not even if we had wings, we couldn't."

The Southerner turned on the speaker, gripping his polished six-gun. "We can, boy, because we got to. Either that, or we set around up here another day, and there's no blessed reason to do that. They paid us for the rest of them cattle, we done collected from off Fessler, give him an' Krause their cut, and now it's time to get on downcountry. You understand me, boy?"

The man who had spoken picked up the bottle instead of replying, and Burdette, who seemed to rock slightly from side to side as he stared into the fire, softly said: "Buried her not three hunnert yards from here with her best smoked tans on, with her iron pots that she treasured, and I made a little fire and prayed into the smoke, then. . . ."

"Shut up, Burdette," the Southerner said harshly. "You an' your god-damned ghost. You made all that up."

"It's the truth, every word of it."

"You're lying. All right, what was her name, Pete?"

Burdette answered so softly the name barely reached out where the lieutenant and the scout were listening. "Her name was Snow Blossom. She was a Crow woman."

XIII

When Lieutenant Winthrop turned to jerk his head, indicating he was ready to jump the rustlers, he was held motionless by the peculiar look on the face of his companion. Morning Gun was staring at Pete Burdette's back as though incapable of moving his eyes away. His entire body was rigid in the cold night gloom. He remained like that for almost sixty seconds, then very slowly faced the lieutenant without changing expression or speaking. Winthrop softly said: "Are you all right?"

Morning Gun continued to stare from unblinking eyes and did not answer. Lieutenant Winthrop frowned; he was certain Burck and Rourke were very close by now. He brushed the sleeve of John Morning Gun. "What is it?"

Finally the Indian let his breath out in a long, uneven rush, and picked up his carbine from the grass. He was ready, he told

Lieutenant Winthrop, in a voice as rattling dry as old cornstalks.

Winthrop looked ahead, then back. He was troubled by the very sudden change in his companion. The reason for his uneasiness was because he did not want to have someone beside him when trouble arrived who for some inexplicable reason could not function properly. He caught Morning Gun by the arm with a gentle shake. "What is it?"

The Indian was gazing in the direction of the five huddled men at their diminishing fire and shook his head. All he said was: "We better move."

Winthrop drew back, still studying his companion, then, as he heard a faint sound from the west, he swore in a whisper and started forward, looking back just once to make certain the tall Indian was with him. He was, pushing his saddle gun through grass and moving without a sound, black eyes fixed upon the lolling cattle thieves.

Lieutenant Winthrop halted within six-gun range, waited for sound off to the west, did not hear anything, and raised his six-gun, looked around at Morning Gun, then cocked the weapon as he called ahead toward the lolling man.

"Not a move! Keep your hands in plain sight!"

It was like jabbing a rattlesnake with a stick. All five of those men seemed to rise from the ground without effort and hurl themselves as far from the firelight as they could, and, as one man landed rolling frantically, he snapped a shot in Winthrop's direction. Two seconds later someone shouted at the man with the gun, then fired twice, very fast. The shooter had been out to the west somewhere, in the eerie darkness. The shooter had hurled himself in that direction before firing toward Lieutenant Winthrop. It was his last earthly mistake.

Gunfire erupted with furious flashes of muzzle blast. Winthrop dropped down and crawled to his right. He heard Morning Gun's carbine firing with an almost rhythmic series of shots.

Rourke shouted from the west, the words indistinguishable, but the meaning clear enough. There were more attackers in that direction. Someone panicked on the far side of the dying fire, sprang up, and fled toward the distant, darkened log houses. For an interval of silence nothing happened, then someone fired a handgun from the northwest, and the runner went down screaming. The noise stopped when other rustlers fired in the direction of that deadly handgun to the northwest.

Lieutenant Winthrop crawled to the east, trying to get around the fire up in that direction, which was where that Texan or whatever he was had been sitting polishing his six-gun and making mean remarks to his companions. Winthrop had already decided the Southerner was one of those people who got disagreeable after drinking. More than that, he had heard every word the Southerner had said, particularly about Lieutenant Fessler and Corporal Krause. He wanted that Southerner alive, and, as he belly-crawled, one of the rustlers bawled at the top of his voice that he'd had enough. What happened next no one ever afterward explained. A hoarse voice answered the cattle thief, telling him to stand up without his gun. Before the man got all the way up, someone shot him. He fell without a sound.

There was so much noise and confusion that what had been an act of deliberate and calculating murder went unnoticed as long as the battle continued. It was until long afterward that someone from the Boston settlement put it all together, detail by detail, and by then it was too late. The killer was never identified.

Winthrop heard that rustler try to surrender, and he heard a gunshot, but at the same time he saw vague movement up ahead where someone was beginning to push backward to get farther into the darkness, and Winthrop changed his own course to make an interception. The grass was badly trampled near the rustler camp. Winthrop could see the moving silhouette increase its rearward pace, and raised up to aim. Someone yelled a warning, then fired. Winthrop felt roiled air pass his head. He was dropping low when he fired—and missed. But the retreating man had discovered now that someone was after him personally. He rolled over, fired, kept rolling, and fired twice more. He was desperate.

The lieutenant felt a bee sting over his left shoulder, then slippery moisture, but the pain did not last more than a couple of minutes. He rested his gun fist upon his other hand against the ground, and fired. The rustler who had been trying to escape made a guttural roar, raised up, hurled his empty six-gun, and launched himself behind it straight at the lieutenant. Winthrop had one moment to catch sight of a greasy, contorted, brutal face in the moonlight, then the rustler landed on him.

Lieutenant Winthrop clubbed twice with his handgun and missed both times. His attacker was not only desperate, he was wild. His strength was almost overpowering as he struggled to right himself and lunge for the lieutenant's gun wrist. But Winthrop understood the deadly fury of his opponent, threw the six-gun overhead behind him, and brought the right hand back forward in a fist. He hit his adversary squarely between the eyes, but with only enough power to make the rustler blink, then duck his head to protect his face. Winthrop arched his back with all his strength and dislodged the rustler. Before clawing hands caught his clothing, the lieutenant rolled twice and sprang upright. The rustler was on his haunches, ready to arise when someone yelled from a considerable distance, his voice deep-rolling like a growl of a large bear.

Winthrop moved ahead quickly. The rustler was a thick-shouldered, deep-chested man with a physique that tapered to a small waist and saddle-warped, spindly legs. He threw up a thick arm as Winthrop came in fast, swinging. The rustler raised his head behind the protective arm, small, enraged eyes peering from under thick bone. Winthrop did not let up. His attack was fast, his aim improved as he kept swinging, and, when the rustler finally brought up his other arm and Winthrop hit him hard in the unprotected parts, the rustler snarled a cry of pain, and lunged ahead. The lieutenant swayed aside, aimed his right fist high, hit the rustler slightly behind the ear, and the man with the gorilla physique dropped to both knees, dazed but still dangerous. He wagged his head and turned cautiously to see where Winthrop was—and caught the full force of a hammer blow that dropped him without a sound.

Otto Burck spoke from fifteen feet away. "Don't shoot him. That's the drover. We need him alive."

The lieutenant did not have anything to shoot with. He watched Burck walk over, drop to his knees, and systematically truss the unconscious drover using the man's own two belts. Burck went about this without a trace of agitation. When he finished and arose, Lieutenant Winthrop had gone in search of his six-gun. He was walking back, holstering the weapon when Burck eyed him steadily as he said: "We got two dead ones. This here son-of-a-bitch and Burdette is what's left. But Burdette don't look real good." Burck cocked his head, then joined the officer in turning northward. There were lighted windows over among the distant log houses, and much closer there was the unmistakable sound of men approaching. The battle of Boston Meadow had not gone unnoticed.

Patrick Rourke walked up, reloading as he approached. He had a fresh cud and turned aside to expectorate, then dropped the weapon into his holster, and joined the other two in facing toward that sound of approaching settlement men. He said: "This is goin' to be like walkin' on eggs, Lieutenant. Me and Otto better fade back and stay out of sight in case they're comin' out here loaded for bear."

Winthrop turned toward the older man. "Where is John?"

Burck jerked his head. "Over yonder on the far side of the fire with Burdette. Pete caught one. Lieutenant, that's quite a mob of those settlers."

Burck was correct. The approaching settlement men were not entirely visible yet, but it was possible to make out that, even walking briskly in a tight formation, there were at least ten or twelve of them, all with star shine reflecting off the weapons in their hands. They were walking right up; the battle was over, there had been no gunfire for ten or fifteen minutes, but, as Albert Winthrop watched them stamping directly toward the dying firelight, his training told him that no Army officer would ever lead men the way those men were being led. He looked around. Burck and Rourke were gone. The bound man at his feet made a choking groan deep in his throat, and feebly struggled. He was coming out of it, but it would be a while yet.

Lieutenant Winthrop moved toward the fire, but to one side of it, and saw a dead man lying on his face, one leg cocked up over the other leg. He was shocked, but it only lasted a moment.

Among the band of armed men approaching the fire someone called out: "What the hell's goin' on out here? You there by the fire . . . who the hell are you?"

Lieutenant Winthrop walked slightly toward the settlers before halting to face them. On his right some distance away he could see John Morning Gun sitting on the ground beside Pete who had been propped up.

The settlement men came up and halted, some with rifles in both hands, some wearing only boots, britches, gun belts, and the visible upper part of their long-handled underwear. Lieutenant Winthrop considered their faces with a feeling of calmness. He told them who he was. He also told them who the rustlers were. He did not elaborate and the silence after he had spoken was not broken until a man with unkempt brown hair pointed to the dead rustler behind Winthrop and said: "Is he done for?"

Winthrop nodded his head. "They all are, but two. Pete Burdette and a man lying over yonder tied with his gun belt and his britches belt."

Winthrop's calmness seemed to have an effect upon the angry settlement men. They stood dumbly for a few moments, looking at the wreckage of the camp with its dying fire and its one visible corpse, then several of them walked westward a few yards, and found another dead man. Now the confusion began subtly to change. Two men walked up to Lieutenant Winthrop and glared at him. One spoke harshly. "You ain't no soldier, not dressed like that. You snuck up here to rob these fellers. Where are your friends?"

Before Winthrop could reply one of the several other settlement men who were over near John Morning Gun, called over. "This here feller is an Indian." Their surprise, followed by swift movement away from the light, infected the others. Several voices called out in alarm about Indians. The men facing Lieutenant Winthrop grabbed him and pulled him with them away from the fire, clumsily pushing him ahead as a shield.

A small-boned man with a high forehead and strange, gold-flecked eyes came over to remove Winthrop's holstered Colt. As he did this, he gave the other two men a curt order that they obeyed without hesitation. He said: "Let go of him. Scatter out. See if those corpses have been robbed." As the two settlement men moved off, the lithe man gazed at Winthrop with his head slightly to one side. "You got any idea what happens to renegades who lead Indians against settlements in these mountains, mister?"

Winthrop answered shortly. "There is one Indian. He was the scout for us."

"Who is us, mister?" demanded the small man. Winthrop ignored the question. "Did you buy cattle from these men?"

The lean, lithe man kept his head slightly to one side and did not answer the question. "I asked you who the other fellers is, who come up here with you, mister. Let me tell you something. In these mountains we got laws and we hang renegades. Now then, for the last time . . . who was with you?"

"Soldiers," said the lieutenant.

The lithe man's odd-colored eyes did not waver. "Where are they, mister? You should have run when your friends did."

Lieutenant Winthrop answered slowly. "No one ran, and these men stole cattle from the Fort Laramie holding ground." He pointed. "That one lying tied on the ground, bring him over here, and we'll see who is lying."

"Mister, you come up onto our meadow to kill folks, and your friends run off and left you. Where is your horse?"

Winthrop had no chance to reply. Morning Gun called to him. He turned, and the lithe man prodded him with a six-gun. Winthrop looked down, then up at the man's face. For a moment they stared at one another, then Morning Gun called again, so Lieutenant Winthrop turned and started walking toward Morning Gun. The smaller man tracked him with a gun barrel, but did not fire; he instead followed Winthrop.

Pete Burdette was bundled in his old bear-skin coat. His hat had been crushed under his head to make a support. His eyes went to Lieutenant Winthrop's face and remained there as Morning Gun raised one side of the coat. Winthrop leaned to look, then straightened up slowly. Blood was pumping out of ragged hole in Burdette's thick body. Morning Gun said: "It hit him from in back, Lieutenant."

Winthrop sank down in the flattened grass. "Why did you shoot Sergeant Flannery?" he asked the still, ruddy face whose eyes were still on him.

Burdette did not open his lips.

Winthrop had another question. "How much money did the

drover pay Lieutenant Fessler and Corporal Krause?"

Burdette remained silent, still staring at Albert Winthrop. The settlement man put up his six-gun and leaned down. Softly he said: "Pete? Who is this feller?"

Burdette finally spoke, but his voice was fading. "Lieutenant Winthrop from Fort Laramie."

Winthrop leaned closer. "Pete . . . did you bushwhack Sergeant Flannery?"

The fading voice came softly: "Yes."

"Why?"

"Because he knew . . . he knew."

"And so did Fessler and Krause, didn't they?"

"Yes. Fessler . . . watched out for us . . . Fred Krause . . . kept the accounts . . . to show the cattle was delivered . . . and paid for."

"How long has this been going on?" the lieutenant asked.

". . . Four, five years . . . since they come to the post."

"Pete, did they know this drover before he brought up the cattle?"

Burdette's eyes wavered, settled upon Morning Gun, and, when next he spoke, it was as though only he and John Morning Gun were there. "I can't show you . . . not now . . . but it's out there. She's out there. I know she is . . . I came up here now and then . . . she never spoke to me . . . but there are old-timers around . . . they saw her . . . they told me they had . . . they saw some of the others, too . . . I told you, John . . . it was where I wanted to bury her . . . it was a sacred place . . . it's always been . . . a sacred place . . . I never knew you was alive . . . John, bury me up here . . . about a couple hunnert yards straight west of here . . . will you . . . ?"

Morning Gun nodded gently, sitting in silence.

Lieutenant Winthrop straightened up to his full height looking at the man in the old moth-eaten coat. The slow shock of final realization hit him hard; it was the answer to that odd look he had seen on Morning Gun's face an hour earlier. John Morning Gun had not been an orphan. *Pete Burdette had been his father.* The *voyageur* who had fled with his grief after the death of John's mother, and who had returned many years later as a scout and hunter for the Army. Could he have found out what had happened to his child after all those years? The Indians were gone, scattered among hide-outs in the mountains or on reservations. He might have been able to, if he made a sincere effort to, but he hadn't, and that, Winthrop told himself, was something he may not have wanted to know. Right or wrong, Burdette was going to take that with him.

The lithe settlement man turned as several of his companions came over. Before they could speak, he shook his head and led them away, out of Winthrop's hearing.

John Morning Gun looked up once, and looked down again without making a sound. Lieutenant Winthrop turned to depart and John said: "He is dead."

Winthrop knew that.

"I want to bury him here."

The officer replied quietly. "Yes. And hide the grave, John."

"I think I shot him, Lieutenant."

Winthrop shook his head. "That wound was made by a six-gun, not a carbine, John." He turned to walk over where the lithe man and several of his friends were talking. They became silent at his approach. They looked at him from expressionless faces until the lithe man said: "We didn't know them was stolen cattle, Lieutenant. The last thing we'd have done was buy critters stole off the Army. There hasn't been no soldiers up here since I've been here an' we got no desire to have 'em come up here."

Lieutenant Winthrop gazed at the smaller man. He was sure of one thing; he had just been lied to. Right at this moment he didn't care. He turned, facing southward, and raised his voice. "Otto, Pat! Come on up!"

The settlement men turned, as did the fine-boned man with the unusual eyes. So did other settlement men over by the fire where they had placed the dead rustlers face up, side-by-side.

Rourke and Burck did not approach from the south; they appeared in dying firelight from the north, carrying their carbines and looking stonily at the men who were watching them. The lieutenant said: "One of them was Pete Burdette. He's over yonder with Morning Gun."

Otto Burck grounded his weapon and gazed over where the Indian was still sitting on the ground. Then he looked back as he said: "Is Pete dead?"

Winthrop nodded.

Burck thought about that briefly before also saying: "What do you want to do now, Lieutenant?"

"Head back to Beeville."

"Now, in the dark?"

"Yes. Take the prisoners with us, including that one you knocked over the head."

"The dead ones, too?"

"Yes."

"Burdette . . . ?"

"No. Morning Gun is going to bury him up here. I'll explain that on the trail."

Patrick Rourke who had been silently listening up to this point made a protesting statement. "Lieutenant, we got to wait for daylight. There's no way to drive them cattle through the timber in the dark."

Lieutenant Winthrop answered that shortly. "Leave 'em. If the Army wants 'em, they can come up and get them. Lieutenant Fessler and his orderly were ringleaders in the rustling ring. I want to get back to the post."

Rourke spat aside, looked around into the faces of the men standing like statues, listening, then blew out a gust of breath and hooked the carbine in the crook of his arm and said: "I'll go bring up our saddle animals." As he walked away, the lithe man addressed Albert Winthrop.

"Lieutenant, what would you have thought if you come onto someone dressed like you are, out here on our meadow shootin' men?"

Lieutenant Winthrop did not answer; he gazed back over where Morning Gun was sitting motionlessly with the beginnings of a new day paleness outlining him, then went over where the settlement men had brought Rufe, whose hair was matted with blood, and who was sitting on the ground near the fire with his head in his hands, and where the other man who had been knocked senseless was also sitting, his face sickly gray.

The drover did not look up when Lieutenant Winthrop halted in front of him and said: "Burdette is dead, along with your hired riders. I counted five of you around the fire when we sneaked up behind Burdette. Where is the one who was sitting near Burdette?"

The Southerner lifted his head, forehead creased. "There wasn't no one sittin' beside Pete," he said. "The firelight fooled you. There was Pete, my two cowboys, and me, that was all, after those boys from the settlement left us. Just the four of us."

Winthrop held the drover's gaze. "I counted five."

The drover's reply was vehement. "Mister, there never was five of us. Not after them fellers from the settlement left us. What's wrong with you? There was me an Pete an' my two riders. That adds up to four." The drover held up four rigid fingers. "Four. You think I wouldn't have known if there was someone else up here, settin' near Pete, for Christ's sake? You didn't see no one else . . . all right, what did he look like?"

It had been dark everywhere except within the ring of the

fire. Winthrop had had firelight in his face. He had had difficulty seeing any of them, but there had been someone sitting not far from Pete Burdette. Suddenly he remembered something. When Pete had finished drinking from the bottle this drover had handed him, Pete had ignored the silhouette sitting beside him to hand the bottle to a man farther to his left. *Pete had not known anyone had been sitting beside him, either!*

Lieutenant Winthrop stood, gazing into the contorted face of the baffled drover a moment longer, then turned to go over where Otto Burck was talking with several settlement men. When he came up, one of the settlement men, old and grizzled and gray as a badger but with bright, intense pale eyes, smiled and said: "We didn't mean no harm, mister. It was just that we been visitin' back an' forth with them fellers for a couple of weeks and when all the shootin' started . . . well, you can see how it would be." The old man spread his hands, palms downward. "We bought them cattle fair and square. Ask the drover. He even give us a bill of sale."

Lieutenant Winthrop watched the old man's lined, wrinkled face without hearing much that the man said. When the words ended, he took the older man gently by the arm and walked out a way with him, then released his arm and turned to ask how long the old man had been up here on the rocky meadow.

The older man laughed a little self-consciously. "I rendezvoused up here before there was anything. I built the first cabin and made the first sluice box lookin' for gold nuggets."

Lieutenant Winthrop said: "Were there Indians around here in those days?"

The old man's smile faded. "Indians! Yes, sir, mister, there was Indians up here. By God, they liked to scairt me off a dozen times, stealin' my horses, smashin' my sluice with boulders."

"But they didn't attack you?" asked Lieutenant Winthrop, and the old man rolled his eyes. "They couldn't do that, mister.

Y'see, this here meadow was an ancient burial ground to 'em. They das'n't commit no killin', not even of game, in a sacred place."

"What did they call this place?"

"Ghost Meadow. Well, mister, in their language it didn't really mean ghost, it meant a spirit, but they're the same, ain't they? Anyway, I never believed that kind of crap no more'n you would."

Winthrop had one more question. "You never saw ghosts up here?"

The old man's eyes crinkled in amusement. "No, and neither did them Indians nor anyone else. That's a lot of hogwash."

Otto Burck came over to say Pat was returning with their saddle animals.

XIV

The sun was climbing by the time Lieutenant Winthrop's cavalcade rode out of the timber behind the peeled-log corrals of Beeville. They were seen the moment they got clear of the trees. Word spread fast; by the time they had reached the corrals Amos Bonnifield was back there with several settlers.

Not a word was said as the horses carrying the living rustler and his dead companions were tethered in shade. Bonnifield watched Burck and Rourke pull Rufe from the saddle, turn him toward Bonnifield, and give him a rough shove.

The big older man with the chestnut beard glared through a moment of silence, then said: "Get out of my sight!" Rufe wasted no time in talk; he scuttled away, avoiding the looks of the other settlers. Then Bonnifield walked up where the drover was standing with both arms tied behind him, and said: "You lied from beginning to end, didn't you?"

The drover looked sullenly at Bonnifield without speaking. The large older man turned his back on the drover and gravely considered the dead men hanging limply over their saddles, belly-down and hatless, then he said to no one in particular that there were no cattle alive worth what they had cost everyone, and turned his perpetually squinted eyes toward the lieutenant. "Where is your Indian?"

Rourke and Burck, who had been told the story on the ride to Beeville, waited for the officer's reply. All Winthrop told Bonnifield was that they had left Morning Gun back on Boston Meadow to bury Pete Burdette, and the older man's brows shot upward. "Pete was one of them?"

Winthrop nodded, saw the handsome big girl approaching, and before she got back there, he told Amos Bonnifield that he and his men would like to change back into their uniforms. Bonnifield nodded as his daughter came up beside him, a faint frown on her face. "Lieutenant, you've been hurt. There's blood on your shoulder."

Winthrop smiled tiredly. Except for that sharp stinging sensation when the bullet had singed his shoulder, he had not been conscious of the injury. Anyway, it was little more than a scratch; blood always made an injury appear worse than it usually was. He said: "I'll owe your pa for ruining his shirt."

She saw no humor in the words and, reaching for his arm, said she would care for the injury, and led him in the direction of the house. Rourke and Burck exchanged a look.

Amos Bonnifield said they should be fed, and helped them care for the animals, and also helped them chain the drover to the corral, then led them over to the house.

Kate was brisk and efficient at cleansing wounds and bandaging them. There were four other women at Beeville; each of them had also been required to learn how to care for injuries. Lieutenant Winthrop sat stripped to the waist as the handsome girl worked on him, as silent as a rock. She finally stepped back to see his face and said: "You look very tired, Lieutenant."

He was in fact tired, so he nodded.

She then said: "And it was a terrible experience." Again he nodded.

The third time she spoke, she was moving in close again to finish the bandaging. "I understand your silence, Lieutenant."

At that incorrect statement he twisted to look up at her. "I doubt that," he told her. "The reason I have nothing to say is because I don't think you like soldiers . . . or maybe this particular soldier."

She took a backward step to meet his gaze. "Why do you think that, Lieutenant?"

"Because the last time we spoke you cut me off and closed the door."

She regarded him for a moment, then said: "Lieutenant, I had a beef roast in the oven and I could smell it beginning to burn. That's why I hurried back to the kitchen. And I didn't close the door on you. It's habit up here because of the flies."

They remained motionless, looking at one another a moment longer, then she stepped close again and completed tying the bandage as she said: "I don't know enough about soldiers to like or dislike them . . . and that also applies to you." She leaned to wash her hands in a pan of warm water. He watched her thick mane of hair tumble forward, saw the strain put upon her blouse as she leaned, and looked elsewhere only when he heard her father bring Rourke and Burck in through the parlor to change back into their uniforms. She straightened up, drying her hands and looking at him. "You need rest," she said briskly. "I'll hang a blanket over the back bedroom window and you can sleep. I'll see that your men are looked after . . . Lieutenant?"

"Yes."

Her eyes moved a little and color rose into her face. "It would be nice if you'd stay for a few days," she said, then turned her back on him and became busy at the stove.

Later, when he was bedded down in the darkened back room, he lay back thinking of all that happened—and the handsome big girl. When he slept, his last conscious thought was of her.

Burck and Rourke declined beds indoors and went back by the corrals to rest in fragrant tree scent. They re-chained the prisoner so that he, too, could lie down if he cared to.

Someone, probably Amos Bonnifield, had covered the dead men with a large old stained tarpaulin and had turned their horses into the corral where they were eating hay.

Otto Burck lay back on soft fir needles. "Old Brewster's jaw will hang slack when we ride in, Pat. And when he finds out Lieutenant Fessler and his orderly were up to their armpits in that cattle stealin' operation, he'll be fit to be tied."

Rourke, lying comfortably a couple of yards distant, was more pragmatic. "The hell with Fessler and Krause, and all the rest. Otto, if we was smart, we'd bury these uniforms and go so far away the Lord himself couldn't find us."

Burck scowled. "That's desertion."

"You dumb Dutchman, what do you think Captain Brewster's goin' to call what we did? Even if he says it's just bein' off the post without permission, that's good for a month in the stockade, then a court martial. Do you like bread and water?"

Burck hitched around until he was lying on his side with his back to Rourke, then he said: "It's a toss up . . . bread and water or the damned buttermilk these folks pour into a man every time he sets down."

Pat Rourke thought about that for a while before he said: "I wish we'd brought that bottle along those bastards was drinkin' out of around the fire."

Burck fidgeted irritably. "It was empty. They had two bottles, and they was both empty. I looked for 'em. Now shut up and go to sleep."

"Otto!" exclaimed Rourke as though he had not heard the admonition. "I always wanted to find me one of those big-built girls with hair like that and. . . ."

"If you don't shut up, I'm goin' to stomp the waddin' out of you. That big girl wouldn't give you the time of day. You seen how she looked at the lieutenant."

Rourke said no more, but he did not close his eyes for a long time, either. By the time he, too, slept, one of the settlement men came hurriedly to the Bonnifield house to drag Amos out front and raise a rigid arm. "This time it ain't just two or three, Amos. I've seen 'em ride like that before, an' any time they got one of those little swallowtail flags out front, it means there's an officer along. Look at 'em. There's got to be a whole damned company of 'em."

Amos stood motionlessly, his narrowed eyes fixed upon the line of soldiers crossing the meadow. His neighbor was right; it was at least a company of soldiers; they had bedrolls and carbines and three pack mules in the drag, while out front was a lanky, slouching civilian, whose bronzed face beneath a disreputable old hat was lean and watchful. The command was not hurrying as it reached the middle of the valley and kept right on coming.

The officer was a few yards behind his scout, and in advance of his column. He was a large man, portly, and red-faced as though this kind of thing was something he had not done in a long while.

And it wasn't. In fact for Captain Brewster, whose custom was to relegate undertakings of this nature to his junior officers, it had been a very long, tedious, and tiring ride. In order to reach Beeville, where he had never been before, he'd had to leave a warm bed in pitch dark.

The heat was mounting, too. His outrider was the lanky Tennessean named Taylor. Captain Brewster had wanted Burdette, but the adjutant had said Burdette was off the post. He had recommended Taylor in his place.

Taylor had been to Beeville a couple of times before, but not recently. He did not have to rely on his memory to find the place; Taylor was a good tracker and Winthrop had left a lot of fresh sign.

Taylor dropped back beside the captain to offer a suggestion. "I could lope on over there first. Looks like quite a bunch of those miners, Captain."

The idea irritated Captain Brewster. "You just stay in point position," he said, then puckered his eyes to study the gathering of settlers over in front of one of the larger log houses. If the men he wanted were not here, he was going to be more than just disappointed.

Taylor raised a hand when the column was no more than two hundred yards out. The response was not enthusiastic; only a few of the waiting miners returned the salute.

Captain Brewster spoke aside to a sergeant, then pushed his horse ahead, passed the scout, and reached the area of tree shade out front of the log house where there was a large old table. He nodded to the silent men nearby, and swung to the ground, began tugging off his gloves, and ranged a bold gaze over the settlement men, decided the large, impressive individual with the chestnut beard was probably as good a man to address as any of them, and introduced himself. He tucked the gloves under his belt and sat down at the old table. "I'm looking for an Indian and three soldiers, one is a lieutenant."

Amos Bonnifield had twice been affronted, once when the portly big officer had dismounted without being invited to, and the second time when the portly officer had sat down at his table, again without an invitation to do so. Amos walked slowly ahead and halted, gazing stonily at his latest guest. "And what might you be lookin' for those gents for, mister?"

"Captain," said Brewster, meeting Bonnifield's gaze, "Captain Brewster. What is your name, sir?"

"Amos Bonnifield, mister. Why do you want those men?"

Brewster reddened. He replied as the column arrived and was dismounted by its sergeant. The men stood with their horses in hot sunlight, watching their officer and the big older man with the thick beard. "I want them," stated Captain Brewster, "for desertion, for stealing government horses and weapons, and for abandoning the post."

Bonnifield thought about that. "Anything about cattle?" he asked, and saw the portly officer blink. "Cattle? What are you talking about?" Bonnifield was silent a long time. What he remembered of the Army helped clear his mind; officers relied on adjutants; adjutants were not always reliable. In fact, in the old Confederate Army, adjutants in Amos Bonnifield's experience had not been reliable at all. He said: "Do you want to talk to your lieutenant, mister?"

Captain Brewster shoved up to his full height. He was not a patient man, unless things were going reasonably well, which they were not at this moment. His face darkened. "Do you have him here?"

"No, I don't have him, but he is here. Come with me . . . and, mister, there's not enough room out back at the corrals for all those horses, but at least there is shade."

He stood waiting. Captain Brewster turned, barked at his sergeant, then turned back, darker in the face.

The little crowd of settlement men parted for them. Captain Brewster ignored them and went up onto the porch where an immensely handsome large woman was leaning in the doorway. He nodded gallantly as she stepped aside. Inside, the log house was ten degrees cooler than the yard. Bonnifield led him through two sparsely furnished rooms and opened a door, beyond which was near darkness and a man who had been

119

awakened on the bed, struggling to sit up before the sleep had left his mind.

Captain Brewster stepped closer, and stared. Lieutenant Winthrop swung feet to the floor and stood up. He said: "Captain. . . ."

Brewster felt the presence of the big man in the doorway behind him as he said: "Lieutenant, you are under arrest."

Winthrop accepted the announcement without even shifting his eyes. "All right," he replied quietly. "Would you like to hear my side of it?"

Amos Bonnifield dragged in a chair and shoved it forward for Captain Brewster to sit upon. Brewster ignored this indication of courtesy as he replied to the lieutenant: "When we get back to the post, Lieutenant. I have a full company outside."

Winthrop smiled a little wanly and sat upon the edge of the bed. "Not when we get back," he said. "Here, Captain." He began a long recitation. Amos Bonnifield left them alone, but returned a half hour later with two crockery mugs of cool buttermilk. Captain Brewster looked up, accepted one of the cups, thanked his host, but did not raise the cup. He watched Lieutenant Winthrop drain his cup and put it aside. Captain Brewster finally spoke through stiff lips. "I just can't believe that of Fessler, Lieutenant."

Amos Bonnifield interrupted. "Captain, your sergeant is outside jumpin' from foot to foot. He wants to tell you about the dead rustler and the prisoner, I expect."

Brewster leaned to place his cup gently aside. "Tell him I'll be along shortly . . . and thank you, Mister Bonnifield." After Amos had departed, the captain arose and paced to the back wall, speaking from over there without turning. "Fessler, for God's sake. He's an *officer.*" Then he wheeled about. "Are you sure you can prove it, Lieutenant?"

"Yes, sir. We have the drover. I heard the man say he had paid

Fessler and Krause."

"Burdette, too? He told you he killed Sergeant Flannery?"

"Yes, sir."

"Jesus! In my command. There will be an investigation. Damn it, Lieutenant, why didn't you come to me the moment you suspected something? Have you any idea what this will do to my record?"

"Captain, if I'd come to you, you wouldn't have listened . . . and George Fessler would have found out."

"Jesus! Lieutenant, I want to get back. When you're dressed, come out back." Captain Brewster reached the door before he remembered something. "Where is Morning Gun?"

"He'll be along in a few days, Captain. And, sir, Burck and Rourke and I don't like the idea of the stockade and a court martial."

Brewster's brows dropped. "What does that mean, Lieutenant?"

"It means, sir, that in your report you could say that you authorized what we did under cover, because you suspected there was cattle stealing going on."

Brewster gazed at the younger man for a moment before speaking. "It would never work, Lieutenant. Army investigators are very experienced."

"In that case, Captain, I doubt that Rourke and Burck will go back with you. And I certainly won't. Captain, if we've been called deserters, we can't be called anything worse if we really desert."

Brewster reddened again. "I told you, I have a full company out there, Lieutenant."

Winthrop met that threat head on. "And you'll have a battle on your hands, sir, in which Mister Bonnifield and some of the other settlement men would likely join in, if you take us back under force. A massacre of settlers would look a lot worse than this other thing."

Brewster's grip on the wooden latch was like steel. "Nobody threatens me, Lieutenant . . . did you hear me?"

"Yes, sir."

"All right, Lieutenant. No charges. My God, I'll crucify Fessler and that damned orderly of his. Are you ready to leave?"

"Yes, sir."

Out back Rourke and Burck were surrounded by sweaty soldiers. They were enjoying every minute of it. When the two officers appeared, some of their cheerfulness departed, to be replaced with sober looks of uncertainty. Captain Brewster passed orders to his sergeant for the company to be mounted. While this order was being relayed, Winthrop strolled over to Burck and Rourke and told them there would be no charges. They went at once to find their horses and rig them out. Lieutenant Winthrop turned and saw Kate Bonnifield in the rear doorway. He went over to her and smiled. "Thank you for everything, especially for the bandage."

She regarded him a trifle pensively. "You are welcome. Will you ever come up this way again?"

"I would like very much to, if I was welcome."

"When, Lieutenant? You would be welcome."

"Next week," he said, smiling a little more assuredly up at her.

"Can you do that?"

"Nothing can keep me from doing it, ma'am."

She smiled into his eyes. "I'll keep watch across the meadow."

He went back to his saddled horse, swung up, held her eyes until the side of the house cut them off, then took his place up beside Captain Brewster. Far back, with the pack animals, Rourke and Burck rode with their prisoner, and the dead men. Out over the meadow sunlight shone like new gold.

Morning Gun never returned to the fort. Nor did any of the

men down there who had known him ever see John Morning Gun again.

★ ★ ★ ★ ★

The Last Gun

★ ★ ★ ★ ★

I

They took the old man out under a leaden sky with a chill wind blowing down off the Tetons and hanged him. The earth was frozen on top and slushy where rain had drenched it three days before, like soft-falling tears. Not many spectators were at the hanging. It was because of the cold and the wind and the fish-belly day, folks said, but that wasn't all of it. In fact, that probably wasn't it at all, because Wyoming folks were accustomed to cold, biting wintertime winds off the mountains. They were used to the bitter, frozen earth and the leaden skies. It was because, in their hearts, the people of Winchester Junction had no heart for it. The old man perhaps had to die. At least the law had proclaimed that he had to, but folks didn't hold wholeheartedly with that kind of law. They never had in the earlier times when murder begot murder, and mostly they didn't hold it to be so now, either.

The old man climbed those plank steps erectly, and he afterward shook his head when Sheriff Logan stepped up with the rope and the black hood. He hadn't said a word, but he'd looked out of his frosty old proud eyes and stared down Tom Logan. He didn't need a black hood to hide his face in; he hadn't done a wrongful thing. He didn't need any ropes, either; he wasn't going to fling up his arms in supplication. Not Old Man Barton. He'd spent his long life in the service of the soil, had learned early how to winnow sickness out of a newborn calf or the wildness out of a mustang's heart. He'd learned well in the service of the soil: Nature took her blessings and her vengeance in equal parts. Old Man Barton had done the same. He was a gentle old man, big and raw-boned, powerful as an ox and oaken in his stance against wrong, against evil, so they hanged him for taking vengeance exactly as Nature had taught him to take it.

The wind whistled through his mane of coarse white hair and Preacher Benedict, standing below with the Book clasped in bony hands tightly against his bony ribs, had gazed in awe, for the old man up there, looking down his scorn, his contempt, showing the full dull fire of his righteousness, seemed like a prophet of old come to his end at the hands of evil, brought low by the jackals of his own tribe in their struggle out of Egypt.

When the trap door had sprung, making its solid thunk in the gusty cold, Preacher Benedict felt a faintness. He heard the solid drop and sudden tearing halt of Old Man Barton's body and could not bring himself to look.

There weren't any more people out back of town where the bleached old scaffold stood than the law absolutely demanded. Sheriff Tom Logan, his deputy Pert Whipple, Preacher Ezra Benedict, undertaker—and liveryman—Will Clampitt. The law demanded three witnesses and one hangman to make it legal. As Tom Logan climbed unsteadily down to peer beneath and be sure the old man's neck had been broken, he wondered just what the law would do if there hadn't been anyone there but the hangman. Hang the old devil over again?

"Cut him down, Pert," Tom Logan said, straightening up to swing his arms and keep the circulation stirring. "He's all yours now, Will. Crate him up and plant him."

"Yeah?" called back the undertaker-liveryman thinly, his long-jawed, hatchet face getting blue with cold. "And where do I collect m'money, Tom?"

But Sheriff Logan was already shuffling away. Preacher Benedict went with him as far as the corner. He said, where he halted: "*God's* will be done, Sheriff. I don't know why he refused to let me say the words for him."

Logan twisted half around showing his darkly mustached, broad, unhandsome face with its small wintry eyes. "You don't, don't you," he growled. "You sanctimonious old faker, you. That wasn't God's will bein' done back there. That was this lousy town's will bein' done. Now I'm going up to the saloon for a big belt of corn likker, and, if I was you, I'd go home and do the same. Good afternoon to you, Preacher. Good afternoon to you!"

There was a rind of hard frost where water stood in the roadway, making a dirty whiteness. Up north of town where the huge, hulking Teton Mountains stood lay dirty clouds halfway up. Above them, immutably ancient and eternal, the peaks were mantled in purest white. The sky was like lead, like oak smoke on a dark day, like the sky would undoubtedly be on Judgment Day, swollen and utterly still and lowering. So close a man could almost reach up and touch it.

Will Clampitt's rickety old rig came grinding along over the crusted roadway bearing Old Man Barton to the dank livery barn where he'd be nailed down firmly into his pitch-pine box to lie cold as ice and stiff until the ground thawed enough for his grave to be dug south of town where potter's field was. There was a lawned-over cemetery over east of town but those lots sold for cash money; they had finely etched and curlicued markers of hewn granite. The *good* people slept out there. Potter's field was also called Boot Hill. Not because it was on a hill, it wasn't; it was in an undesirable place that flooded winter and spring, land no one wanted. It was called Boot Hill for a simple enough reason. The men who went into that soggy earth died with their boots on, died violently as Old Man Barton had died. Hanged, yes, but mostly those unknowns out there had died with gun flame around them, and, while folks recalled their various, violent passings from time to time, they didn't know which grave was which any more, because Will Clampitt's inexpensive wooden crosses rarely survived more than one or two fierce Wyoming winters. Anyway, since nearly all those graves out there belonged to drifters, gunfighters, outlaws, or renegades of some kind or another, no one admitted ever being related to them even if they were related. Mostly, though, no local people even knew those strangers.

But Old Man Barton was different. They all knew *him*. Not a man or woman in Winchester Junction lived or breathed who hadn't known Old Man Barton. It would have been impossible *not* to have known him. He'd been in the Winchester country, as he'd had a habit of saying with a twinkle, since the Great Spirit molded the Tetons, since the first Indian buck rode onto the foothills northeast of town, threw back his head, and bawled out his challenge to the white skins.

Maybe he hadn't actually been around *that* long, but he'd been there when the first log houses had been cobbled together because the other oldsters vividly recalled him in those days, a tall, raw-boned man with a chest like a barrel and arms like logs, who acted more Indian than white, with a droopy old notched feather sticking out of his hatband and a fringed, smoke-tanned soft buckskin scabbard over his gun, riding a big black horse with slit ears in the Crow fashion, and smelling like a hundred campfires.

There were legends, too. Folks remembered them. Some of them were almost beyond credibility, but then, unless other men had lived close to the earth like Old Man Barton had lived, they couldn't have the greatness of spirit to comprehend, or for that matter, even to believe. But, when you killed a man, you had also to kill his legends. It wouldn't do to have those great old stories still kicking around because they made an awkward pause every time they came up. Some stranger was sure to ask—whatever became of this Barton? We hanged him, you had to say, and immediately you felt the chill settle; you felt the incredulity of the stranger and there was no genuine defense against it. What kind of a man didn't kill in defense of his own? What sort of a legend would Old Man Barton have been if *he* hadn't killed like that? No kind of a man at all, and in your heart you knew it to be so. And yet when he'd killed, you'd hanged him. So, you had also to kill the legends. But there was one thing you couldn't kill. The spirit—it walked the roadways when the icy blasts came down from Old Man Barton's beloved Tetons. It rattled the shutters and sighed under the eaves. It walked out upon the frozen tundra and frightened livestock. It left its place in Boot Hill and set the town hounds to wailing at the scudding sky and at the cold, big, old, sightless moon.

"A man," Old Man Barton had once said to Tom Logan in the last good summer they'd known together with the sap running strong and the earth yielding up its emerald wealth, "a man don't quit this world with his last breath. He takes his leave a little at a time, sort of like leaves tumbling from the trees in the fall, one at a time, like the blades of grass curling up one at a time ahead of winter. A man's spirit waits just a little while, Tom, because all the things that a man has been, has lived through, trail along, and none of that can just tear itself away and disappear because a man's drawn his last breath."

So, Old Man Barton's spirit lingered. Logan heard it in the sharp tinkle of falling icicles as it passed by. He saw it in the gray smoke rising above Winchester Junction in the leaden, winter nights when darkness came swiftly. He felt it around him a dozen ways, and once, when he was entirely alone after the New Year in his log jail house, he poured a glass full of whiskey, and he lifted the glass, saying: "When spring comes, you'll likely be gone, but there's something you forgot, that day we talked. A man's spirit doesn't really leave altogether until everyone who remembers him goes, too. Here's to the better days. Here's to the craven hearts in this lousy land . . . may they have their damned sleepless nights!"

Tom Logan was a bachelor. So was Will Clampitt down at the livery barn, but there the similarity ended. Will Clampitt was over six feet tall, built like a fence rail stood on end and had an Adam's apple that jerked up and down like a turkey wattle. It was just about that red, too. Logan was shorter, broader, and rounder. He was a bulldog of a man in appearance. Generally he was like a bulldog in other ways as well. When he had something to say, he said it, like when he told Preacher Benedict he was a sanctimonious old fraud. He'd meant it. Every word of it. But still, as people whispered, it had been Tom Logan's hand that had pulled the pin that dropped the trap door under Old Man Barton, so he remained exactly what he'd been all his life—controversial.

It had been just ahead of Christmas when they'd hanged Old Man Barton. It had been just after New Year when the worst blizzard of the year came crashing down over the range and town from the Tetons, burying everything under layers of beautiful snow. The Junction was like a graveyard. Cattlemen stayed out on their ranches anxiously to break ground ahead of wagons laden with hay. Coaches didn't run because drifts across the stage road got to be, in some places, six to eight feet deep. Even the usual wagons heading up into the mountains from town with woodcutters didn't try it.

Not that there was any real danger to the folks at Winchester Junction. There wasn't. They'd been through blizzards before, and usually before October was out they had cord wood racked up under eaves around back, inside woodsheds, and even in barns, to last them through if they never split another piece. Food was plentiful, also. The Junction had three general stores, all well stocked, all thriving. It also had the same number of saloons—three—so a man's innards could be pleasantly oiled from time to time. The blizzard came and swirled and screamed itself down to a long wind wail Old Man Barton had said was the death chant of a big Crow medicine man, and, when the wind finally died, there it was—snow hip-pocket high to a tall Indian anywhere you looked.

The days were lead-colored, slaty, with diaphanous clouds that changed shape but never seemed to pass over. The air had a metallic smell to it, like the inside of an old cannon, but most of all, like those filmy clouds up there, nothing changed. Morning came, noon came, night came—nothing changed. Smoke rose up in the gun metal days from dozens of stovepipes. Paths came into existence and the more energetic merchants shoveled off their lengths of the rough old board walkway on both sides of the treacherous roadway. Will Clampitt wailed, after the ninth day of it, that unless a Chinook wind came to melt that dratted snow so as folks would rent his rigs and horses instead of making little bird tracks from woodshed to kitchen, he was going to sell out his livery barn and move somewhere else—somewhere a man didn't have to gird himself up to the knees just to tramp across the road to a saloon for a drink.

II

The Chinook wind Will Clampitt wished for didn't come. On the eleventh day, in fact, another frigid blast came, starting around suppertime, and by morning of the twelfth day there was another eight inches of snow over the previous crusted pack.

"That," stated Tom Logan's tough and rugged deputy, Pert Whipple, as he stamped into George Henry's Big Eagle Saloon, "is all we needed. Another lousy foot of snow." Pert was, in many ways, a worthwhile individual; he was stupid enough to be uncomplicated, naïve enough to be absolutely fair, and because he was six feet tall and weighed better than a hundred and a half he was wiry and tough as old rawhide. He wasn't the most astute sleuth in Wyoming Territory by a long shot, but on the other hand Wyoming had no real need of clever lawmen; all it needed was tough ones. Pert was tough; he had scars over both eyes from his share of brawls. He also had a knife nick or two and some bullet marks. Currently he was acquiring a new kind of experience. Pert had been married eight months. A lot of his earlier thoughts about females were undergoing serious alterations. Not that Pert wasn't happy, he was; it was simply that he'd never, in all his twenty-six years, made any point of eating on time, or for that matter doing anything else on time. Well, that was changing. So was Pert's clothing. It was changing, too. And now he shaved every day—or at the least every other day. But Pert could assert himself, and did the first time his bride mentioned offhand that too many visits to the Big Eagle Saloon could, her staunchly Baptist parents had assured her, lead a man down the terrible road to degradation and ruin.

Pert had over the years seen a lot of good men, including Tom Logan, sit an hour or two of nearly every blessed day at George Henry's bar, and as near as he could detect there wasn't any indication of degradation or ruin overtaking them, so he laid down the law. He'd go to the Big Eagle when he felt like it. He'd provide for his bride; he'd also provide as long as he was able for anyone else who came out of their blissful union, but also he'd go to the Big Eagle. And that was that.

That was that, too. Pert's wife was Henry Poole's daughter. Henry ran the mercantile, the biggest, best-stocked, and most thriving general store in Winchester Junction. Henry was a wispy, bird-like man somewhere in his indeterminate fifties. He was a lay preacher of the Baptist faith, a real hellfire-and-brimstone preacher, too. But Henry was profit-motivated, whatever else he was, so when Pert laid down the law and his wife went to her widowed father with an unshed tear and bruised feelings, Henry sagaciously suggested that, if you can't always best the devil, then the next best thing was to learn how to live with him. In other words, if Pert put his foot down about the Big Eagle and an occasional drink, then Pert's wife should be wise enough to use other means for saving his soul from the downward trail. Evidently she did, because Pert wasn't the steady customer he'd once been, or, as cynical, swarthy, and stocky George Henry observed to Tom Logan: "Old Henry's girl's got ways about her no saloon on earth could compete with."

Tom's reply to that was laconic. "Take what you can get and be damned glad you got it."

George Henry had been foreman of the twelve good and true men who'd brought in the hanging verdict against Old Man Barton. George was a fearless, short, and burly man, as dark as a half-breed and, some said, as mean and vicious when he got roiled up. But George never got angry at Tom Logan. Some men know to whom to show their fangs and to whom not to show them. George Henry was forty-five years old; he hadn't got to that respectable age by making mistakes about men in a land where tempers and erupting guns went hand in hand— *literally* hand in hand. Still, it bothered him that Tom Logan hadn't looked squarely at him since the hanging, so the afternoon of the twelfth day of the snow-in, he took a bottle, two glasses, and a very business-like expression, over to Sheriff Logan's table, sat down firmly, filled both glasses, and pushed one across at Tom. Then he gripped his own glass like it was a club of some kind, looked Tom straight in the face, and said: "Listen, I didn't like my part in that any better'n you liked yours. But the judge give us our instructions. Barton couldn't make it come out his way, so what was we supposed to do?"

135

"Forget it," growled Logan, flinging back his head, swallowing that straight shot, and afterward furiously blinking his eyes as he braced in the chair against the ultimate impact when that buffalo bile hit bottom. It hit, Logan shuddered, blew out a flammable breath, and said: "No one's blaming you. No one's blaming anyone, I reckon. Or if they are, they're blaming me. All I did was my duty, just like you did. But who do folks ordinarily blame for everything in this tarnal country from blizzards to incipient pregnancy? Me! You just naturally blame a sheriff. He's the offspring of a she-dog the second he puts on a badge, just naturally. Fill it up again. What's Pert doing over by the stove?"

"Bellyaching about the weather." George refilled Logan's glass. "I knew Old Man Barton as well as anyone hereabouts. I recall him with a notched feather in his hat thirty years back. I'd have rather cut off my right hand than see him hang."

"You don't have to cut your hand off," muttered Tom, reaching for the glass again. "Because you weren't out there to see him hang. Weren't none of you jurymen out there." Logan downed this straight shot, too, went through the same pantomime again, but after this one his eyes began to grow pleasantly warm and cloudy. "No one was out there 'cept Will Clampitt, waiting to clean out the corpse's pockets, Preacher Benedict, and me. Make a note of something, George. If I die ahead of you, take a stick an', if Ezra Benedict shows up, whang the hell out of him."

George downed his drink, too. "Sure," he said, meaning sure he'd run Ezra Benedict off if Logan died first. "You know, Tom, I don't know what this town's comin' to, hangin' a feller like Old Man Barton. Why, hell, he's taught more kids how to make fires without matches, how to read sign, how to. . . ."

"Oh, shut up," snarled the sheriff, peering straight over at the burly bar owner. "You make me sick. Don't tell *me* how good a man Old Barton was. I know how good a man he was. But I released the trap door an' you put the knot under his ear, an' all those folks, when they were kids he taught that stuff to, they sat at home in out of the wind, the cold, and let him go like he was a common felon. Don't go getting sanctimonious with me, George. You're at fault, I'm at fault, this whole lousy town's at fault. I'm sick of myself and all the rest of us, too."

George Henry refilled the glasses again. This time Tom was courteous to wait until George lifted his glass, too. George said: "To Old Man Barton . . . wherever in hell he is."

Tom drank and he very slowly, very slyly smiled. "Wherever in *hell* he is, George?"

"Ah," muttered George, wiping his mouth and looking apologetic. "That's just a figure of speech. You know that, Tom. I didn't mean. . . ."

"He's not in hell, George. He's right here in Winchester Junction."

George reflected on that a moment, decided it really wasn't worth disputing, and refilled the glasses again. "Have a drink," he said, sounding like he was making this offer from deep down in a well, the words blurring together pleasantly.

Tom did. He no longer even batted an eyelid when that rotgut hit bottom, either. "Barton had that piece of land west of town, y'know," he said, speaking very gravely. "Lived out there with his horses . . . he always called full-growed horses ponies . . . and raised his food, hunted, fished a little, used to sit out there, cross-legged, naked to the waist on summertime full-moon nights, wailing at the sky like a danged Crow. He never hurt anybody. Left folks alone and asked only that they leave him alone."

"I know," murmured George Henry, one big, round tear forming in each dark eye. "Have another drink." He poured a little unsteadily and Tom watched the pouring as he went on speaking.

"I used to ride out and supper with him now an' then. We talked. Y'know how fellers'll talk. He told me yarns from 'way back before you 'n' I come to the territory. I swear, George, some of 'em'd fair make your hair stand straight up. Old Man Barton was a pure bit of holy terror in those old-time hell-roaring days." Tom desisted from his rambling recital long enough to down his fourth straight shot, then resumed speaking. He wasn't especially talking to George Henry, though, he was just talking.

"Then, by God, there I am, standing up there with that lousy cold wind congealing m'blood, looking him straight in the eye with that trap door yank rope in my hand, and he's gazing right into my face sayin' . . . 'Go ahead and pull it, Tom. As well first as last. I ask no favors. A man outlives his times. I got regrets . . . plenty of 'em, but I'll be around long enough to undo some of them, so go ahead and pull. Don't stand there like you're ten years old and on the edge of blubberin'. You got your duty. Now do it!' " Logan paused, his head fell forward, he raised it with an effort, and, when George pushed forth his refilled glass for the last time, Logan didn't even see it. "I pulled that god-damned yank rope," he whispered. "I killed the man I valued most in this place. I went down and looked underneath. There he was, turning gently forth an' back, his head canted over in an unnatural way, his fierce old eyes looking at me, right through me, like he could see something almighty interestin' that I couldn't see."

"Did he look accusin' at you?" breathed George Henry, and Sheriff Logan had to come back from a long distance to realize who'd asked that and where he was. A looseness was on him. A faint roaring filled his head.

"Naw. He wasn't mad at me, George. He didn't even look

sad. You know how he looked?"

"I got no idea how he looked," George Henry said very solemnly. "No idea at all. You haven't touched your drink, Tom. Drain it off an' we'll have another one."

"He looked," said Sheriff Logan, dropping his voice and leaning across the table the better to bring George into focus, "like he'd just discovered that something he always thought would happen was happening. You understand that, George?"

George didn't understand it because the table was proving that it had a life of its own and would not hold still, and in order to keep his old friend from being inconvenienced, even hurt if the damned table should suddenly veer away, George was mightily concentrating upon holding the confounded thing steady.

Tom scowled, he screwed up his lips in an ugly way, he glared, then he reared in his chair and said fiercely: "You wouldn't understand it, anyway. You were the foreman of that lousy, yellow-bellied jury. You sentenced him to death, didn't you?"

George looked helplessly around. His shoulder muscles were straining and still the table writhed in his powerful grasp. He'd never before in his entire lifetime seen such a strong table. He called desperately.

"Pert, come over here and mind this cussed table, will you? Mind it until I can find a hammer an' some nails. I'll fix it so's it won't prance around when folks are seriously conver—, conser—, speakin'."

Pert Whipple came over, looked at George, looked at Tom Logan, set aside his glass of beer, and swung his head. Over at the bar, around at the other tables, men were looking and grinning. The big iron stove was merrily popping. Outside it was gray and slaty with ragged puffs of soiled clouds boiling down from the glisteningly white high peaks. There was a little skiff of fresh snow falling. Will Clampitt, over with his nose glued to the frosted front window, rubbed a clear place, looked out, and groaned.

"I swear I'm pullin' out the second the roads are firm in the spring. I swear I am. Isn't a man born got to put up with what I've put up with in this stinkin' country. I say give it back to the dirty Injuns."

Someone over along the bar glanced around and said: "They won't take it back and that's what we get for educatin' 'em. You send a Indian to school an' he wouldn't take this land back. Not now."

Pert had Tom Logan hoisted to his feet. Tom lived in a two-roomed lean-to off the back of his jail house. Being a bachelor he didn't need more than one room to cook and eat in, and another room to sit or sleep in. A sturdy man in a checkered wool-blanket coat asked Pert if he needed a hand. Pert allowed that he didn't. He also allowed that in four years of being under-sheriff, deputy, and turnkey for Tom Logan, he'd never before seen him in such a fluid state.

Pert got Tom outside. The wind was knife-like. It made Tom gasp and stagger, but it also had a somewhat sobering effect, too, so by the time Pert and Tom were halfway along, Sheriff Logan could, with only a minimum of help, navigate the treacherous roadway with its ice and dirty puddles.

They made it to the jail house and Pert departed, more embarrassed than disgusted. Maybe, like his wife had said many times, there really was a degradation and ruin in strong drink. But Sheriff Logan found his sobering condition intolerable. He went to a backroom cupboard, found his private bottle, and took a long drink from it. He then unsteadily lit a fire in his stove and tripped over a little bench someone had carelessly left in the center of the room. Even before he hit the floor he was flailing away.

"L'go my legs you . . . you horse-stealin' devils!" he roared.

"L'go my legs or I'll drive you into the ground like a nail, the whole danged bunch of you. Steal horses in my bailiwick, will you? So help me Hannah, I'll learn you!"

The little stool took a violent punch and crashed into the wall. Next it was the swivel chair. It put up a better fight because it was on casters, but Tom Logan in wrath was a fury and a terror. He vanquished it, too, in time, then, with the stove sending forth its warming glow, he fell back, panting, triumphant but tired with a sprained hand, and fell asleep with a snatch of an old chant on his lips he'd learned from Old Man Barton.

III

The thirteenth day was a corker. Six inches of fresh snow had fallen in the night, covering all the old tracks and filling in most of the stamped-down trails. Henry Poole met George Henry outside where Poole was supervising the shoveling of snow off his stretch of plank walk. Henry didn't actually expect much business on a day as frigidly cold as this one, but not being prepared should any business happen along nagged at him.

George, who lived east of town, came slogging along with a shawl over his head, his hat over the shawl, wearing a fire-red big Hudson's Bay woolen coat, and looking a little less darkly swarthy than usual, especially around the gills where he was putty-gray. His eyes, too, Henry noticed sharply, were bloodshot. Henry could take pleasant comfort in poor George's appearance because he'd never been hung-over from drink in his life. He was a healthy, if not a robust man; his little blue eyes sparkled with a quick, hard shrewdness. In his own opinion he'd lived an exemplary life. There was one small blight. Poole, like George Henry and ten others, had sat on Old Man Barton's sentencing jury. Still, Henry Poole was a law-abiding man like many a pirating merchant was; he would never, as long as he could draw a breath, agree with a lawbreaker. On top of that he was a lay preacher in Ezra Benedict's church. He could hand-ily rationalize surreptitiously raising his prices on tinned goods daily as the snowed-in condition of Winchester Junction continued—that was business—but with lawlessness in any guise, seemingly justified or not, he could not compromise.

He took a deep breath of the bitterly cold morning air and let it out savoringly as the swarthy saloon man came along. "Good to be alive," he said heartily, maliciously. "Taste that air, George. God's own bounty to man."

George stopped with both hands pushed far down into coat pockets, looked disapprovingly at Henry Poole, and grunted. It was a lousy day, black and terribly cold and as gray as an old abandoned body.

Henry sucked back another big breath and heaved it out. "Makes a man's corpuscles expand!" he exclaimed. "Makes folks glad to be alive to see all His vast majesty."

"I hope," said George raspingly, "you slip and bust your hind end on the ice." He stamped on past, and Henry Poole smiled after him.

"Next time drink less of it or drink it slower," he softly called.

George stopped, turned fully around, and glared. Anger made his throbbing head hurt the more. "What d'you know about how men drink?" he growled.

"The demon rum has many friends in your shape, George. They suffer and sometimes they repent. I read of a feller back in New York who fell sick, and, when they opened him up, his liver was full of whiskey flukes. The poor man died."

George fisted both hands, jammed them deeper, and said: "Liver flukes! You damned old. . . . Oh, forget it. You wouldn't understand anyway." George turned and went shuffling along toward his saloon.

Across the road Will Clampitt was pushing fresh snow out of his barn's entry way as though he expected riders to lope up.

He didn't really expect any horsemen but habit is a powerful factor in every liveryman's life. You can't be around animals like horses that are almost exclusively creatures of habit for ten, twenty hours a day, without becoming a little like them.

Tom Logan came along looking like he'd spent a bad night, which he had, and keeping his aching right fist tucked inside his sheepskin coat. Tom's eyes copiously watered. He stopped every once in a while to dash away the run-over. Will paused at his labor for a breather, leaned upon his snow shovel, and said: " 'Morning, Sheriff. Another foot of the damned stuff last night. When's it going to quit? I never seen such lousy weather, did you?"

Tom wiped his eyes, hunched down deeper inside his coat, and shook his head. "Not in a long time," he conceded. "But we got it coming."

"Huh? You mean we *deserve* this blizzard? Now just how'n the devil do you come to a belief like that, I'd like to know."

"Never mind," muttered Logan, looking at the frosted window of the café up the road, and looking swiftly away as his stomach gave a queasy lurch. "Never mind how we deserve it."

Clampitt put his head a little to one side. "You feelin' all right this morning, Tom?"

"I feel lousy. Does that sound good to you, Will?"

Clampitt straightened up. He didn't want any argument. Particularly he didn't want any argument with Sheriff Logan before he'd even had breakfast. "No, it doesn't sound good. I was just bein' sympathetic, that's all."

"Well," mumbled Logan, wiping a stiff sleeve across his upper face, "save your lousy sympathy. By the way, how much did you take off Old Man Barton before you planted him?"

Clampitt shifted his stance, looked down the runway of his barn, looked northward up the roadway, then southward, and eventually said: "Three dollars an' a watch older'n I am, worth

143

no more'n another three dollars. If you're askin' because you want to know how much I got comin' for the embalmin' and planting, it'll cipher up to about. . . ."

"You're a liar," said Sheriff Logan, his swimming dark eyes turning suddenly fierce. "Barton had eleven dollars on him. I saw it, Will. Eleven dollars. Your charge for a pine box and planting is ten dollars for the kind of a job you did on him."

Clampitt's red Adam's apple jumped up and down, his white face turned splotchily red. "Eleven dollars . . . ?" he said, looking guilty and chagrined both.

"Yes, eleven dollars. He showed it to me. He had eleven dollars in his pants pocket. Will . . . ?"

"Yes."

"You make me want to throw up," said Sheriff Logan, and stepped down into the icy slush to go tramping on up toward the Big Eagle Saloon for a little of the hair of the dog that had bitten him the night before. He got to the bar and banged on it with his left hand. He still had his sprained right hand tucked inside his coat where the cold wouldn't make it pain him so much.

George had stoked up a big fire in the iron stove and was out back tying a fresh apron around his sturdy middle. He growled: "Hold your damned horses, will you?" And took his own sweet time about getting ready for the day's business.

When he passed back again into the outer room, though, and saw who his first customer was, his face lost most of its naked hostility. He fumbled under the backbar for two glasses, lifted down a bottle, and wordlessly poured two stiff jolts. "Drink," he grumbled. "And the next time you want to get drunk find someone else to do it with. My head feels like someone's inside it, walkin' up and down with caulked boots on."

They drank and set aside their glasses and gazed at one another. George lifted the bottle, held it poised without speaking. Tom shook his head, turned, and paced over where the stove was beginning to radiate pleasant warmth. "How the hell did we get started last night?" he asked.

"How? Old Man Barton, how else?" grumbled George. "That's all that's on this town's mind now. It's the snow. Being snowed-in does funny things to folks. It's worse'n being locked in a jail house. Everything's the same. No new faces, nothin' happening, everyone's standin' around like they're awaitin' the crack of doom. The lousy snow." George turned to replace the bottle. That drink had made him feel a lot better. "It's the damned waitin' that does it. But I'll be dog-goned if I know what we're all waitin' for."

"For the storm to pass," said Sheriff Logan, bending to push his swollen, battered right hand closer to the stove. "You've seen these blizzards before. Every four or five winters we get 'em. If we *didn't* get 'em, how long do you reckon we'd have creek water and green grass in the summertime? Without grass an' water . . . no cattle. No ranches. This town'd curl up an' die without the cattle money to keep its arteries pumping."

"Of course I've seen blizzards before," snapped George, his irritability returning. "But not like this one. And neither have you. This is the thirteenth day of it. They usually only last maybe two, three days. Sedge an' the other cowmen'll be fit to be tied. Bad enough haulin' hay out on wagons, but when the snow's this deep on the range, no one takes wagons through it. They'll be feedin' right out of their barn lots. They'll be madder'n a nest of roiled scorpions."

"Mad," said Sheriff Logan, looking over his shoulder. "Mad at who? I didn't order this lousy blizzard."

"Don't be ridiculous."

"Well? Do I or don't I get blamed for everything that happens around here?"

"You're talkin' like a damned fool. Come over here and have

another drink."

"Oh, no. Not on your tintype," averred the doughty lawman. "The way I feel this morning I'm about to join Henry Poole's temperance movement."

"That," exclaimed George Henry with a snort, "will be the day!"

Will Clampitt stamped in and closed the storm doors, looked around, and headed immediately for the stove. His face was red from exertion. Redder than usual. He started to say something, saw Logan's purple-swollen knuckles, and blinked owlishly. "You been in a fight?" he asked.

"No," growled Tom, "I haven't been in a fight."

"Well, what'd you do? That's your fightin' hand ain't it . . . the right one?"

"How the hell do *I* know what I did," snarled Logan, checked himself as Will's eyes lifted uncomprehendingly to his face, and burned a deep brick red as he swung away from the liveryman. "You're the nosiest critter I ever saw. Besides, you smell of your barn. Don't get so close to the stove."

George, looking on during this exchange, said: "Will, you want a drink?"

Clampitt shook his head. "I just come over to tell you the damnedest thing. A rider just come into my place."

Logan slowly turned and fixed an unbelieving stare upon Will. George, pushing his flat belly against the backbar, also stared. "A stranger?" he asked.

"Perfect stranger. He come ridin' out of the west through that danged thirty inches of snow like it was somethin' he did every day. Rode in the back alleyway door, got down, handed me his reins as cool as you please, an' said . . . 'Feed him up, rub him down, stall him with plenty of beddin', and bait him with a half gallon of oats.' Just like that."

Logan and the barman exchanged a look. Logan flexed his

aching right hand. "From the west, you say, Will, from the due west?"

"Straight as an arrow. An' that reminds me. He's a big, dark-lookin' feller. Looks like maybe he's some kind of a 'breed Injun. About your coloring, George."

Probably, under other circumstances and at another time, George Henry would have taken exception to that, but now he didn't. In fact, George *was* a third Indian. It never bothered him and it never bothered anyone else, so perhaps he wouldn't have taken exception. George was not an inward, a self-conscious man in any sense.

"Westerly," mused Tom Logan, his diminishing headache nearly forgotten at this bizarre piece of news, "lie all the big cow outfits. Maybe he was a rider for one of them, got fed up and quit."

George and Will chewed that over. It wasn't the best judgment, but on the other hand no one could truly blame a cowboy for being sick of Wyoming after thirteen days or nights of snow and thirty-below weather. Still, walking off the job and heading for town wasn't going to make things any better for a range man. But you could never tell; no two range men ever appeared to be of a like mind about anything.

"Where is he now?" Tom asked.

"Went over to the café to eat," stated Will. "Pretty big man, Sheriff. Looks like he might be mean, too, although he smiled, even chuckled when I stood there gawkin' with m'mouth hangin' down at the sight of him ploddin' through that snow."

"Cowboy?" Logan asked.

Will nodded. "Cowboy, I'd say, from the looks of him. Well set up, nice-lookin' feller . . . except that he's a dark cuss, needs a shave and a haircut."

"Well, he can get them here," George said quietly. "One thing . . . did he say where he came from . . . say anythin' about the storm?"

"No. Like I just told you, he rode in, got down, give me his reins, and told me what to do about his horse. Then he grinned when I stammered around about him ridin' in through the blizzard, paid me in advance, and walked right on across toward the café."

George slowly poured a shot glass full, inched it over to the edge of the bar, and gazed at the liveryman. "On the house," he said. "Can't sell it this early in the mornin' anyway." As Clampitt shuffled gratefully forward, George turned and lifted his eyebrows at Tom Logan. "Well, at least we don't have to look at each other's faces now. Maybe he's a good drinkin' man or enjoys a game of poker. If he just got paid off, he'll have a little silver in his poke."

Pert Whipple came stumbling in, caught his balance, uttered an annoyed small curse, and stamped snow off his boots before looking around. When he saw Tom Logan over by the stove, he tentatively grinned. "Looked in at the jail house for you, straightened up the furniture, an' figured you might be up here. There's a big stranger in town. He's standin' out front of the café, suckin' on a toothpick. I didn't see him come in. Looks like maybe one of Sedge Horton's riders. Anyway, he looks like *someone's* cowboy."

Will explained to Pert about the stranger. Then, as his trouser pocket jingled from the stranger's silver money, Will sighed and smiled. "It's an omen," he said. "Things'll change now. We'll get our Chinook sure."

"We'll likely get something," agreed Tom Logan, and studied his loosening, pleasantly warm but still badly swollen right hand. "What the devil would make a man ride across a prairie through thirty inches of snow, just to reach a place like Winchester Junction?"

"He had to go somewhere, didn't he?" Will asked brightly, his whiskey working.

"No," said Tom, scowling at the liveryman. "He could've stayed right where he was until the storm passed. Most men would have."

IV

Pert and Tom, George and Will made up a poker game. There wasn't a blessed other thing to do. George had no customers, Will's chores were done over at the barn, and for all the lawlessness likely to erupt in Winchester Junction this day, or, from the looks of that outside sky, for some days yet to come, Tom and Pert might just as well have hung up their guns and tossed away their badges. But poker in a hot room with restlessness hanging over everyone like a bomb with a short fuse didn't help tempers any, and, actually, it didn't even seem to make the time pass too pleasantly. Not for Will and George because they began to lose steadily to Tom and Pert.

George, an old poker player, just got grimmer and grimmer in the face as the pots were swept across the table by either one of the lawmen. But he wouldn't say anything. George had won and lost a small fortune at poker. If he could never quite reach that happy state of philosophical acceptance over steady losses, he at least kept his mouth closed. But Will Clampitt was different. After Pert had swept in the silver Will had got from the big stranger, Clampitt began muttering under his breath. After three straight losses to Tom Logan, Will began squirming on his chair. Finally he blurted out a string of oaths and bitterly complained about his luck. Everyone else took that in stride; Will Clampitt was not a man the others admired. He was devious, underhanded, stingy, and prone to whine. Still, four-handed poker was much better to play than three-handed, so the others took up their fresh cards and ignored Clampitt. The hand went to George. His swarthy countenance brightened faintly; he was still down $3, but it seemed that the worm might be turning.

Will's Adam's apple bobbed up and down like he was an old stag turkey getting set to gobble. He tossed in his cards and said: "George, lemme rub your back for some of that luck."

George glowered. "You keep your damned hands to yourself," he growled. "It's your deal . . . pick up the cards."

But at that moment the storm doors opened and a large, black-hatted, sheepskin-coated man stamped inside, cast a quick look around, barely nodded at the poker players, and carefully closed the doors behind him. Without a word passing, the card players knew exactly who that big man was—the big stranger. To Tom Logan, sitting down, that man looked seven feet tall and perhaps a solid, powerful two hundred and fifty pounds. He wasn't actually either that tall or that hefty, but there was no mistaking one thing: he was the broadest, if not the tallest, man in that room. Only Pert Whipple could look him squarely in the eye without tilting his head, and Will Clampitt, who was also a tall man, although quite skinny, only lacked possibly an inch of meeting the stranger's height.

"You want a drink?" George asked, getting heavily up from the table and turning to cross over to his bar. "Whiskey or beer?"

"Whiskey," replied the big man, putting a slower look at them all before following George on across. "Better make it a double shot."

Will smiled upward and said ingratiatingly: "Feller needs a double shot this kind of weather. Colder'n a witch's kiss out there."

The big man considered Will without nodding or smiling or even mumbling agreement. Just stared, and walked away.

Tom put his cards down. It wasn't a full hand anyway. He gazed at Pert, then they both looked at Will, who'd slumped down in his chair after that cold, hard look from the stranger.

Will rolled up his eyes. He leaned far across the table and whispered: "I told you he was a mean-lookin' cuss, Tom."

Logan made a low snort. "You told me he chuckled. That he grinned at you."

"Well, look for yourself. He ain't grinnin' now. He looks mean. Like maybe somethin' just happened he don't like."

"Ice water splashed inside his boot," muttered Pert. "Deal, if you're goin' to. I got to win back anything I lose. My wife doesn't approve of gamblin', an' she knows exactly how much money I had on me when I left the house this morning."

But Will didn't pick up the cards to finish his deal. He shoved back his chair and stood up. "I got work to do. Can't be sittin' around here all day losin' my money." He turned and hastened over to the door, passed through out into the leaden day, and was lost from sight. Pert swore, racked up the cards, and pushed his chips forward to cash them in from the pot. Logan swept up the rest of the money and also stood up.

"Treat you to a beer," he said, gazing over where the big stranger was standing loosely, both elbows hooked over the bar, moodily gazing down into his glass. He and Pert went on over. Tom called for two beers and turned sideways to consider the stranger. "That feller who just left . . . he's the liveryman. He told us about you riding in this morning." Tom paused and awaited the stranger's reaction. He expected the man to make some comment. So did Pert, and George, also waiting. But the big man acted like he hadn't heard at all. He pushed his glass forward with one broad finger and said to George: "Refill."

Tom and George exchanged a glance. George went ahead to pour another double shot. Pert, standing on Tom's left, tried his luck.

"Big country you came across, mister. Big and empty. A man could freeze to death at night out there, unless he could dig down thirty inches for firewood."

151

The stranger held his glass, turned only his head, and gazed at Pert. "I reckon folks dig deeper than that in this country, mister. A lot deeper." He tossed off that second drink and shook his head at George, who was poised behind his bar to refill the glass again. The big man quietly belched, dragged a big-knuckled, work-hardened hand across his lips, and shifted position. He studied Tom Logan for a moment and there was no trace of any smile at all. "You're curious," he stated in that soft, deep, rumbling voice of his. "Why don't you just jump right in an' ask, Sheriff?"

Tom made a little brittle nod. "All right, mister. Where'd you come from?"

The big man raised an arm and gestured vaguely toward the north with it. "Up there."

George's eyes popped wide. "You mean to say you come across the mountains in this blizzard?" he asked.

"Well, barkeep, to tell you the truth, I did. But there's ways, when a man's used to big mountains. Anyway, it hasn't snowed on the far side. Just on top and down on your side."

"But the passes up there," responded George. "Hell, they must have thirty-foot drifts by now."

The big man shrugged. "You start early, you take your time, you walk ahead, an' break trail for your horse. It's a matter of not gettin' scairt, and keepin' in the right direction."

"Where'd you camp last night?" Pert Whipple asked, leaning there full of sharp interest about this stranger, about his quiet voice, his powerful size, his steadily unsmiling, inward-looking eyes.

"West six, seven miles. At a little ranch out there where no one was around and the critters hadn't been fed for a spell."

Tom Logan said softly: "The Barton place."

"Yeah, the Barton place," murmured the stranger, looking at each of them in turn. "Seems odd a stockman like Barton must have been would up and go off and leave his critters to paw through three feet of snow."

George Henry licked his lips, turned, and picked up a turkey-feather duster with which he began flicking away a non-existent film of dust from the backbar shelves and bottles.

Pert turned, looked down into his empty beer glass, and said to George: "You better give me another one. How about you, Sheriff?"

Tom shook his head. He was like a stone. A bad premonition gripped him. He and the big stranger steadily regarded one another. Finally the stranger said: "Sheriff, if you're lookin' at me like that because you reckon I'm wanted somewhere, forget it. You won't find my picture on any Reward poster. I'm just a feller passin' along. Thought I might rest a spell in Winchester Junction. Been thinkin' I'd drift over this way one of these days for a mighty long time. But you know how that goes, a feller never quite makes a lot of those dates he has in mind. Or else he makes them . . . too late."

The liquor was changing the big man right before Tom's eyes. Two double shots of George Henry's mountain dew were enough to bring forth speech from a brass monkey. The stranger quietly surveyed the whole room from its backbar shelves to its scattered tables, over to the crackling iron stove, and finally to the frosted front windows with their lacings of obscurity around small central clear places through which he had an excellent view of the empty, snow-piled, dirty roadway. His face was broad with high, flat planes and angles. His chin was prominent, his jaw square. He had a long mouth that seemed, ordinarily at least, to have little laughter wrinkles around its tilted outer edges. His shoulders were wide and packed with muscle. His waist was tiny and his long, sturdy legs were encased in stout black cowhide boots. His spurs, snow-washed, were heavily silver inlaid, and his holstered six-gun was noticeable because of its intricately carved walnut stocks. He was, plainly, a man who knew his way around, who was big and powerful enough to laugh off most challenges. With or without his gun, in Tom Logan's eyes—and Tom knew men—this one was the kind that made a good friend and a mighty fine enemy.

But that wasn't what was absorbing Tom's attention now. The big man's eyes were a slaty gray with flecks of gold in their depths. They were large, liquid eyes that took in a lot of territory without seeming to move at all. Tom had seen eyes like that before. There was no fear in this stranger. There was no laughter now, either, although he obviously was a man who liked to laugh.

"One on the house?" asked George Henry, gazing up at his large customer. George made a little weak smile. "Like I said before, this morning, when you can't sell it, you might as well give it away."

The stranger shook his head without returning George's smile. "Quite a town you've got here, barkeep. You get many blizzards as bad as this one usually?"

"No. In fact, this is the longest one I've ever seen here, and I've been at the Junction a long time."

The big man leaned forward again, putting his whole attention upon George. "Been here a long time, have you," he murmured in that rumbling, deep-down quiet voice. "Then maybe you can settle somethin' for me that came up a little while ago when I was down the road, eatin' breakfast. There were two, three fellers eatin', too. One of them was named Benedict. Some kind of a sky-pilot. Another was named Poole. They were discussin' a recent hangin' here in your town, barkeep. They said this old feller got hanged for shootin' a horse thief."

George bent, brought up a shot glass, carefully poured it full, and tossed off the whiskey. He afterward straightened up and waited for the stranger to speak on.

"Now, barkeep, I've lived thirty years. I've punched cows from Mexico to Montana, from California east to the Nebraska plains, and this is the first time I ever heard of a man bein' hanged for killing a horse thief." The big man's long lips lifted in a mechanical, mirthless little smile. "I'm real curious about that. Maybe, you bein' an old-timer in these parts, you could sort of explain it to me. I'm not a book-learned man, and I figure any time a feller can improve his store of knowledge, he surely ought to. Well, barkeep, how about it? Why do they hang folks in Winchester Junction for somethin' they give a medal for anywhere else on earth?"

George reached for the bottle to pour himself another shot. Pert and Tom, drawn by this movement, saw the stranger's thick hand and wrist move; George's arm was caught in a strong grip. He didn't fight it; he simply looked up, his swarthy face paling a little, his dark eyes showing pain that did not come from that hand hold.

"I'm waitin', barkeep."

"You're asking the wrong man," said Sheriff Logan. "I'm the law here. I cut the rope that sprung that damned trap door."

The stranger's head slowly turned. He didn't release George's right arm but he said to Logan: "*Damned* trap door? You sound like a man who did somethin' he didn't like doing, Sheriff?"

"Did you ever hang a man?" Tom demanded thinly.

Now the stranger released George to swing half around. "Never did, Sheriff. Never would, because I wouldn't get myself in a position where I had to."

"Then you wouldn't understand why I said damned trap door, mister. Hanging's the worst thing a lawman ever has to do. It's the vilest way to snuff out a life. But when you follow my calling, you take an oath to perform your duty. I performed mine."

"You hung that old man, Sheriff?"

"I did, and the good Lord knows it tore my guts loose to do it, too. Now, stranger, let me ask you a question."

"Sure. Turn about's fair play, Sheriff. Shoot," said the stranger, his wintry eyes with their bright flecks of gold turning mocking, turning sardonically assessing. "You want to know my name. Isn't that it?"

"You're plumb right. Or, maybe I ought to say I know what your name is, stranger. I only want you to confirm it for me."

The stranger gently inclined his head. "What is it, Sheriff?"

"It's Barton."

Pert Whipple spilled the last of his beer in the act of putting the glass aside. George Henry's jaw muscles bulged low along his face, his gaze flicked from Tom to the stranger and hung there. He said in a low, low whisper: "No!"

The stranger gazed mildly at George. "Why not, barkeep? Something wrong with the name Barton in this town? Well, I reckon there must be. Anyway . . . yes, you're right, Sheriff. It's Frank Barton."

"You're his son?" Tom asked.

"His grandson, Sheriff. My folks are dead. I came here to see my only livin' blood kin. But like I said . . . got here too late."

V

Business picked up a little at the Big Eagle later, on that thirteenth day of the blizzard that would go down in Wyoming history as the one that broke the back of hundreds of cattlemen, and others, too, for that matter. George, though, snaffled a part-time bartender he knew and put him on the counter while he shrugged into his Hudson's Bay woolen coat and sloshed on down to Logan's jail house. He passed Henry Poole without even seeing him. He didn't see Will Clampitt over in the door of his livery barn, either. Will was talking to a big, tousle-headed range rider over there who looked, in a casual way at least, like

Old Man Barton's grandson, only he wasn't. He was big Sedge Horton, the biggest, most powerful cowman in all the Winchester country. George didn't see Will; he didn't see Horton. He trudged along until it was necessary to cross over, then he didn't pause like most folks did, to pick the likeliest place. He just stepped off the sidewalk, sank to his hocks in icy mud, and kept right on going. George had something powerfully bothering him.

Tom knew what it was the moment the barman walked in, too. Tom and Pert were brewing a pot of coffee on their little heating stove. The jail house was warm but nevertheless Tom stood beside the stove with his bruised right hand held close to the shimmering heat. The hand was unusually sensitive to cold, for some reason. He had trouble opening and closing it outdoors. Indoors, it worked fairly well, however, even though it pained Tom a good deal. There were no broken knuckles, nothing like that, but those small oaken benches like the one Tom had belted the previous night with that hand didn't have a whole lot of give in them.

"What are you goin' to do?" George asked, unbuttoning his coat and looking uneasily at Logan. "You'll have to tell him, have to explain it all to him."

Tom looked down his nose skeptically. "Tell him, George? Tell him what? He knows. He's been listening to those two sanctimonious jackasses Benedict and Poole. He'll know as much as you and I . . . as the whole blessed town knows." Logan worked his hand and gazed at it. "*Telling* him isn't the point, George. The point is . . . what'll he do when he gets it all sorted out."

"Start a war," muttered Pert Whipple, heading for the stove with a crockery cup. "George, you want some java?"

"No. Tom . . . ?"

"George, there's nothing *to* do. Anyway, since I'm the law . . .

if he comes after anyone, it'll be me. Where is he now?"

"Up at my place, sittin' alone at a corner table with a bottle and a glass. That's all he does . . . sits there. Watches fellers come and go like a damned tomcat watches a mouse hole. Sits back there half in shadow with those eyes of his hardly ever movin', but let me tell you somethin', he's not missin' a thing. He's lookin' for something, for someone, and it gives me the creeps. Tom, can you get him out of there?"

Logan stopped flexing his right hand and turned. "It's a public saloon, George. I can't do anything unless he does something. Breaks a window, picks a fight, busts some furniture."

"Well, dammit, I can do somethin'!"

"Hold it, George. Just hold on a minute. What's he actually done today? Nothing, just sit up there. Well, listen to me a minute. Old Man Barton was all the kinfolk he had left in this world. Today, for the first time, he found out the old man's dead. He also found out just why Old Man Barton died. Now then, just how would you feel under those circumstances? Leave him be. Keep clear of him, don't go around scowlin' at him. He's got some tall questions to answer for himself. Don't go pushing him into the wrong decisions."

George rolled his eyes and he uttered a flat, blistering curse. "Are you tellin' me you don't think he's goin' to want Winchester Junction to pay him back for Old Man Barton? Tom, you're not that simple-minded. Sure I'll leave him alone. He's got a gun and he's got the look of a man who knows how to use one. I never wear guns. Besides that, he's twenty years younger and sixty pounds heavier. *I'm* not goin' to push him into any decisions at all, right or wrong. But *I'm* not goin' to have to. That's what I'm tryin' to get over to you. He's makin' them all by himself back there in that damned dark corner of my saloon, and *that's* what I'm tellin' you. I don't like it."

Pert Whipple sipped coffee throughout this exchange, watching first one of the older men, then the other one. Now he said: "Maybe he's just grievin', Tom. Maybe he's. . . ."

"Oh, for gosh sakes," groaned the saloon man. "Pert, stick to your coffee. Grievin'? That big devil? You ever see one like him before, Pert? Well I have, so has Tom. They don't grieve . . . they get even."

Tom Logan, watching George Henry's aggravated expression, thought of something George had said many hours earlier that same morning. The snowed-in situation of them all was getting their nerves jumpy—the deadly monotony, the constant sameness. "Go on back and take it easy," he said quietly. "Pert and I'll drift up a little later."

George departed. He had accomplished, in his own view, just exactly nothing at all. As he waded back through the icy roadway mud and paused in front of Poole's emporium to kick gobbets of cloying mud off his boots, he asked himself what, precisely, he'd hoped to accomplish? Aloud he said: "Nothin'. Not a lousy thing. How can you when you got no idea what you're hopin' for?"

Behind him a voice said, almost pleasantly but not quite: "Talkin' to yourself, George? If you're cursing the weather, I can tell you my water glass is clearin', which means the storm's over."

George turned. Henry Poole was standing in his doorway. George made a slow, malicious smile. "Got a piece of news for you," he said, stepping over closer to the rosy-cheeked merchant. "You remember Old Man Barton, don't you, Henry?"

"What kind of a question is that?" demanded the merchant, losing his smallest vestige of condescending superiority.

"Thought you'd remember him, Henry. Well, have you seen a big cowboy in town this mornin'? Big, dark-faced man with a carved grip to his Forty-Five?"

"Yes," stated Poole. "I saw such a man at the café when I got my breakfast. What of . . . ?"

"Henry, that's Old Man Barton's grandson," said George, and hesitated just for a moment to watch the slow look of congealing apprehension obscure Poole's stricken eyes. Then George smiled at him and started on up toward the Big Eagle.

Evening came at 4:00. It was totally dark by 4:30. For the first time in thirteen days, when the moon eerily arose later on, stars could be seen. There wasn't a breeze stirring, not a visible cloud in the sky, and the thermometer dropped down like a plummet. Where there were pines and firs, limbs would pop like pistol shots throughout this bitterly frigid night. There were no trees worthy of the name in Winchester Junction, though. Once, so they said, there had been, but even the trunks had rotted away by now.

Tom and Pert walked up the east side of the road after supper, bundled in their coats. Tom had his right hand shoved deep into the pile of his sheepskin. Ezra Benedict came out of Henry Poole's store, saw those two pacing along, and waited for them to come even with him. Preacher Benedict was a gaunt, scarecrow of a man, somewhere in his fifties, with thick curly hair and myopic eyes that had a stubbornly righteous, fanatically unintelligent glint to them. Once, when Tom Logan had chided Benedict about having a fee for every service he performed from baptizing to burying, Benedict had said the Lord's will was that his servants should be provided for. Tom's answer to that had been typically laconic: "The God I believe in doesn't use money." There were other things, all of which contributed to a bristling attitude on Tom's part and a stubbornly righteous attitude on Benedict's part, which stood between these two men in their middle years who were so vastly different. But, as with Will Clampitt and others in Winchester Junction, Tom Logan had to get along, so he mostly kept his mouth closed.

Benedict said: " 'Evening, Sheriff. 'Evening, Pert. Henry was just telling me Old Man Barton's grandson's in town. The ways of the Lord are indeed inscrutable, aren't they?"

Pert kept silent; he had no use for Ezra Benedict, but his wife was Henry Poole's daughter; she'd been raised in the faith and one of the fascinating things Pert was learning was that reasoning with bigotry in any form was about like stepping outside on a stormy night and whistling at the moon.

Tom, though, had an answer. He said dryly: "I'm not near as fretful about *His* ways as I am about Frank Barton's ways. Come along, Pert."

"Wait," called the minister. "Sheriff, Sedge Horton's in town." Benedict had let that drop as though he'd known in advance it would stop Logan in his tracks. He was correct; Tom stopped and faced stiffly around.

"Where did you see Sedge?" he roughly demanded.

"I didn't see him, but Henry did. He was over talking to Brother Clampitt. Now, Henry said, he's up at the Big Eagle. Mark my word, Sheriff, no good comes of men spending idle time in places like. . . ."

"For once, Ezra, you might be right," broke in Tom, and jerked his head at Pert. The pair of them walked off, moving more briskly than before.

Halfway along they saw the liveryman in conversation up on the plank walk ahead. "Who's that he's talking to?" asked Logan, peering through the settling night. "Looks like . . ."

"It's Toughy Hammond," muttered Pert, speaking Hammond's name like it was a bad word. "How'd he get to town?"

"Flew," growled Sheriff Logan, and walked along. "This is getting to be a bad night, Pert. Sedge and Toughy in town. I kind of hoped the snow drifts'd keep 'em out for another week or so."

"Why? Because you also hope Frank Barton'll get tired of doing nothing and drift on?"

"Something like that."

"Sheriff, I got Frank sized up different. He's not going to drift on. Not until he gets blamed good and ready."

Tom blew out a long sigh. "I expect not," he muttered, his tone full of dull resignation.

They came even with Will and Hammond. Toughy was a compactly put-together, hard-eyed cowman from the eastern plains. He was young and hard-fisted, which is how he'd got that name of Toughy. Actually his first name was Cliveden. Years back folks had called him Clive. He was an even six feet tall and stood a rock-hard hundred and ninety pounds of gristle. He was a blunt man and, sometimes, he was also a bully, but none of this was on Tom's mind as he came to a slow halt and nodded at Hammond and Clampitt. What he was soberly recalling now was that Toughy Hammond had also been in that jury box with Henry Poole and George Henry.

"How'd you get into town?" Tom asked impassively. "Snow's pretty deep out your way, isn't it?"

Hammond shrugged and made a nonchalant gesture. "Felt like a drink. Ain't enough snow this side of hell to keep me away if I feel like ridin'." Toughy paused a moment and puckered his eyes a little at Logan. "Will's just been tellin' me we got Old Man Barton's grandson in town. How about it, Sheriff?"

Tom looked reprovingly at Will, who faintly winced. "He's here, Toughy. Up at the Big Eagle I'm told. In fact, that's where Pert and I are bound for right now."

"Why, Sheriff, to protect him if he gets to mouthin' off?"

"No, Toughy. To protect *you* if *you* get to mouthing off." Hammond's weathered features turned a little sour. Tom shook his head to cut off anything bitter or scornful Hammond had in mind to say. "Go take a long look before you sound off," he cautioned. "And Will . . . what's in this for you?"

"What, Sheriff? What d'you mean? I'm only. . . ."

"I know what you're *only* doing. I've seen you *only* do it before. You stir this up into a fight and so help me I'll punch enough holes in your scrawny carcass to drive a herd of cattle through. Let's go, Pert."

They strode on. Overhead, the sky was like black glass; every star up there was brilliant. Even the ancient moon was sharp in every detail. The air was so cold it had to be taken inward slowly, a little at a time. If for no other reason than that, the freeze was going to establish some kind of a record. Winchester Junction was going to remember this night for a long time.

Outside the Big Eagle several townsmen were stamping feet and frostily speaking back and forth in little grunts. They peered stiffly around as Logan and Pert Whipple pushed on into the saloon; for a moment afterward only their eyes moved. Then one of them said: "Not I, boys. I can get into enough danger without leavin' the house, without bargin' in there tonight. You see how Sedge's been drinkin'?"

The others agreed that Horton was taking on a load. One of them said: "You fellers get a look at the old man's grandson? Hell, he's big enough to eat hay."

This little party dispersed, finally, each man shuffling off on his homeward way. There was wood smoke in the air with a biting tang to it. Not a breath of air stirred to sweep it away. Inside George Henry's place, though, the stove, which had been working hard all day, since early morning, plus the restless movement of nearly two dozen bundled-up drinkers and idlers, kept the place warm. Almost too warm, Tom Logan thought, as he stepped in out of the hushed cold, loosened his sheepskin, and brought forth his aching right hand into the good heat.

He saw big Sedge Horton at once, over at the bar, drinking

with several other men. He stepped aside to permit Pert room to pass along toward the bar. Over in a southward corner of the room, seemingly totally oblivious to the steady hum of masculine talk, the tinkle of a glass over wood, and the less noticeable abrasive rub of heavy clothing, sat Old Man Barton's grandson, exactly as George had said. He exchanged a long look with Tom. There was a nearly empty quart bottle and one glass in front of him. Tom wondered dispassionately about the big man's capacity. A quart of liquor, even granting that it took all day to kill it, was a sizeable amount of whiskey. It took a real man to down that much of George Henry's whiskey and still be able to stand up, let alone do anything else—such as starting a fight.

Tom let his muscles loose and started on over to the bar. He didn't want a drink; in fact, what he really wanted was something he had doubt about getting—that was a good night's sleep. The previous evening he hadn't slept very well at all.

VI

Sedgewick Horton was any man's match. It was said in the Winchester country that if the devil himself ever popped up through the floor and Sedge Horton was standing around, those two could sit down and drink, or they could square off and fight, and either way Sedge would come out top dog. And that wasn't altogether idle talk, either. Sedge Horton stood two inches above six feet tall. He weighed a powerful two hundred pounds or better. He was gray-eyed and sorrel-haired and he owned eight thousand head of cattle from the Tetons to the southward Colorado plains. He never hired a rider he didn't believe was as tough as he was, and because of this exceptional selectivity he had some of the most rugged range men in the Northwest working for him at the home place or in his cow camps.

Sedge had married once, when he was still in his teens, but it hadn't stuck, and there were some thoughtful folks who had no difficulty understanding why it hadn't, either. Tom Logan was one of them. He'd had his run-ins with Sedge. Upon occasion he'd jugged Sedge's hard crew; once he'd pistol-whipped three of them at the same time, which was no small feat at all, and he'd stood up to Sedge about posting the bail. There wasn't any love lost between these two, but there definitely was a sort of grudging respect. At least there had been up to a few months back, then something had happened that had killed Tom's feelings about Horton.

Sedge had a son from that early marriage. He was like his father—big and rough and inclined to trample over lesser folks, and things he and men like him considered unimportant. It had been Sedge's son—dead now—who had brought Old Man Barton to the gallows. It had been something a lot less than heroic in proportion that had brought Sedge's son to his death, and that had also killed Tom Logan's bleak respect for the big man beside him at the bar. Sedge was somewhere in his late thirties or early forties. He didn't look it, though. In fact, as far as Tom Logan could see, Sedge Horton hadn't changed at all in ten years—up until that day Old Man Barton had driven into Horton's yard in his rickety old wagon, had silently got down, gone around to lower the tailgate, and dragged out the blanket-shrouded body of Sedge's dead, hell-raising son. Sedge hadn't been at the ranch that day, which was all that kept Old Man Barton alive to hang later. He'd been down on the Colorado plains. But when Sedge returned, saw the lumpy grave, heard the story from his men, he'd started changing from that day on.

On the far side of him, now, stood Toughy Hammond, also drinking, also morosely standing there with his smoldering thoughts. Toughy didn't even bother to turn his head when Logan said to Horton: "Pretty bad storm. I expect you've had your share of it out on the ranch."

It was an opener, neither important nor pertinent to what was uppermost in all their minds this night. Behind them over in his southward corner sat Old Man Barton's grandson, who was, so far as Tom had casually noticed, the only other man in George Henry's place who could match Sedge Horton in size, in heft, and probably in hating. Sedge stirred, tossed back his head, and downed his drink. He set the glass down, hard, and turned. "Lost about a hundred head so far," he stated coldly. "But that's only a preliminary count. It'll likely run closer to six, seven hundred. Yes, Logan, it's a pretty bad storm."

"Thirteenth day of it, today," said Logan, shaking his head when George walked up behind the bar and raised his eyebrows, in this silent fashion inquiring whether or not Tom wished a drink.

"Kind of prophetic, isn't it?" said Horton softly. "The thirteenth day." Sedge wasn't talking about the storm and Logan knew it.

"If a man's superstitious, which I'm not," replied Tom, "and which I don't believe you are, either."

Horton drew in a big breath. Logan heard the deep-down sweep of that sucked-back air. Horton said: "I wonder, Tom, if *he's* superstitious?"

Logan, knowing exactly to whom the cattleman was referring, said: "Who?"

"Who? Don't play games with me, Sheriff. You know who."

Toughy Hammond, who'd been listening all along, now spoke without looking up. "You boys know how to skin a polecat? First you make him rear up, then you cut him down, an' go to work on him."

"I gave you some good advice outside," Logan said quietly, "when I saw you with Clampitt tonight, Toughy. Take a good long look first."

"I've took my long look, Sheriff. I've cut down a dozen as big as he is. I'll cut down a dozen more after this one, too. Don't you never doubt it."

Tom's dislike of Hammond firmed up and swayed his otherwise cool judgment. He almost wished those two *would* tangle. But it wouldn't do for him, as local law enforcement official, to be an idle bystander when that happened. Still, his dislike of Hammond was influencing him toward doing just exactly that. If ever two men needed humbling, it was these two beside him at the bar. He had no idea at all whether or not Frank Barton was raw enough to do that, but if looks were any indication, Tom thought Barton just possibly might be. One thing he knew for a fact—there were no other men in the Winchester country who could accomplish it, and some mighty good men had tried it.

But Tom's disapproval of those two went deeper than just his vindictive urge to encourage this battle. Of all the men on the jury who had turned thumbs down on Old Man Barton, Toughy Hammond was, Tom suspected, the only one who had done so for dishonest reasons. Henry Poole had done it because he was a legalized-pirate; the law favored his kind. George Henry had done it because, as jury foreman, he'd had no alternative, once the balloting was completed demanding the death penalty. But Toughy Hammond had done it because Sedge Horton had either paid him to do it, or because, being a cattleman, too, Toughy had been sympathetic to the wishes of another cattleman. In either case, Hammond hadn't voted to hang the old man out of any sense of outraged justice. On the contrary, Tom Logan had himself heard Toughy growl threats against horse thieves a dozen times right here in George Henry's barroom. If Ezra Benedict was a hypocrite in Tom's eyes, then a man who'd done what Toughy Hammond had done was even lower; he hadn't even tried hypocritically to justify what he'd done.

"Tom," said Sedge Horton, "you get that feller out of this town. I don't want any arguments. Just get him out of here. If you don't, so help me I'll do it myself, and my way won't be as clean as yours would be."

"You've been drinking," said Logan, and looked around to see where Pert was. Pert was farther down the bar, talking with a pair of townsmen, but Pert was watching Logan, which was all Tom wished to be certain of because trouble was coming. "A man's got to do something before I can order him out, Sedge. You know that. As for you running Barton off . . . I wouldn't advise it."

Horton stared for a long time at Logan. Beyond Horton, Toughy Hammond flagged for a refill of his shot glass. He was acting casually, which fooled Tom Logan not one bit. These two cowmen were hand-in-glove. Toughy wasn't the man Sedge Horton was, and in Logan's view this made him more treacherously dangerous. Sedge would never make any secret of where he stood. Hammond would, to achieve his ends he'd lie or bushwhack or do whatever he wished to do. George walked up with a wooden face and refilled Hammond's glass.

"I could bait him into a gunfight right here an' now," remarked Sedge, still staring at Sheriff Logan.

"You could," agreed Tom. "But like I told Toughy, you'd better look him over before you try it. Your money's bought you a lot of things, Sedge. It won't stop a bullet."

Hammond, having downed his drink, pushed over closer and said, giving Logan a venomous glare: "I told you how to skin a polecat. Now watch how it's done." As Hammond drew back, he lifted his lips in a cruel smile.

Tom felt something hard pushing into his ribs and looked down, knowing even before he saw the little Derringer in Sedge's hand what was down there. Sedge wasn't drunk. It struck Tom, too, that this had happened too easily, too smoothly.

That's exactly what these two had been waiting at the bar for. They could have started their play an hour earlier. They hadn't because they'd wanted first to neutralize Tom Logan. He raised his eyes to Sedge's flushed face and bitter stare. "You've skirted around pretty close to breaking the law a lot of times, Sedge," he said. "But if you go through with this, you'll be making a personal thing out of it between just you and me. Not Barton. Just you and me. Think it over."

"I've already thought it over, Tom, and this is the way it's going to be. Now, if you think for a minute you're a big enough man to go up against Sedge Horton with your two-bit badge, you just try it. All you've got to do is sing out to Pert."

"And George behind the bar with his scatter-gun, or the rest of the men in this room, Sedge? Don't be a damned fool. No man's bigger than the law. I'm just an enforcer. The law's this whole territory. It's the whole damned federal Union. You think you're that big?"

"Call down there for Pert to interfere and find out," snarled Horton, pushing that hidden little big-bored gun harder into Logan's side. "You'll get Pert killed and maybe some others as well." Horton paused, then said in a softer tone: "All I want is for that old devil's grandson to get out of this town. That's all. That old devil killed my son, Tom."

"He paid for it, Sedge. You rigged that jury and he paid for it."

"Sure he did. But this other one's here to make trouble. By God, he isn't going to do it. Now then . . . you goin' to get Pert killed, or are you going to tell Pert to keep out of it when Toughy goes to work on Barton?"

Beyond Sedge, Toughy Hammond was staring straight at Logan. He was waiting. All three of them were waiting, and for Tom Logan this was a bad moment. He knew Horton wasn't drunk; his hand on that little concealed gun was too steady. He also knew, though, that a man didn't have to be drunk for liquor to have affected his judgment. Sedge wasn't bluffing. He'd pull that trigger and, afterward, either he or Toughy Hammond would catch Pert Whipple exactly as unprepared as they'd caught Tom. A vision of Pert's wife floated briefly across the sheriff's mind. A vision of George Henry lunging for his back-bar shotgun, and catching lead as he did so, also crossed his mind. On the other side, the worst thing that probably would happen to young Barton was a bad beating. Tom lifted his shoulders and dropped them. Two lives, perhaps three or four if anyone else tried to interfere, against one man possibly getting fist whipped. It was not a difficult decision, really, and in Tom's heart he earnestly hoped Barton would reverse things; he'd thought like that only moments earlier. But there was one other thing—never before had a man got the drop on Tom Logan, and it rankled.

"Time's up," said Horton. "What d'you say, Tom?"

Logan looked past to Toughy Hammond's brutal, weathered face with its arrogant lips and cruel eyes. "I don't have much choice. All right, you two. This time it's your play. Toughy, I hope he stamps you into the floor."

Hammond put both hands atop the bar, rocked there a second, then pushed off and turned around. He looked straight across into that faint-lighted gloomy corner where Frank Barton was sitting. Before he moved, Horton spoke. Sedge was able to see the upper bar. "Pert's coming," he said. "Wait a minute, Toughy." Hammond rocked back down on his heels. Horton smiled disarmingly at Tom Logan. It was a false smile but it served its purpose; Pert saw it and wasn't suspicious. "Think of something right quick," said Horton softly. "Get him out of here."

Tom eased around as his deputy came up. Without a stammer or a faltering look Logan said: "Pert, go on up to the jail house and wait for me. I'll be along in a little while. I think we're going to have callers. One of us ought to be up there when they come."

Pert's expression showed slow surprise, wonder. He looked first at Horton then on over at Toughy Hammond. "Something special?" he asked. Logan nodded. Pert gave his head a little wag and turned to start through the tables and moving men toward the door.

"You did fine," Horton said. "Now step around on the other side of me, Tom, so's while I got an eye on you, I can also see what happens over in that corner."

Logan obeyed and Horton turned with him, still holding that hidden little double-barreled pistol against the sheriff's yielding flesh. "One more thing, Tom," murmured the flush-faced cattleman. "If George or anyone else tries to interfere, use your authority to make them butt out."

Toughy stepped away from the bar, balanced forward on his toes to permit a pair of arguing customers to pass in front, then he started across the room. Tom had to twist from the waist in order to see Hammond. It was an awkward position. He also saw Frank Barton over there with his bottle. Tom's heart sank a little. He'd forgotten about that quart of raw whiskey Barton had been sipping since morning. Unless Barton was one hell of a good man, he wasn't going to be able to navigate very well. An ordinary man, in fact, would not by this time be able to find his head with both hands after consuming that much liquor.

"You thinkin' what I'm thinkin'?" asked Sedge Horton almost amiably. "We noticed that bottle when we first come in, Tom. I'd like to lay you odds Barton can't even stand up straight."

Logan said nothing. His own misgivings were serious.

Elsewhere in George Henry's saloon, men were laughing, talking, scuffling, and drinking. They not only had no inkling of what was about to erupt in their midst, they didn't even seem concerned about the bitter cold outside or the tedious duration of this unreasoning storm that had kept them all more or less hearth-bound for just short of two full weeks. It was like any other night in the Big Eagle, except for the purposeful manner in which Toughy Hammond was approaching Frank Barton's shadowy corner table.

VII

"Turn around an' you'll be able to watch better," said Sedge Horton to Sheriff Logan. But that wasn't the only reason he said it; with Tom's back to him Horton made it less likely that the lawman would try anything. Horton had that little concealed, big-bored gun on Tom from behind. In order to resist Tom would have to turn and also draw. He might be able to do one or the other before he got shot, but he'd never be able to accomplish both and he knew it as well as Sedge Horton also knew it.

"Turn, I said," ordered Horton, and Tom turned. He had no idea at all about trying anything. Only a fool bucked a cocked gun and Tom Logan was no fool.

Toughy cleared the last table, got past the farthest patrons of the Big Eagle, halted in front of Frank Barton, and placed his left hand lightly upon the back of a vacant chair. Neither Tom nor Sedge could hear what Toughy was saying. Neither could they see Frank Barton's face in the shadows over there, but they did see Hammond's hand on that chair back suddenly convulse into a set of gripping talons as though whatever Barton had said to him had caught him off guard.

Then Toughy moved both his hands. Behind Tom, Sedge said wonderingly: "Hell, Toughy's taking off his gun belt."

Tom, with a lot of experience in affairs like this, made a caustic little grunt. "Toughy just made his first mistake, Sedge. Barton saw him coming, guessed what he wanted, and pushed his Forty-Five under the table, pointing up at Toughy's middle."

"But he's going to fight," breathed the big cowman. "He's getting up."

Tom said nothing. What Horton had commented upon was too obvious now to speak about. Barton slowly unwound up out of his chair. He holstered his six-gun, dropped the little leather tie-down over the hammer to keep his gun from falling from its holster, and he motioned toward the table top. Toughy dumped his shell belt and holstered pistol between the pair of them.

"He's bigger'n I figured," muttered Sedge. Tom felt the pressure of that Derringer in his back slack off a little.

"I warned the pair of you," muttered Logan, raising his left arm, using it to lean upon beside the bar. "It was dark over there and he was sitting down. I warned you, Sedge."

Hammond did the obvious thing; he raised his knee swiftly, struck the table, and tipped it violently over against Barton. By all rights Frank Barton should have staggered at the very least or perhaps been diverted. He did neither; the table struck him, but whereas the table couldn't have weighed more than fifteen pounds, big Frank Barton weighed a lot more. The table struck him and rolled aside. Toughy's maneuver after kicking the table was prescribed, too, by all the rules of saloon brawling. He hurled himself straight at his adversary while the table was supposedly diverting him. What actually happened was different. Barton whipped sideways and sucked back from Toughy's hurtling form. He swung a rocky fist—not upward—but straight downward like it was a club. Toughy disappeared down behind the table in a crashing fall.

That brought the saloon's patrons around in surprise. It also brought George Henry from the far north end of his bar with an indignant bawl. As George swept up and reached down under the bar, Sheriff Logan turned his head and, without any prompting from Sedge who was straining toward the battlers as though Sheriff Logan wasn't even there, Tom said: "Let them go, George. I'll see you get paid for any damage, but just leave them be."

George's black eyes were full of dull fire for the moment he balanced there between intervening and just watching. He did not appear to Tom fully to recognize who it was Barton had been attacked by, so Tom told him. "Toughy Hammond wants to chalk up another notch. Let's give him the chance, George. He's been spoiling for this for the last five years. I want to see him get it . . . damned good."

George switched his gaze to Tom, to rigid big Sedge Horton. He removed his empty hands from below the bar and slowly shrugged. He didn't say anything, which was just as well because now his customers, stampeding closer to see Toughy roll clear and jackknife up onto his feet again, were hooting and gesturing. They didn't seem to be the least bit partial. This promised to be a fine fight, which was all any of them cared about after thirteen days of crushing boredom.

Toughy proved that his name had not been idly bestowed. After that overhand blow had put him down, and should have kept him down, he got away, pushed the table over against Barton's moving legs, got back to his feet, and, as Barton hurled the table clear with one hand, Toughy went for him again. This time Barton didn't side-step. He spread his legs, dropped over into a head-down crouch, and met Toughy's rush with a blasting right hand that ripped through Hammond's guard, sizzled up alongside Hammond's right cheek, and knocked Toughy's hat half across the room as that big fist raked up the side of Toughy's head. It had been a paralyzing blow, and, even though it nearly missed, it still heaved Hammond off balance, sent him stumbling to the left.

Now it was Barton's turn. He went over onto the offensive by stalking Hammond, by stepping close and springing away, by drawing Toughy out and by easily avoiding his blows. Barton was making a fool of Hammond, was making him look clumsy and stiff and boyish in front of that roomful of cat-calling, red-faced, and wild-eyed men. He was, Tom thought, deliberately doing that to Hammond. He was making Hammond's acquaintances shrill their derisive taunts at the cattleman who most of them had stepped lightly around for many years.

Tom smiled a little. He even turned to look up at Sedge. Horton showed no trace of the whiskey he'd consumed. He dropped his eyes. "I told you two fools," Tom murmured exultantly. "I warned you to look first, before you jumped."

"Toughy'll kill him," snarled Horton.

Tom, still softly smiling, turned back. He didn't say a word.

Barton stepped away, dropped both arms, and put his hands upon his lean hips. He said something. Tom saw his lips move, but there was too much noise to hear what it was he'd said. Toughy stepped gingerly forward, jabbing lightly with his left, holding his right up and cocked. Barton didn't move away; he simply turned his head this way and that to avoid those stinging little jabs. Toughy got bolder; he took a long forward step and swung. Barton finally moved. He jumped back, ducked, and jumped in. But Toughy desperately whipped sideways and avoided the murderous strike at his middle. He tried to chop one of those overhand strikes down atop Barton's head. It missed. Toughy roared a curse and aimed a kick at Barton's groin. The big man got swiveled around in time to take that pointed boot toe alongside one leg. Tom saw Barton wince, saw his face reflect quick anguish. Then Barton limped clear.

Hammond bawled out another curse. He'd hurt his man and knew it. Like an old wolf he charged in for the kill. Barton shifted, threw his weight upon his uninjured leg, and met Hammond head-on. They were both big men, powerful and

175

rugged. For perhaps ten seconds they slugged it out toe-to-toe before Barton, twisting his body to the right, got all the heft of his right shoulder in behind a sledge-hammer strike that knocked Toughy Hammond backward, and which would have knocked most other men quite senseless.

Hammond was stunned. He back-pedaled, twisted and turned, used all his little tricks to keep from being struck down. He was successful only because Barton could no longer rely upon his injured leg and therefore dared not plunge ahead. But Hammond didn't entirely escape. Barton herded him back toward the far gloomy corner. The window was fifteen feet to Toughy's left. He didn't realize how he'd been maneuvered until his shoulders touched the cornering wall. Then he tried to slide off to the left, but Barton was too close. Toughy had to fight now with his back to the wall, Barton blocking any escape.

The tumult inside George Henry's saloon was so loud now, what with the agitated onlookers screaming and stamping, that a surge of newcomers came bursting through the roadside door, drawn from as far southward as Poole's store by the bedlam. Toughy bobbed and weaved. He slammed hard punches into Barton's unprotected chest and stomach. He rolled his head and swung from side to side. He was desperate.

Barton took the best punches Hammond could throw. He stood with most of his weight on one leg while he parried, blocked, and counter-punched. Tom Logan had by this time entirely forgotten the conditions under which this battle had begun. He was no longer even conscious of big Sedge Horton behind him, or of George Henry across the bar from him.

Frank Barton's intake of liquor hadn't phased him. Also, in Tom's seasoned experience, he didn't believe he'd ever seen a man as clever and deadly with his fists before. Barton seemed to anticipate most of Toughy Hammond's moves. The blows he didn't block and avoid, he appeared to absorb with his body in order that he might throw more telling blows.

"It's an art," George Henry said in loud awe from across his bar. "By golly, boys, it's an art."

Toughy Hammond seemed to be coming to that same conclusion now. He was no longer fighting with a clear head. He was trying to use his knee, his head, his fingernails. He was fighting with rising panic, making his sweat-shiny face twisted and ugly. He caught a punch flush across the lips. Claret spewed over both battlers. He took another high one across the bridge of the nose. He punched wildly, kept his arms working like pump handles. Barton hitched himself in closer with a limping stride. He seemed now to be as cold about this as when the battle had started. He began relaxing his guard, began absorbing more of Hammond's punches. Tom thought—correctly—that the reason Barton was doing this was because Toughy's blows no longer had any power behind them.

Barton lowered his sights, went to work on Hammond's unprotected middle. Across the bar George said: "He's not tryin' to finish him, Tom. He's playin' with him. Whittlin' him down a rib at a time."

The crowd, too, began to realize this. For the first time since the fight started, the noise began to diminish. Barton was systematically beating Toughy Hammond to death. The room was almost silent. Men's flushed faces began to mirror an appalled understanding of Frank Barton's tactic.

Barton could have put Hammond away with one punch now. He wasn't doing that, though; he was hitting with most of his power held back. He was beating the stricken man from the chest down. He was flicking aside Hammond's futile, pawing blows and making mincemeat out of Toughy. There were no more than one or two men in that room who wouldn't rejoice, long and loud, at seeing Toughy Hammond humbled, but this—this was very near to cold-blooded murder.

"Stop him!" someone cried out. "Sheriff Logan, make him quit!"

Tom heaved upright off the bar. He twisted to look at Sedge Horton. The big cowman was standing like he couldn't believe what he was watching. He didn't heed Tom Logan at all. As Tom turned back, he heard George Henry give a long, growling sigh. He looked over. Hammond was reeling in the corner, was beginning to go down. His arms fell, his knees sprung, blood dripped from his smashed lips and trickled also from his cracked nose. He went down in a soggy heap. The saloon became silent as a tomb.

Frank Barton stood over there, breathing hard and gazing straight down. He had a purple welt alongside his face up near the hairline. His big chest rose and fell like bellows. He slowly bent, caught hold of Toughy, lifted him in both hands like a sack of meal, and hurled him bodily through George Henry's roadside front window. George, at the last moment, started to move. He was much too late. Glass tinkled, woodwork snapped, cold outside night air rushed into the room, making the lamps whip and flicker.

Barton turned to face the onlookers. He was dark with sweat and had trouble standing, but he did not unclench his large fists. "Anyone else?" he croaked, and stared straight at big Sedge Horton. "How about you, big man? You're Horton, aren't you, the one who bribed a jury to hang my grandfather because he caught your rotten lousy son tryin' to steal one of his horses. Step out, Horton. You're armed. Step out. You can have it fists, guns, or knives. Step out, you yellow son-of-a-bitch."

"That's enough!" bellowed George Henry, lifting a sawed-off shotgun from below his bar. "Mister Barton, that window'll cost you fifteen dollars! Get out of here, all of you but Sheriff Logan and Mister Barton. Out I said!"

They went, those nearest the door moving out first, the others trudging after them. There was some low growling, some black looks thrown over at Frank Barton, the same man these spectators had been so vociferously shouting favorably toward only a minute before.

"Out, dammit! All of you . . . out!"

Tom turned on Sedge Horton. He held out his hand. "Give me that Derringer," he said softly. Horton acted dazed. He handed across the little gun. Tom balanced it in his hand and made a snap decision. "Leave town, Sedge. Stay at the ranch. Don't come back here. I'll overlook this because it ended the way it did. The next time you come here like you did tonight, I promise you . . . it's going to be a lot different. Now go on."

Horton went. He paused at the roadside door to look outside, down where Toughy Hammond was lying, senseless and bloody. Logan said: "Never mind him. He'll be taken care of . . . at my jail house. Go on."

Horton passed out into the freezing night and shouldered through the clutch of men out there who were turning up their coats, pulling on their gloves, and talking up to one another. Tom could hear them in the ensuing silence as he pocketed Horton's little hide-out gun and stood with George Henry gazing over where big Frank Barton was gingerly working his right leg back and forth.

The thirteenth day of the blizzard had ended just about as Sheriff Logan had feared that it might. Someone had once said, so Tom'd been told, that it was an ill wind that brought no good with it. He doubted like all hell that this blizzard was any such a wind at all; Barton was still on his feet and the deep-down apprehension and hatred that had muddied the atmosphere since Old Man Barton's passing was, if anything, worse now than it had been the day that blizzard had struck, which had just happened also to be the same day Old Man Barton had been hanged.

"Give him a drink," Logan muttered to George. "We better nail a blanket or some planking over that window, too. It's colder'n the devil in here."

George put down his shotgun, gazed at Tom, wagged his head, and blew out a breath. He was scowling and kept right on scowling while he filled a shot glass, and turned to go shuffling on around to where Frank Barton was now shoving his shirt tail back down inside his trousers.

"Drink this," growled George, "then fork over fifteen bucks for that window. Then you better go out back an' wash up. You're a sight."

Barton impassively took the glass, drained it, handed it back, and dug into a trouser pocket for a roll of bills. He peeled off two green backs and handed them to George, still showing nothing, saying nothing, and returned the roll to his pocket. Afterward, he limped over to the bar near Tom and leaned there with his head hanging.

"Which one was he?" he hoarsely asked.

"Toughy Hammond?" said Logan. "He was one of the jurymen."

"One down and half a town yet to go," mumbled Barton.

George, behind the bar, gave Tom a quick look. Tom nodded. He'd thought that was about how Frank Barton was going to feel about the hanging of his grandfather.

VIII

Pert acted like he didn't believe his own ears when Tom Logan explained what had happened. They were standing above the wreckage of Toughy Hammond in a jail cell, and the men who had helped Logan carry Hammond there were gone. Pert had some coffee boiling on the little heating stove. Tom said: "You better go turn down the damper. It'll all boil away." As Pert moved off, Tom continued to stand stonily considering Toughy.

"He'll need a doctor to patch up his face, I expect," Logan said aloud, and the fact Pert couldn't hear didn't seem to make any difference. "Brother, that was a fight! All the bullyin' Hammond's done for the past five years got settled up for tonight."

Pert returned as Sheriff Logan was leaving the cell, locking the door behind himself. "What about Horton, throwin' down on you like that, Tom? Is he still in town? I could go round him up. . . ."

"Let him go. No, he's not still in town. I told him to go on back to the ranch and to stay there."

"He won't do it, Tom."

"Of course he won't. I didn't expect him to. But I'll tell you one thing, Pert. Before he comes back to the Junction again, he's going to do a heap of thinking."

"What kind of thinkin'?"

Tom, heading over for a cup of Pert's black Java, said: "That's strictly up to Sedge, m'boy. It's strictly up to him. A wise man would come alone, an' he'd come to make his peace with Frank Barton. A fool will push for trouble, and that will put Sedge in fact where he's always been in theory . . . outside my kind of law."

Pert sank down on a little bench and tipped his shoulders back onto the wall. He watched Tom, still faintly smiling, fill a mug and sip it. "You got any idea what you're implyin'?" Pert plaintively inquired. "If Sedge Horton ever hit this town all fired up with that big crew he's got, there wouldn't be enough left of Winchester Junction to sweep into the stove."

Tom didn't comment. He went over to his desk, sat down with his cup of coffee, and thoughtfully considered his swollen right hand. After a time he pushed back his hat, owlishly looked across at Pert, and broadly smiled. "I'm sorry you missed it, boy. That was the finest battle I've ever seen. I tell you, though, Frank Barton's no novice. He's not even a run-of-the-mill, top-notch saloon brawler. He's a genuine. . . ."

The roadside door opened and Preacher Benedict stamped in out of the bitter cold accompanied by Henry Poole. Pert's father-in-law was wearing a soft hat and crumpled old coat. He looked wan and worried. Benedict, holding his lean, horsy face tilted back so that he had to look down the full length of his nose, said: "Sheriff, do you know what malfeasance means?"

Tom swished his coffee, gradually lost his faint smile, and gazed steadily up. "I know what it means," he said very softly. "I also know something else, you fraud. I know I'm going to grab you by the seat of the britches and by the scruff of the neck and heave you headfirst into a snowbank if you come in here tonight to start rawhiding me. And, Ezra, you better believe that."

Preacher Benedict had obviously hardly expected to have his attack met head-on with a more potent attack. He wilted, lowered his head slightly, and rolled his eyes around until they rested uncertainly upon Henry Poole.

Tom sipped his coffee and also gazed at Poole. He had an idea this was going to be an awkward meeting as far as his deputy was concerned, what with Henry being Pert's father-in-law, so he said, without taking his eyes off the two visitors: "Pert, go hunt up the doctor. Fetch him back here to sew up Toughy's mouth and bandage his nose."

Pert got up and headed straight for the door, looking enormously relieved. As he passed out into the cold, Tom Logan peered into his cup, found it quite empty, and put it aside, saying as he did so: "Henry, something Barton said tonight might interest you. He asked me who Hammond was. I told him Toughy was on his grandfather's jury. He said . . . 'One down and half a town to go.' Does that mean anything to you?"

Poole stepped around Ezra Benedict, located a slat-bottomed chair, and eased down into it. "I knew even before you said that why young Barton was here. Tom, I only did my duty, the same as you. The same as all the rest of us did it."

"Yeah," murmured Logan, his dark eyes bitterly alight. "Like Toughy did it. Like Sedge Horton did it . . . from behind the scenes. I'm not blamin' any of you any more'n I'm blaming myself. I'm only saying . . . Barton's here, I can't stop him unless he back-shoots one of you . . . so maybe Preacher Benedict'll salve your soul a little, Henry. I've got a hunch you're going to need some salving before Frank Barton rides on."

Poole clasped his hands and gazed silently down at them in his lap. He was not a brave man, a shrewd one, yes, a successful one, yes—a brave one, no.

Ezra Benedict went over to the doorway front wall and gently leaned there while he considered Tom Logan. "You must be the tool of divine intercession," he insisted. "Sheriff, it's your duty!"

Tom glanced up. "I've told you before . . . stick your long nose into my affairs, Benedict, and I'll run your head into a snowbank up to the shoulders. You get out of here. Go on now. Henry doesn't need you and neither do I."

"I came here to minister to the injured," said Benedict, his stubborn streak up. "You have no authority to deny me that."

Logan got up, took his cup back over to the stove, and wordlessly refilled it. He then returned to his desk, put the cup down, and lifted a ring of keys that he held out. "Go on in an' see him," he said. "Lock yourself in and, when you come out, lock yourself out. Toughy's not going anywhere, though. Not for maybe a week. Preacher, all the lousy things Hammond's done for the past five years caught up with him tonight in one sitting. By not stepping foot inside George's saloon you missed the damnedest fight you'll ever see. Well, don't stand there looking like that at me. You said you wanted to minister to him . . . go do your ministerin'."

Tom sat down, leaned back, and watched Benedict stiffly stride across to the cell room. Henry Poole lifted his head.

Henry's colorless, thin features looked gray and old and frightened. "I can't cope with a man like Frank Barton," he whispered. "I never wore a gun in my life, Tom."

"Well, that's what I'm paid for," responded Logan. "But I can't do anything to protect you, Henry, until Barton does something that makes me think you need protection."

"Yes," muttered Poole in a quavering voice. "Like shooting me in the back . . . and after that I won't need your protection."

"He won't shoot you in the back. Barton's not that kind."

Pert returned with the disgruntled local doctor in tow. Tom smiled, not in greeting particularly but because the doctor was swaddled in an old blue Army coat that dragged across his instep and looked as bitterly resentful as men look only after being routed out of a warm bed in the middle of a bitterly cold night. Tom inclined his head toward the cell room. "He's in there, Doc. If you need anything, just sing out."

Pert guided the medical man along. The pair of them looked briefly at Henry Poole as they passed across in front of him, and moments later Henry jumped when the doctor roared out an angry curse from out of sight beyond the cell-room door. Moments later Pert and Preacher Benedict came out. Pert was looking wry.

"He dang' near bit the preacher's arm off when he saw him in there with Hammond," Pert reported. Benedict stalked across to the door and reached down for the latch. He was angry.

"Ezra," murmured Logan, "do the town a favor, will you? Go on home and go to bed."

Benedict snorted, hauled open the door, and stamped out. A frigid blast of roadway air came in, driving Pert over to the wood box where he got some kindling for the stove. Henry Poole sat through all this like he was part of his chair.

Tom sipped coffee. He thought he knew what Frank Barton would do next. He didn't mention it for a number of reasons, but primarily because he was tired, his hand hurt, and, if he said any more, Pert and Henry would start talking all over again, and all Tom wanted right now was to go to bed. There was always another day. There always had been another day and Frank Barton, Toughy Hammond, Sedge Horton notwithstanding, there would *still* be another day. He put aside the coffee cup and stood up. "Go home, Henry. We'll just have to wait and see."

Pert came forward as though to assist his father-in-law out of the chair. Henry got up by himself and ignored Pert to look glassily at Logan and repeat what he'd earlier, plaintively said: "It was my duty. It was everyone's duty. The old man shot and killed young Horton."

"I know, Henry. Now go on. . . ."

"How could Old Man Barton expect us to believe a lad like that, with all his father's wealth and all his father's horses, would deliberately try to steal another man's horse? I tell you, Sheriff, we *had* to bring in that. . . ."

"Take him home," said Tom to Pert. "Then you go on home, too." Logan passed across and held the door for Poole and Pert to pass through. He afterward gently closed the door and leaned upon it and was still leaning upon it when the doctor came out into the office and tossed down Tom's keys.

"I locked him in, but he couldn't get out of there if he had to crawl on his hands and knees. Tom; did you see him get that beating?"

"I did."

"Couldn't you stop it, man? Hammond's nose is broken, he is minus two teeth, his lower lip is a mess, and, if that's not enough, he's got three cracked ribs. I tell you frankly, I've seen men run over by wagons without half his contusions and bruises."

"But he'll live," muttered Logan. "Doc, you believe in that

there law of retribution?"

The medical man squinted his eyes nearly closed. "If all I'm going to get out of you is philosophy," he growled, "I might as well go home. But I want to tell you something, Tom. A thing as serious as standing by and watching a man get beaten as bad as Hammond has been beaten cannot possibly do your official standing any good in this town. You can take my word for that."

"Doc, Sedge Horton had a gun in my back when that brawl started. Sedge and Hammond had that all cooked up before I even showed up. It backfired on them. If the town wants to blame me for that, then it can go right ahead because I'm sick of Winchester Junction anyway."

The doctor pursed his lips and thoughtfully considered Logan for a moment before he said: "You mean to tell me Sedge Horton is that big a fool, holding a gun in a peace officer's back?"

"You've got no idea how big a fool . . . and a louse . . . Sedge Horton is, Doctor. Now, you'd better go on home and try to catch up on your sleep. I've got a feeling, too, that you hadn't better leave town for a day or two, even if the snow melts. Frank Barton's not leaving, which probably means more work for you."

"Ahh, yes," the medical practitioner murmured. "I heard a rumor about Old Man Barton having a stepson or something who showed up here. Was it him that did that to Toughy Hammond?"

"It was."

"He must be a very powerful man, Sheriff. Very powerful."

Tom opened the door for the doctor. "It takes more than just power, Doc, it also takes savvy. Barton had to know how to use his fists like that. A man doesn't learn that in saloon brawls, either. He learns it some other way."

The doctor passed out, paused to tug up his collar, then went hiking northward up the empty roadway with his footfalls emptily echoing upon the frozen planking. Tom watched his retreating figure a moment before he raised his eyes and glanced along the roadway. There were no forgotten or neglected saddle horses left at any of the tie racks, which was one of his jobs to look after. There were no drunks lying in the roadway, which was another little chore he was responsible for, and up the way and across the road only one turned-down lamp glowed through only one window at the Big Eagle Saloon. The other window had been boarded up with a large piece of planking. Tom sighed, closed the door, went over to the stove, and held forth his right hand for a moment, until the heat winnowed out all the ache, then he headed on through to his own quarters. It had been a very enlightening night, very enlightening indeed.

He looked in on Toughy Hammond, saw that his prisoner hadn't moved, and left the lantern burning outside Toughy's cell. Sometime in the night Hammond was going to wake up, and, when he did, that light might seem like the friend he was sorely going to need.

IX

When Logan awoke the next morning just at sunrise, there was a steady, warm wind blowing. He got up, freshened up, went along to see how his locked-up guest was, and found Toughy sitting there, trying to smoke a cigarette with battered hands and a swollen face. The Chinook wind was blowing steadily out of the north and worrying along at the eaves of the jail house roof, making a little scratchy, moaning sound. Hammond's smoke smelled especially strong to Logan. He stopped and gazed through the bars. Instead of offering the customary new day greeting he said: "Boy, you're a mess."

Toughy looked up. "You don't look exactly pretty yourself," he grunted, his words difficult to understand. "Why'n hell'd you have stitches taken in my mouth? It'd have healed all right without 'em."

Tom shrugged. He was not in an argumentative mood even though Hammond obviously was. "You want some mush?" he inquired, and Toughy kept staring at him.

"What I want," he thickly said, "is another crack at Barton as soon as I'm able."

"You never learn, do you?" responded Tom Logan. "I reckon next time you'll want to try it with guns. Take my advice, Toughy, and call it quits while you're still alive. I tried to talk sense into you 'n' Sedge last night, but, no, you two are just too cussed smart. Well, I won't stop either of you. If you want to try it with guns . . . go right ahead. It'll ease a lot of my headaches if Barton kills the pair of you. You know what I think, Toughy? I think he can do it, too. Now, do you want some breakfast or not?"

"When you goin' to let me out of here, Tom?"

Logan turned and abruptly strode off to get his own breakfast.

Outside, that steady warm wind had evidently been blowing for several hours, perhaps for half the previous night, because there were strong rivulets of dirty water flooding the roadway, the snowbanks at the sidewalk's edge were beginning to cave in, out upon the distant plain bare patches showed darkly through a white blanket, and even far up the distant slopes the trees showed black against their eerie background.

Over at the café two men were glumly eating. There was steam on the front windows. Tom ordered fried potatoes and a small breakfast-size steak for himself and a bowl of mush for his prisoner. One of the other early diners was Will Clampitt. Will hadn't shaved; in fact, he didn't look like he'd washed, either, and his hat did not quite hide his rumpled hair. Tom made a little sniffing sound of disapproval.

The other diner was Pert. He gave Logan a funny little look

and said: "Women need more sleep'n men. Anyway, I don't mind eatin' out."

"Sure," Tom murmured.

At the break in their otherwise silence, Will Clampitt raised up from his hunched position and looked at Logan. "How's Toughy?" he asked.

Tom's breakfast came. He considered it a moment, then said: "He'll live." Then, as he picked up his tools, he added: "If he changes his attitude, I mean."

Clampitt twisted as the roadside door opened and the hulking big frame of Frank Barton came in out of the gray morning. Clampitt seemed to be thinking of something to say, but in the end he evidently decided against speaking and hunched over his plate again. The counterman came forth and asked Barton what he wanted to eat. The big man looked at Logan's plate and nodded. The counterman went away.

"How's the leg?" Sheriff Logan asked, tossing a look around, then falling on his meal with both hands.

"It'll do," stated Barton. "How's Hammond?"

"I reckon he'll also do," returned Logan. "But he's got an awful hard head."

"In more ways than one," grunted the big man, easing down at the counter between Pert and Tom.

"Tell me something, Sheriff. Did Horton and Hammond have that set up between them?"

"They did. Horton wants you out of Winchester Junction."

"I see."

The counterman returned, set a platter before Frank Barton, and went after Barton's coffee. For a while there was only the sound of men eating, then Barton put down his knife and fork to lean there, sipping coffee. He said: "I've heard two versions of the hangin', Sheriff. Mind tellin' me your version?"

Tom straightened up. "I'm eating," he growled. "There's a

189

time and a place for everything. Not now."

Pert turned to see how Barton might take this rebuff. Barton's dark face showed nothing. He went back to eating. So did Pert.

But the atmosphere seemed to turn a little sour, and, as though he felt this strongly, Will Clampitt stood up, counted out some silver, put it atop the counter, turned, and walked out of the café without glancing back. Tom waited until Will had closed the roadside door, then he pushed his plate away, hooked his coffee cup in closer, and started speaking.

"Horton's kid went out to your grandfather's place. That much no one's in doubt about. After that, there are two sides to what happened. The local side is that Sedge's kid might've been wild and arrogant and sort of a bully, but he didn't have to steal a horse."

Barton quietly said: "What was the old man's side of it?"

"Your grandfather said the kid was in his barn, rigging out a gelding the old man'd trained for a couple of years into the best cow horse in the country, when the old man walked down there to do his chores. The kid fired at him. The old man wasn't armed so he run back to the house. The kid was making a run for it. The old man picked him off with his rifle at two hundred yards. Killed him."

Barton called for a refill of his cup. He didn't speak again until this order had been complied with, then he said: "Did you find a bullet hole where the kid shot at him?"

"Nope," stated Tom. "And that's one thing that weighed against your grandpappy, Mister Barton."

"If he was in the doorway of his barn, you wouldn't have found one anyway, would you have, Sheriff?"

"No," replied Logan candidly. "The slug wouldn't have hit anything. It would've just sped on out over the plain."

"And on that . . . you folks hung the old man?"

"Mister Barton," said Sheriff Logan flatly, "the kid was hit in the back. He hadn't. . . ."

"Sheriff, how about his gun? If he shot at the old man, there'd have been an empty shell casin'."

"That's what I was coming to. There were six shells in his gun, none fired." Tom shifted on his seat under Pert Whipple's look. "All right," he grumbled. "When his paw brought the gun to me four days later, it could've been swabbed out and re-loaded. That's what came out at the trial. But still, except for your grandfather's word, there wasn't a lick of evidence that Old Man Barton hadn't shot the kid in the back without provocation."

Barton said, over the lip of his raised cup: "Do you believe that, Logan?"

Tom's dark brows dropped and he fidgeted on the bench. Pert was watching him impassively. "What I believe didn't carry much weight, Mister Barton. I told 'em I'd known the old man since I first came here. I told 'em they also knew him that well. He wasn't a back-shooter."

Pert spoke up, softly, to Frank Barton. "Something you got to understand about your old grandpappy, Mister Barton. He's been tellin' tall tales around Winchester Junction since I was a little kid, about how he fought Injuns, and later on how he knocked over his share of badmen. He never seemed to make any secret that all his fights didn't end in face-to-face shoot-outs."

"That's how they fought in his day," stated Barton, putting down the empty cup. "My father was mostly Crow. He used to tell me about his father. I reckon the stories he told me are the same stories the old man told you fellers. My father heard them from the old man many years ago, before my folks got married and the old man drifted on because, as he said, there wasn't any teepee big enough for two families." Barton stood up, dug in

191

one pocket for some coins, and, as he slapped the money down, he said: "But the old man wouldn't shoot someone unless he had to. I never knew him, but I knew my paw. The old man raised him an' *he* raised me. The same rules were handed down. You kill when you have to, *how* you have to, but you never kill for sport. So . . . my judgment is that Horton's kid was stealin' the damned horse."

"Well," Tom Logan stated, "that isn't going to change anything, Mister Barton. Times change. Folks change with them. Except for a couple of things I'd say that the old man's trial was reasonably fair. I told the court I didn't want to be the one to trip that damned trap door. You got any idea what the judge told me? He said it was my sworn duty and he wouldn't appoint a substitute. Then your grandpappy, who happened to be an old friend of mine, said . . . and I remember his words like it was yesterday. He said . . . 'It's better for a man to die looking at the face of a friend, Tom, even like this. I'm askin' you to do this for me. I want you up there on the scaffold with me. It's my last request, from an old friend to an old friend.' "

Logan also stood up. He and big Frank Barton faced one another. Pert turned on the bench but did not stand up. In his kitchen the café man was rattling pots and pans. Outside that warm Chinook wind was steadily blowing. Tom said: "You believe what you want to, Mister Barton. If you feel I got to be punished like Hammond and the others, why you just go ahead and do what you got to do. I'm asking no favors an' I wouldn't accept any if you offered 'em. In a way I'm sort of like the old man. I've lived a good while. I've seen my share of life an' people. I'm not so damned fond of either that I can't bear the thought of leaving 'em."

Frank Barton's dark-liquid gaze hung on Logan for a long time. He made a quiet little sigh, then turned and walked on out of the café without a word.

Pert strolled through the roadway mud back toward the jail house with Toughy Hammond's mush in his hand, and with Logan beside him. He didn't speak until Tom was reaching out to open the jail house front door. "Tom, that big devil's more Injun than white. He doesn't say what he's thinkin'. Frankly he gives me the creeps."

They went inside, Pert got the keys, and went along to give Toughy his breakfast. Tom stood in the doorway with that good warmth against his face, watching Winchester Junction come sluggishly to life. Henry Poole came briskly along to open his place of business. He had a spring to his step he hadn't had the day before.

Will Clampitt was ditching the run-off snow water so that it wouldn't flow across the entrance to his barn. Up the road and across it, George Henry was standing in front of his plank-patched window with both hands on his hips, looking at his handiwork. Two women in shawls and bonnets came down the northward sidewalk holding their skirts above the mud and slush, with baskets on their arms, the first shoppers to pump silver into the town's economic arteries of this new day. Overhead, the sky was cloudless and a very pale, faded shade of blue. The sun was brightening the world in the east; where its dawn rays struck upon Teton snowfields high up and far off, a soft pinkness resulted.

Tom relaxed. It looked like the beginning of a good day, except for the muddy undercurrent of what had happened the day before. Tom shrugged. Maybe Sedge would do as Tom had told him. Maybe. Tom wasn't that naïve. He'd known Horton a long time, too. Men didn't change very much from cradle to grave. The older they got, the more they reverted to their youthful convictions. When things got complicated, they turned inward, turned hard and resentful and sometimes unrelenting in their vindictiveness. In his earlier years Sedge Horton had always triumphed. He would revert to the same tactics now, which he had used then. That was how men were made.

Pert came across to stand in the doorway, also without speaking, gazing up and down the roadway. South and west of town someone was ringing a small bell. Pert took out his watch and flicked open its case. "That's the school bell," he observed. "But she's ringin' it an hour early." He put away the watch and made a low grunt as Ezra Benedict came striding down the yonder plank walk bound for Henry Poole's emporium. Pert turned back into the office and went over to the stove to make a little fire and put the coffee pot on.

The sight of Preacher Benedict curdled Logan's thoughts a little, too, so he stepped back, closed the door, and strolled to his desk, his earlier hopes for a lull before the next storm dwindling. Sedge would return; he'd come this time with men and guns. He had an abundance of both. He also had his hard-headedness and his violent temper.

Tom rummaged his desk, found a dry old cigar someone had given him, bit off the end, and lit the thing. It smelled like old barnyard rope burning but it had the good tang of strong tobacco, so he smoked it and went over by the stove to push out his right hand and consider it. The bruises were still there, but most of the swelling had departed. He could work the fingers without any great difficulty, but, as Pert watched, Tom read his doubtfulness. "It'll do," Tom said in reply to Pert's expression.

"Not against Barton it won't," contradicted Pert. "Not against Horton, either. Next time, use your left hand. A feller never knows when he's goin' to have to rely on his gun hand, Tom."

Logan said smoothly—"How's the missus?"—but it didn't fool Pert any.

"If there's need for gun work, you'd better let me handle it, Tom. Not that I'm as good as you are, but with those fingers gettin' stiff every time you get 'em cold. . . ."

"Gun work?" mused Logan, chewing his stogie. "If there's any of that, it won't be Barton who starts it. I've got an idea about him, Pert. I've got a feeling he's going to whittle Sedge down one man at a time . . . and with his fists."

"He's sure good with 'em, all right."

"It's more'n that, boy. Barton's a trained fist fighter. He's been professional at it somewhere. I've seen too many brawlers not to recognize the real skilled professional when he comes along."

Pert ran this through his mind while he took down two crockery mugs and carefully filled them. Finally Pert said: "In that case, if that's what he's plannin', then he'd better quit wearin' that gun, because Horton's men'll figure that out soon enough. Then they'll challenge him to shoot it out."

X

The wind was beginning to come in warm gusts by the time Logan sauntered up to the Big Eagle. Pert had made the earlier round of town and had come back to report that some of the outlying cattlemen had drifted in. It was a safe bet that these ranchers, after two weeks of isolation, were bubbling with restlessness. It was also a safe bet that they'd head for George's place, because they always did; the Big Eagle had long been the cowmen's favorite hang-out.

The sun was aiding in melting off the drifts. Creeks would be swollen for a month after this. Winchester Junction's roadway was a morass. An enterprising saddle maker up the roadway, in conjunction with another storekeeper, had devised what, upon first view, seemed like a mighty clever method for folks to get from one plank walk across to the other one without sinking to their hocks in mud. They had laboriously put down two long planks atop the mud. The trouble was, as Logan came along to try this innovation, at the same time a ranch rig came skittering along behind a team of thousand-pound horses and after all four big wheels had passed along, the planks were out of sight somewhere down below, in the mud. Logan had to make the crossing without aid. Upon the far sidewalk, when he paused to hold to an upright post and kick off the clinging gumbo, a sympathetic cowboy with his spurs out a notch so as they'd jangle on the sidewalk the way cocky young buckaroos often did, said: "Sheriff, there are times when it just don't pay to visit cities."

Up at the Big Eagle Logan got a surprise. George had his substitute barman running the place while he and Frank Barton were at that same gloomy corner in the south end of the place, playing two-handed casino. The last time Logan had seen these two they'd been far from friendly. He walked on over. When the barman signaled inquiringly to him, Tom shook his head, drew out a chair, and dropped down. George looked over his cards at Logan. So did Frank Barton. Logan shrugged.

"Nothin' else to do," he muttered, and fished out some silver to plunk down. "Three-handed is better anyway."

George looked at Barton. The big man shrugged and returned to adding up his cards. The object was to see who could get closest to the number twenty-one. If you went above twenty-one, you were busted. If you stayed under it, and your opposition stayed even lower than you did, then you won the pot. It was not a complicated game, but it was an old favorite among range men. It was also called twenty-one, or blackjack.

George and Barton finished drawing against each other. George won, and the next hand they dealt Logan in. While George dealt—the winner of each pot also got the deal—he said: "I told Barton who was foreman of the old man's jury, Tom. I also told him where Toughy Hammond fit in."

Logan picked up his cards impassively, wondering exactly how George meant that. Had he told Barton what the gossip was—Hammond had sold his juryman's vote to Sedge Horton? George cleared that up when next he spoke.

"He's got a right to know, Tom. He guessed about Toughy, anyway."

Logan added up his cards. The total was eighteen, never a good number. He glanced across at Frank Barton. The big man was studying his cards with a wooden face. "Well . . . ?" Tom said.

Barton rapped the table top. George flicked him another card. Barton took it up, added it to his hand, and slowly shook his head. He then folded his cards and looked squarely at Logan.

"A man learns something in every fresh situation, doesn't he, Sheriff? For instance, Hammond's the kind to condemn an old man to death who never hurt him . . . for cash or its equivalent. Henry here . . . he's the kind who fights to the last ditch, then gives in when he's overwhelmed. And you . . . well, you're harder to figure, but in the end you did your duty, so I reckon you can sleep easy, too."

"No," objected Sheriff Logan, "you're oversimplifying things, Frank. No man sleeps easy just because he's done his duty, not if it required him to hang another man. And no man sleeps easy after he's been swept along and snowed under by the vote of others. As for Hammond. . . ." Logan looked hard at his cards, then threw them down. His total score was eighteen. He gazed across at George, but Henry shook his head. He'd stood pat on seventeen. Frank Barton tossed down a black ace and a black-jack.

"Twenty-one," he murmured, and swept in the pot. "How about a man like Henry Poole?" he inquired. "Does he stay awake nights, too?"

Logan and George exchanged a sulphurous glance. Logan pushed the cards over to Barton. "Henry's kind isn't new in the world," he explained tartly. "They may be sort of new this far

West, but elsewhere they've always constituted a majority, so they've had their say, and it's usually been in some way that favored their interests."

"That's a fair appraisal," said Barton, dealing, "but it doesn't answer my question."

"He was in my office last night, scairt stiff," stated Logan gruffly. "Does that answer your question?"

"Maybe," murmured Barton, and picked up his cards. "What should I do about Poole?"

"Kill him if you want to," said Logan acidly. "He doesn't wear a gun and he's probably never been in a real fist fight in his life."

"I'd have to kill your deputy, too, then, wouldn't I? The way folks have told me, Whipple is Poole's son-in-law. He'd stand up for Poole, wouldn't he?"

"Would you," asked Logan, frowning bleakly at his cards, "if Poole was your daddy-in-law?"

Barton didn't answer. He put aside his hand and picked up the deck. "You want a hit?" he asked. Tom shook his head. "How about you?" Barton asked George. The saloon man nodded, caught the card, looked at it, and threw down his hand in disgust. He was busted with a score of twenty-seven. He leaned back and looked from Barton to Logan and back again.

"Poole's not the one responsible," he stated. "I figure you know that by now, Barton. He did what he figured was right. If you're going to start thinnin' out the folks in this lousy world who do things they're convinced are right, you're goin' to have to work at it day and night. In fact, you're goin' to need a big army of helpers. Poole's kind looks at things a heap different from some of us. He's for his own particular kind of law 'n' order. He's got to be, otherwise folks'd never pay their bills or respect his property, or even act like they was civilized. I'm not sayin' his kind of right doesn't leave a bad taste in my mouth. I do say, since his kind runs things an' out-numbers all other kinds . . . at least for now . . . that's how things are an' how they're goin' to continue to be."

Logan put his cards down face up. He had twenty. Barton placed his cards down, also face up. He had eighteen. Tom raked in the pot.

"What about Horton . . . who wasn't on that jury?" asked Barton.

Tom answered him. "The law's got nothing on Horton. Even if Hammond told the truth . . . that he'd sold his vote and worked like hell at browbeatin' the other jurymen to bring in that guilty verdict against your grandpappy, the law still couldn't do a whole lot."

"But I can do something," said Frank Barton, handing Logan the deck to shuffle and re-deal. "And you two've already guessed that I reckon to."

"You'll just get killed," mumbled George Henry.

Tom held up dealing for a moment while he gazed at the big cowboy. "Something interests me about you," he said quietly. So quietly his companions had to sift out the other noises within the barroom to hear him. "Where did you learn to fight, Frank? Last night . . . that wasn't luck, it was skill. You've fought with your hands for money, somewhere."

Barton's dark gaze brightened with sardonic amusement toward Sheriff Logan. "Funny you should mention that," he drawled. "As a matter of fact, Sheriff, that's how I've made my living through the winters for the past four years when there weren't any ridin' jobs to be had."

"You done a lot of it?"

"Quite a lot, yes. I've fought under a dozen names all the way from Montana to Texas, and back again."

George leaned back and watched Tom slowly deal out their cards. He had nothing to say until he'd picked up his cards, added up their total, and decided, on the strength of what he was holding, to stand pat. As he folded the cards, he said: "Barton, if you figure to thin 'em out with your fists, you'd better quit wearin' that gun. Horton's boys'll salt you down with lead."

Barton called for a hit. Tom dealt him the card and Barton dropped the hand, busted with a total of thirty-three. "I thought about that last night," he said. "What's your advice, Logan?"

But Tom was gazing over at George. "What you got?" he demanded. George spread out his cards. He had a ten of hearts and a black jack, which was twenty-one because face cards counted eleven. Logan looked and waggled his head. "You're winnin' too much," he grumbled. "You ought to have to stand the drinks."

"I asked your advice," said Barton, tossing away his hand.

Tom shrugged. "I'm paid to keep the peace. You wouldn't heed my advice, Frank. But since you asked for it, I'll give it. Your grandpappy's dead. He wouldn't want to see you get killed over that fact. I knew him, I reckon, as well as anyone around. He was a wise old misfit. A good man. Don't bother taking off the gun, Frank, saddle up and ride on. You asked for it and there it is. You can't whip Horton by yourself. Not in a million years." Logan scooped up the deck and riffled it. He slowly dealt and did not look at Frank Barton again until the three of them were counting their spots. Barton's face was darkly unreadable, but in the depths of his oddly gold-flecked eyes a flinty light lay smoldering. Logan sighed. Barton wasn't going to take his advice. He hadn't expected him to, any more that he'd expected Sedge Horton to take his advice after Hammond was vanquished the night before.

Pert came into the saloon, saw those three over in their shadowy corner playing cards together, and, after recovering from his surprise, Pert sauntered over, bent down to whisper something into Logan's ear, then walked stiffly on over to the bar for a drink.

Neither Barton nor George Henry said anything. They acted as though Pert hadn't come over at all. That pot went to George and the next one went to Frank Barton. He was dealing when Logan twisted to gaze around. There were more than a dozen men in the room, none of them seriously drinking yet because it was only noon, but mostly just playing with glasses of beer, which gave them the right to be congregated in the saloon, talking a little, mostly about the break in the weather. Logan squared back around and reached for his fresh cards.

"You expectin' someone?" Barton asked casually.

"You never know," muttered Tom, concentrating on his hand of cards. "The roads and trails are melting off pretty fast now. The range men've been cooped up a long time. You never know what to expect in a situation like this."

Will Clampitt came, and paused to stamp mud off his boots. George saw this and made an unpleasant face. In a near whisper he called Will a fierce name. "Most folks do that at the edge of the walk, but not Will. He's goin' to cadge a beer or maybe pry himself loose of a five-cent piece and buy his own, which gives him the right to bring his dirt in here. Someday . . . someday. . . ."

"What've you got?" Barton asked, and George bent skeptically to consider his hand.

"Twenty," he said. "How about you?"

"Eighteen."

George made a little clucking sound and gazed at Logan. "Busted," Tom said, throwing his cards down. "Barton, on second thought maybe you'd better keep that gun on. Providin' you're fast with it. Y'see, I hurt my right hand the other night an' can't draw right fast now."

Barton looked over, not quite comprehending. "Are you deputizin' me?" he asked.

"No. Nothing like that. What Pert came in to tell me a minute ago was that Sedge Horton's on his way to town with seven of his men . . . and Jack Forester."

"Who's Jack Forester?"

"Horton's range boss."

George put down his cards. "A Texan," he growled. "A big, mean Texan. They say he's one of the best cowmen in Wyoming Territory. I wouldn't know about that, but you see that planked-up window you flung Toughy Hammond through last night? Well, the last time it got busted, it was Jack Forester who did it. He hurled two east-country cowboys through it. *Two* of 'em."

Frank leaned over, counted Logan's cards, George Henry's cards, and swept in the pot with another twenty-one. All he said in response to George's description of Sedge Horton's range boss was: "Interesting." He dealt out the cards and waited for the other two to pick them up. Neither Logan nor George Henry did. They were looking straight at Barton. They were waiting.

Barton lowered his hand and looked back. He said: "All right. I've been expecting this. You didn't figure I was so dumb I didn't think Horton would be back, did you?"

"You're one man," said George. "I don't give a damn how big you are, Barton. No man's *that* big. Sedge Horton by himself is bad enough. With seven of his men . . . and Jack Forester . . . you're done for."

Barton put down the cards, glanced around the saloon and relaxed, pushed his long legs far under the table, and gently inclined his head. "Like I just said, I figured he'd be back. I figured a man who'd get someone else to do his fightin' once, would do the same thing again. I'm ready."

George stared a moment longer, then gripped both arms of his chair and leaned forward to shoot upright to his feet. "Buy you both a drink at the bar," he said, springing up.

Logan arose, but Barton shook his head at them. "A mite early for me," he said. "I'll just deal out a hand of solitaire." He looked at the pair of grave, older faces above him and made a slow, soft little wolfish smile. "You're a good guesser, Sheriff, about my experience at one kind of fighting. Now just go on over and have your drink . . . and stay out of the way so's you can find out what experience I've had at this other kind of fighting. I give you my word that I won't shoot first. I won't break your law."

George said, gruffly: "Come along, Tom. The fool's got a right to defend himself. I need a drink."

Logan walked away with a troubled expression.

XI

Men constantly passed in and out of the saloon. Some went down to the café for their midday meal, and some went reluctantly to Poole's store with their lists of things for the ranches. But other men came to take their vacated places along George's bar. Mostly these were cattlemen swathed in heavy sheepskin coats and with heavy woolen mufflers around their throats. There were even a few of the older men with those hairy old-time Angora chaps over their legs; for all that gusty warm wind and the dazzling sunlight, it was still below zero outside. The air was so crisp the smallest sound carried a goodly distance. Sunlight bouncing back off white drifts nearly blinded men, so generally they rode into town with their hats tugged low above their eyes.

It was unsteady going for the ranch wagons, out in the muddy roadway. Horses pulled but wheels did not always obediently follow. Some parts of Wyoming had a unique soil; it was like the adobe plains of the far Southwest. When it was wet, it got as greasy as a peeled onion. Men's curses bristled in the roadway as much from trying to avoid collisions under these circumstances as from being splattered when they had to navigate it on foot.

At the bar Will Clampitt had a suggestion that he confided to Tom Logan. "Fetch down maybe a couple dozen big loads of fine rock from the dry washes at the base of the Tetons, and fill the roadway in with the stuff."

"Sure," grumbled Pert on Will's far side. "Then the danged slush'd ooze up over the boardwalks and we'd be stepping into stores full of muddy water. Will, you got any more real clever ideas?"

Clampitt subsided. After a decent interval had passed, he took his beer glass and went farther down the bar where he'd be appreciated.

Henry Poole walked in. Tom and Pert didn't notice him. They instead saw the look of surprise cross George's face. George was standing in front of them. They both turned. Henry looked entirely without confidence, standing over there in the doorway, glancing owlishly around.

"Make him take a drink," said George caustically. Henry spied Tom and Pert, struck out for them, and halted with that guilty, self-conscious expression teetotalers invariably show when they visit a saloon. "Sedge just rode in," he blurted out at Logan. "He's tying up outside right this minute."

"Yeah," said Pert to his father-in-law. "With seven riders. We know."

"Well, do something. Don't just stand in here drinking. Do something!"

Logan growled: "What's worrying you, Henry? Sedge is here to polish off Frank Barton. You should be happy about that. Barton's no friend of yours."

Poole's expression turned desperate. "No man deserves to die from odds like these, Sheriff. Not even Frank Barton."

"He'd like to hear that from you," said Logan. "Go on back

to the store and keep low." Tom put his back upon Poole and lifted his beer glass to gaze thoughtfully at its amber contents. Across from him George became busy under the bar where he had a bucket of greasy water for sluicing out whiskey glasses. Only Pert didn't show contempt; Pert took his father-in-law by the arm and piloted him out of the saloon, then returned to his place at the bar.

"What do you figure we ought to do?" he asked Logan.

"Nothing yet," growled Logan. "No one's forced to do anything yet, boy. Relax. Hey, George, you got that blunderbuss of yours underneath the bar full-choked with lead slugs?"

George nodded. "I have. But I'm not right set on bucking the Horton bunch, Tom."

"No? You like killing old men with hang ropes better?"

George's head shot up, his nostrils flared, and his dark eyes turned fierce. "You had no call to say that, Tom Logan. Whose side you on anyway?"

"Damned if I know for sure," muttered Tom, turning his glass between both hands. "Damned if I know, George. And maybe you're right. I shouldn't have said that. Still, the odds do sort of stick in my craw."

"Well, are you an' Pert an' me supposed to get killed, too, just because that big Injun over there think's he's a match for Horton's guns?"

Tom went on turning the glass slowly as he answered that. "I reckon not. But we did do the dirty work that's got young Barton into this fix, George. We did hang the old man."

"So do we owe Frank Barton something?"

Tom shrugged again, looking morose. "That's what I can't figure out, exactly. Do we, George?"

"We might owe Old Man Barton something, but this one, hell's bells, didn't any of us set sights on him until. . . ."

"But he's the same flesh an' blood, George."

Pert, on the sheriff's right, cleared his throat loudly and turned with his back to the bar. Over at the doorway several coated men in hats and gloves were pushing on inside out of the golden cold. They were all large men; none of them was smiling. Sedge was in the lead. Behind him was another man, perhaps an inch shorter than Horton, but also a few pounds heavier. Jack Forester. In his sheepskin coat and black hat, Forester looked as large as a bull moose. He looked as mean and cruel as a rutting bull moose usually is, too. He had a ruddy face and light blue eyes. His mouth drooped at its outer edges, his nose high-bridged and somewhat hawk-like. Any place in this world Jack Forester would have inspired hard men to step widely around him. He exuded menace as some men exude the odors of horse sweat and strong, shag tobacco.

Horton saw the pair of lawmen opposite him at the bar. He stepped farther into the saloon so that all his riders could push in behind him. Along the bar other men, sensing something, also turned as Pert had done and as Sheriff Logan was now doing to stare. Horton had eyes only for the lawmen. He didn't look triumphant or even exultant; he simply looked business-like, as though he'd come here for one job alone and meant for nothing to obstruct him.

Tom Logan knew that look. He'd seen it many other times on Sedge Horton's rugged, square-set face. In fact, he'd pictured Horton coming at him looking like that for the past twenty-four hours. It made all his senses sharpen, made his nerves sing tautly. He and Horton had never openly clashed like this before. They'd had their growling arguments and their frequent differences, but this wasn't like it had been before— this was for keeps.

Forester, swinging to consider everyone in the saloon, spotted big Frank Barton playing solitaire over in his dark corner and said something low out of the corner of his mouth. Sedge looked over at Barton, too, and nodded his head.

Behind Logan something made of steel scraped the bar top. George Henry stepped clear and pushed his shotgun straight out. He cocked it. Those twin, harsh sounds brought complete silence in their wake. At that range George's riot gun would chew up Horton and his men.

"You don't start anything in here," growled the burly barman. "If you're here to make war, Sedge . . . you, Jack 'n' the rest of you . . . go on back outside for it."

Not a man was moving except down where Frank Barton leaned over to gaze at the lay of cards in front of him. Without deigning even to glance at Horton, Barton drawled: "Like the man says, Horton . . . outside."

Jack Forester tilted back his head and put a fierce, bold look upon the card player. "After you, mister," he said thinly.

Barton put down his cards, jackknifed up out of his chair, and studied Forester for a silent moment before he nodded and moved around the table in the direction of the door. Each of his heavy footfalls made a hollow echo in the hushed saloon. Tom Logan dropped his right hand straight down. So did Pert. Off on their right George was closely watching from a hunched-over position above his scatter-gun. Tom thought he had an idea about how Barton was going to work this. Tom had seen these scenes acted out before. But he was dead wrong.

Barton didn't push on through the stiffly standing Horton cowboys and go out into the muddy roadway to make his stand. He walked straight toward Sedge, turned at the very last second as though to shoulder between Horton and massive Jack Forester, and let drive with a sledging fist that traveled from no farther than his belt buckle. Horton wasn't expecting it. The fist cracked under his jaw like a tree limb breaking.

Then Barton was on Jack Forester, this time with both fists. Forester, too, was unsuspecting, but he took the first two slamming blows without more than gasping and staggering. He was, obviously, tougher than his employer. Horton had crashed over backward across a card table, from there to the sawdust floor, and was completely out of it.

The other Horton riders bumped one another in their frantic effort to get clear. They swore and jumped this way and that. Probably none of them saw Forester go down, but Logan and Whipple and George Henry did. It was odd how the powerful Texan did it; he didn't collapse as Sedge Horton had done. He tried to protect his face and middle, pawing with mighty arms at Barton, then fell to one knee and tried blindly to catch hold of the other big man.

Tom sighed, almost feeling sorry. Barton sucked back, dropped his right shoulder, pivoted on his right foot, and struck Forester on the side of the head. Jack's arms flailed, his eyes aimlessly rolled, he pitched forward, and fell on his face.

It hadn't taken more than twenty seconds from start to finish. Horton's men were beginning to recover, to turn back. Barton stood there with his .45 out and slowly swinging. It was cocked, his trigger finger was snugged back; all it would take would be the weight of an expelled breath and men would start dying.

One of the heavily dressed cowboys, in the act of sweeping back the lower length of his coat to bare the holstered gun underneath, froze in mid-motion. Barton's black barrel was looking him straight in the eye. "Hold it," this man said harshly. "Hold it now, fellers. Just hold it."

This man had no authority. He was simply a common range rider. Yet his advice was sound; the other men balancing upon the verge of violence took his words verbatim because that rock-steady, blue-black barrel seemed to be covering them all, and no one could match it now, so no one completed a draw.

"Five of you," said Barton, gazing at the bunched-up riders.

"I never took on five men at one time. Suppose we all shed our guns and put it to the test?"

Tom Logan said, from farther back: "No! That ends it, Barton. You riders, pick up Sedge and Forester and haul them outside, rub some snow in their faces, then get to hell out of this town—all of you. Move!"

The cowboys glanced briefly across at Logan, but their primary interest was in big Frank Barton. They were watching him as rabbits would eye a circling hawk.

"Barton!" George Henry called out from behind his bar. "Put up the gun. You've made your point, so put up the gun."

Barton kept his back to Logan and the others over at the bar. They couldn't see his expression. But he slowly put up his gun. Tom stepped away and hiked across to the doorway. "Haul 'em out of here," he snarled, motioning downward. "An' you tell 'em, when you get 'em back to the ranch, that smart men don't need more'n two warnings. Get moving!"

The sheepskin-coated riders bent and hoisted up their employer and his foreman. They staggered outside with them. Over at the bar George eased off the dogs of his riot gun, put the thing below the bar, heaved a big sigh, caught hold of a full quart, and started along the bar pouring each glass full. "On the house," he growled as he moved along. "And you boys better drink to m'shotgun. Otherwise some of you'd be goin' out of here feet first, too."

Tom and Pert followed Frank Barton out to watch the Horton cowboys drag their range boss and employer over as far as the tie rack that held their horses. Tom said without looking around: "Frank, that was a risky move."

"Any move would have been risky, Sheriff. I just figured this one would be the least risky." Barton turned, showed big white teeth in a cold grin, and said: "Anyway, I didn't rightly cherish the idea of takin' 'em on one at a time out in that roadway mud. It's too cold."

The range men got astride with two on each side of their injured companions. They gave Logan and Whipple and big Frank Barton venomous glances as they wheeled away, but none of them said anything.

Logan watched them ride out of town. "They'll be back," he mused. "Frank, you better grow an eye in the back of your head."

"I did that a long time ago, Sheriff. And a nose, too, so I can smell skunks." Barton turned and walked back into the saloon.

Tom and Pert exchanged a wry look, head shake, and wordlessly struck out for the jail house.

XII

That evening Henry Poole had a visitor just ahead of closing time when the store was empty, and, the way he afterward described it to Logan and his son-in-law over at the jail house, it looked as though Barton had made a study of Poole's place so as to know exactly when Henry would be alone. "There I was, totaling up the receipts," explained Henry, "without a customer in the place, and he steps in. Moved so quiet I didn't even know it until he said right over my shoulder. 'Let's have a little palaver, Mister Poole.' I liked to jumped out of my skin."

"What'd you talk about?" Pert asked.

"A fancy granite headstone," replied Poole, looking sharply at his son-in-law. "He had the guts to ask me to donate . . . contribute, he called it . . . to a fund for a fine granite headstone for Old Man Barton."

Tom Logan, seated at his desk, rummaged for another of those cigars people invariably gave him, and which, because he wasn't an habitual smoker, he tucked away like a pack rat until they were so dry and stale only he could stand the taste of them. He found one, lit it, leaned back with both hands clasped behind his head, and said: "Well, go on. Did you contribute?"

Henry Poole looked indignant. "What would you have done . . . that big, solemn, ham-handed 'breed lookin' into your face from less than ten inches away?"

"I'd have donated," replied Tom candidly. "How much, Henry?"

"A hundred dollars. One . . . hundred . . . dollars!"

Tom looked at Pert. "Mighty fine headstone, wouldn't you say, Deputy?"

"Finest in town, Sheriff," gravely answered Pert.

Poole glared. "Are you two trying to make fun of me?" he waspishly demanded.

Logan shook his head. "Where'd you ever get such an idea?" he murmured, poker-faced and puffing on his rank cigar.

"Well, what're you going to do, Sheriff?"

"Nothing, Henry. Did he twist your arm and point his gun at you, or ball up a fist?"

"No. But he. . . ."

"Well, then, did he verbally threaten you, or so much as make a threatening gesture of any kind, or look like he might be on the verge of . . . ?"

"No! No! No! I've already told you, confound it. He did not threaten me at all."

"Henry," said the sheriff, removing his stogie and looking at its bone-dry ash. "Just why did you come over here? Barton only asked you for a donation. You agreed to give it to him. That's no crime. Hell's bells, Henry, every Sunday you pitch something into Ezra Benedict's offering plate, don't you? Well, that's to sort of keep the skids greased so's you can slide into heaven, isn't it? Now then, I sort of view this other contribution as an even better investment. Anyway, since no threat was used, Barton broke no law. Besides, I figure maybe we all owe Old Man Barton a fine stone. Don't you?"

Poole got red in the face. He sprang out of his chair and rushed out of the jail house. Neither Logan nor Pert Whipple commented additionally upon his purpose in being there, but Tom said: "Go fetch Toughy in here, Pert. We might as well set him loose."

"He'll head straight for the Big Eagle, Sheriff," Pert mildly protested as he crossed over to take the cell keys.

"Maybe," agreed Logan mildly. "He's stupid enough. Still, we've got nothing to hold him for except maybe disturbing the peace, and, hell, everyone does that."

Pert went as far as the cell-block door and dryly said: "You've got something more'n that in mind, Sheriff."

Tom smiled. "Maybe I have at that. Maybe I figure, since Barton's willing to face 'em all, the least we can do for the memory of Old Man Barton is feed 'em to him one at a time. Go ahead, Pert, fetch him out here."

Toughy's face was a mess but the testy fire of his angry glance indicated that otherwise he'd rapidly recovered from his beating. He snarled at Logan. "Give me my gun."

Logan handed the weapon over without removing the cigar from his mouth or more than coolly glancing at the cattleman.

Toughy dropped his weapon into its holster and glared. At that moment the office door opened, Frank Barton stepped in, and for a moment or two, as he and Toughy eyed one another, Pert feared that Tom had accidentally made a bad mistake by selecting this most inopportune of moments to release his prisoner. Then the sheriff softly spoke and his quiet words dispelled all the heightened tension.

"Toughy, in case you're gettin' any war-like notions . . . that gun of yours isn't loaded. I always unload the ones I take off fellers I lock up in here."

Barton turned toward the sheriff. His odd-colored smoky eyes smoldered with ironic humor. He said nothing, though; he just stepped over a chair, hooked both mighty arms across its back, and sat down slowly, running his glance back where Toughy Hammond was stiffly standing.

"I'm leavin'," growled Hammond, and that, at long last, elicited a comment from Barton.

"Don't stop," he said. "Or else go get some slugs and wait for me up at the Big Eagle. If you're around when I walk out of here, I'll kill you, Hammond. You'd better believe that."

Hammond left, and Pert closed the door after him. Tom Logan considered the smoke drifting above his head for a moment. "Always figured someday I'd be glad I unloaded those things when I brought 'em in here." He lowered his head. "What can I do for you, Frank?"

"Tell me what you know about Sedge Horton's son."

"Well, not a whale of a lot to tell. One thing you can say for him . . . he was consistent, eh, Pert?"

The deputy made a grimace and nodded.

"Like his father?" Barton asked.

"Spitting image," concurred Logan. "Only meaner in some ways. Spoiled rotten all his lousy life. Mean an' cruel an' a bully."

"That's what I wanted to know," said Barton quietly. "In fact, that's all I wanted to know," Barton said, pushing up to his feet. "George gave me some answers, but he said you and Pert knew more, said in fact that a couple of times you had run-ins with the kid, and later with his father for pickin' up the kid."

Logan put aside his frayed cigar. "You're trying to satisfy yourself your old grandpappy was justified in shooting him."

"That's about it, Sheriff."

"I'd say that he was. The trouble lay in a new direction. The trouble was, Frank, that your grandpappy killed him like men killed thieves and other low types fifty, seventy-five years back. With straight shooting and not too much attention paid to where it hit. But, nowadays, if you shoot a man in the back, you've got to have fifty church-goin' witnesses . . . and even then you'll likely hang." Logan got up, yawned, and stretched. He considered Frank Barton wryly for a moment. He bent, opened a desk drawer, and brought forth a six-gun that he handed over. Barton examined the gun. It was fully loaded. He ran the tip of his smallest finger inside the barrel and brought it out shiny with oil. He looked inquiringly upward.

"That was the kid's weapon," explained Logan. "The one your grandpaw said was fired at him. You see that oil on your finger? Well, Pert and I knew that kid. He wouldn't take that good care of a gun if it'd been made of gold. Yet there it is, and it was good enough when offered in evidence to help hang Old Man Barton." Logan took back the gun, dropped it into the drawer, and slammed the drawer closed with unnecessary harshness. "Now, then, Frank, you need any more contributions for your grandpappy's headstone?"

Barton came near to smiling. "So Poole told you," he said. "Well, Sheriff, as I told you before, I wouldn't break any of your laws. I haven't. I asked, Poole gave. That's all there was to it."

Tom went over, opened the door, and waited until Barton was passing through it before saying: "I know what you're doing. I think I do anyway. Good luck." As he closed the door behind Barton and turned, Pert was gazing at him with a puzzled expression.

Tom went back and picked up his ragged stogie, coaxed it back to life, and said: "He said Winchester Junction was going to even up with him for the old man. He gave your daddy-in-law the break of his life, even if that danged old skinflint doesn't think so. He let Henry buy his way out, with that headstone, rather than kill him."

Pert's eyes got perfectly round. "You mean . . . he's going to make everyone pay who was connected with the hangin'?"

"One way or another, Pert. One way or another. I can't quite see him taking money from Hammond or Horton, but he sure took it from Henry. And that was shrewd. What does Henry dislike losing above everything else?"

Pert made a slow, wide smile. "Money," he stated. "Say, Sheriff. I think I'm beginnin' to understand Barton. Maybe even admire his way of thinkin' a little."

Logan chewed thoughtfully upon his cigar as he said softly: "I wonder what he's got in store for me, Pert? What he's got in store for George, for the rest of us who were involved in the old man's passing?"

A long time later, Will Clampitt came in out of the cold, gave each lawman a hurried little nod, and rushed over to put his back to the stove. "Dog-gone sun ain't got no warmth in it. To a feller with no more meat on his bones'n I've got, this here cold weather is pure hell."

"You walked a long distance just to get warm," Logan tartly stated. "Why didn't you hike on up to the gun shop? There's a stove up there, too."

"Someday," mumbled Will, "you're goin' to insult me once too often an' lose as good a friend as you got in this country."

Tom sighed. "With friends like you, I don't need enemies," he retorted. "What brought you down here?"

Clampitt's prominent Adam's apple bobbed like a cork on water. "Ezra Benedict went out a-prosyletin' this mornin' and on his way back he saw Jack Forester and two other Horton riders circling around to come into town from the east."

Pert abruptly looked interested. So did Tom Logan. "What kept you quiet about it so long?" he growled at the liveryman/undertaker. "What time did Benedict see 'em?"

"He never said, but he was usin' a rig of mine an' he got back to town maybe a couple hours ago, so I'd guess he seen

215

'em maybe an hour ahead of that. Make it three hours, Sheriff."

"Make it three hours," snarled Logan, and bit the words off. "I ought to crack your damned skull, Will." Logan's earlier lethargy fell away. He reached for his hat. "Come on, Pert."

The pair of them left the jail house with Clampitt still standing back there in front of the stove. They went immediately up to the Big Eagle, but Barton wasn't there. George was, though, and he wanted to know what was going on.

"You two look like you've just seen a ghost," he said.

"Trying to keep from seeing one. Forester's on the loose heading this way . . . or at least he was three, four hours ago . . . so maybe he's already here. George, where's Frank Barton?"

George didn't know. "He walked out about an hour back. Been sittin' back there in his corner, sippin' a beer and sort of smilin' like he. . . ."

"You take the other side of the road," Logan barked at his deputy. "I'll take this side. If you see Forester or Barton, use your gun if you have to, but take 'em to the jail house and keep 'em there until I show up."

"Hey," squawked George, rushing from behind his bar, "what's this all about?"

Logan looked exasperated as he said: "If I knew, it likely wouldn't worry me so much, but my guess is that Jack's burning up over getting smacked silly and has come back to do a little bushwhackin'. If I knew which riders of Sedge's he's got with him, I'd know for sure."

"Well, listen," protested George, "wait'll I get my shotgun and we'll both. . . ."

"You mind your danged bar," declared Logan, and rushed out of the saloon behind his deputy. At the plank walk's edge, as Pert was stepping down, Logan said: "Look close now, and be damned careful. Forester's no man to take chances with, especially after he got made a fool of in front of others."

Pert went on across the road and turned right to go toward the initial northward stores and intersecting little roadways before beginning his search. Logan didn't bother being that thorough. He tried to imagine where Barton might be, decided to try the hotel first, and went down there. On his way he also peered into each store along his route. There was no sign at all of Frank Barton. At the hotel the clerk had a negative report, too. He hadn't seen Barton since Frank had left the hotel earlier that day. But the clerk said one thing that brought Logan up short.

"When Barton left, he had his saddlebags over one shoulder. He didn't check out though, Sheriff, so I figure he'll be back. Maybe he just aims to remain out one night is all."

Logan returned to the roadway, looked for Pert, and, when he failed to see him, crossed to the livery barn with orders for Will Clampitt, long since returned from the jail house, to saddle up two horses. Will, detecting Logan's anxiety and surmising the cause, said: "Sheriff, if Forester'd been huntin' Barton for a gunfight, we'd have heard the firin' by now."

"Just get the damned horses," snarled Logan, spying Pert stepping forth from a northward doorway. He caught his deputy's attention with an arm wave, and commanded Pert to hasten forward with the same gesturing, upraised arm. Pert came on the run.

"Barton left the hotel," explained Logan, "with his saddlebags. My guess is that Forester's skulking around here somewhere, or maybe he's sent his friends into town for Barton while he waits out on the plain somewhere. But I got a hunch they aren't going to find him. I got a hunch Barton's gone out to the ranch. We're going out an' have a look."

"The old man's ranch?" inquired Pert, and stung Logan into an irascible reply.

"What ranch would he be interested in, you idiot? Come

217

along, confound it!"

Will had their animals ready. They left the Junction in a hurry, riding straight west.

XIII

It was a seven-mile ride by the most direct route, but, because the land was slippery and still snow-coated in places, they took as much time getting out to the Barton place as though the ranch had been ten miles from town. In fact, by the time they came within sight of the buildings and saw a pencil-thin drift of oak smoke rising straight up into the still air from a stovepipe, the sun was beginning to redden off toward the snowcapped, craggy west.

"That's real smart," grumbled Logan, pointing at the smoke. "Horton's men'll spot that danged smoke from five miles off."

"He doesn't know Jack's after him," murmured Pert.

"Well, damn it, he ought to know!"

They came down into the yard, noticed the number of horse tracks in the mud around the barn, and put up their horses before passing over to the house where Tom Logan pushed on inside without any ceremony, and stopped dead still. Sedge Horton and five of his cowboys were gazing at him from over by Old Man Barton's iron heating stove. Logan and Pert still had their sheepskin coats buttoned, still had their gloves on. The men silently regarding them not only were ungloved but had their coats open for quick access to the guns they wore. There was no question of who was holding the top cards in this meeting, but Logan didn't show that he was conscious of this.

He said gruffly to Horton: "What you doing here?"

Sedge's cold-reddened face was stony. "The same thing I expect you are, Sheriff. Lookin' for Frank Barton."

"You've got no right in this house, Sedge, and you know it. Where's Jack?"

Horton raised his eyebrows. "Forester? Darned if I know."

Logan's expression hardened toward the cattleman. He didn't believe that about Horton's not knowing where Forester was. The longer he stood in the doorway with Pert beside him, the more this all began to fit an old pattern. Forester was out hunting Barton. Horton was here, in case Barton wasn't in town. Either way, wherever Frank Barton was, these men—and Forester—were waiting his appearance.

The riders with Horton were all familiar to Sheriff Logan. They were part of his home ranch crew, his best hired men, most loyal and least likely to have compunction when Horton ordered something done, including a killing, even a murder. They were standing across the room with their backs to the stove, impassively watching Logan and Pert Whipple, their faces hard and willing.

"So you built the fire to make Barton curious, and you put your horses out of sight so he'd think, maybe, he'd find only some drifter in here." Logan shook his head, kicked the door closed, and started to unbutton his coat.

"Never mind that," said Horton. "You're not going to stay long, Sheriff. You came here lookin' for Barton. He's not here. You better head right on back."

Logan's dark eyes turned sulphurous. "I'm staying," he growled, and went right on unbuttoning his coat. It was warm in the cabin, which meant that Sedge and his men had been here at least an hour, perhaps more than an hour. The stove was crackling, which was the only sound as Horton and his men stonily eyed Sheriff Logan and Deputy Whipple. In the mind of them all was the possibility of eventual violence, but, also, Logan was banking on his badge and his official status to heighten his position in this antagonistic stand-off.

It seemed to be working out that way too. At least big Sedge Horton made no further argument about Logan and Pert staying. He was, Tom thought, considering the other facet of this affair; if Forester was successful, there'd really be no need for him to make an open issue with Tom Logan. In fact, it would be far better if he didn't push for trouble with the law, if Forester found Barton and killed him. That was a big if. Horton wouldn't have any way of knowing what luck Jack had had until they met again at the home ranch.

Logan stalked over and roughly shouldered in to get closer to the stove. Horton's men grudgingly gave way, but, when they looked at Sedge, he only made a very faint shrug in reply to their unasked question. Pert brought forth his makings and went to work manufacturing a cigarette. He lit up, turned his back, and steadily gazed out of the window. "It's goin' to be dark in another hour," he said, breaking the stiff, alien silence in the room. "You reckon we'd ought to bed down out here, Sheriff?"

Logan's eyes flintily glistened with tough approval of Pert's attitude. "I reckon," he answered, making a slow drawl of it. "Sedge was decent enough to fill the wood box." He looked at Horton. "How about grub? You didn't happen to fetch along some coffee, did you?"

Horton's neck got red. He glared, then looked away. He was losing face here in front of his own men. But the last thing he'd expected was for the law to ride in, and now that Logan was here, whatever else he'd had planned, he obviously could not go through with it, unless of course he should make up his mind also to shoot Logan and Whipple, and that was not something he cherished doing. Not because he had any use for either lawman, but simply because there was a world of difference between shooting Frank Barton, who no one in the Winchester country knew, and shooting two lawmen who were not only widely known but who just happened also to be widely respected.

"Dammit," he growled to his men, "let's go."

Logan said nothing. Over by the window Pert slowly turned and watched Horton and his riders stalk on out of the house. He took a long drag off his cigarette, watched through the window as Horton led his men on around the house toward a grove of second-growth old cottonwoods, and said: "They had their saddle horses around back, Sheriff. If ever I saw a carefully laid murder plan, this was it."

"Close," muttered Logan, strolling over also to gaze out the window. "Damned close. I wonder what became of Barton?"

They remained indoors for a while. It was warm and snug in Old Man Barton's cabin. There were three rooms and a fourth, lean-to room had once been begun, but something had kept the old man from ever finishing it. There were the mementoes in this place of a long, colorful lifetime. Logan picked up a coup stick leaning in a corner and counted the notched feathers hanging from it, layered over now with dust. As he replaced the thing, he wondered whether all those kills had been made by Old Man Barton. It was entirely possible. He went back over to the window where Pert was still standing. Outside, the land was beginning to roughen with gloom, to turn coldly stiff and shadowy. The air was utterly still, the way it sometimes becomes when a fierce freeze is building.

"We better get back," said Logan, knowing how Pert's thoughts were running. In eight months, since his marriage, Pert hadn't been away all night.

They left the house, got their animals rigged out down in the barn, and struck out back toward Winchester Junction. Because of the congealing cold the ground was turning hard, making better footing possible for their mounts. It also made their passage noisy, for in the bitter hush each time freezing mud broke and chipped, the sounds carried.

"Be a lousy night to try 'n' slip up on anyone, wouldn't it?"

Logan asked, trying to make conversation.

Pert nodded. He was squinting ahead for sight of town lights. He said: "Wonder what Forester eventually did, Sheriff? Sort of wonder whatever became of Barton, too. Where would he be ridin' to, if not out to his grandfather's place with his saddle-bags?"

Logan shifted in his saddle. The cold didn't bother his upper body because it was warmly concealed in the sheepskin coat, but it was beginning to seep into the marrow of his leg bones, which was usually the first place horsemen felt the cold. "I've been puzzling over that, too," he replied. "He maybe went down to Horton's place, Pert."

Whipple's head whipped around. "You mean . . . while Horton and Forester were layin' for him, he was also layin' for them?"

Logan shrugged, a scarcely noticeable gesture in his heavy coat in the settling early winter night. "Maybe. I can't come up with anything better."

They got back to town with full night swiftly falling. It wasn't very late, though. In fact, when they stiffly dismounted down at Will's livery barn, it was not quite 7:00.

Clampitt wasn't there. He had a night hawk who he occasion-ally used, but because Will was a hard man with a dollar, he used this night man only very rarely. Because he was aware of this, Sheriff Logan asked the man where Will was.

"Him an' one or two other fellers was told there was some elk north of town an' went out to see couldn't they maybe get a couple," explained the hostler, taking the reins from Logan and Pert Whipple. "Reckon them elk got drove down outen the Tetons by snowdrifts. Probably hungry and come down here lookin' for willow bark or new shoots."

Logan waited until the night hawk had departed with their animals, then said, gazing across where warm light showed from the Big Eagle: "I'll buy you a drink to get the icicles out of your belly, Pert, then you'd better head for home. We don't want the little woman worrying."

They crossed over a rind of thin ice that popped like distant gunfire with each step they took, kicked off the clinging particles at the walk's far edge, and proceeded on into George Henry's bar. The first thing they saw was Frank Barton. He was sitting, relaxed and comfortable, at that gloomy corner table he'd more or less homesteaded since arriving in town.

Logan darkly scowled and uttered an irritated oath. Barton gravely nodded at them. Pert nodded back, but Logan didn't. He stamped on over and pushed in at the bar where a number of men were pleasantly standing. It was warm in the saloon. Orange lamplight somewhat obscured by tobacco smoke heightened the atmosphere's relaxing mood, and George came along to look inquiringly at Sheriff Logan.

Tom jerked a thumb backward. "How long's he been sitting over there, George?"

Henry looked toward Barton's corner and back. "Couple hours, Tom. Right after you fellers rushed out of town, I saw him ridin' back in from the north, but he must've went to his room at the hotel because he didn't show up here right away. I told him I thought you were lookin' for him."

"What'd he say?"

"Nothin'. He just smiled."

Logan saw Pert fidgeting from the corner of his eye. "Give us a couple of double shots," he growled at George. "It's colder'n a schoolmarm's love out there tonight and Pert's got to get home."

Logan fell to thinking, still scowling, and, until George returned with their whiskey, he didn't move. As he picked up his drink, he asked a question: "George, you heard of any elk north of town that've come down from the mountains?"

George gazed straight at Logan. "It sure must be cold out," he dryly said. "No elk come down here, Tom. You know that. They never have."

"Well that's odd, George. Someone told Will Clampitt there were elk north of town. He went out to see if he couldn't bag one."

George scoffed. "Who told you that yarn, Tom?"

"Will's hostler."

Pert touched Logan's arm. "Obliged for the drink. Now I've got to head for home, Sheriff."

Tom nodded without looking away from George. He absently said: "Sure, Pert. See you in the morning." To the bar owner he said: "Didn't you say you saw Barton ride in from the north?"

George nodded, looking puzzled. "What's that got to do with elk comin' down out of the mountains?" he wanted to know.

"You real curious, George?"

"Yes, I'm curious."

"Then take off that apron, go out the back door into the alleyway, and wait for me to saunter around an' meet you there."

George's brows dropped straight down. "Are you up to something?" he demanded.

"I don't know yet," answered Logan. "But why would anyone tell Will such a yarn?"

George neither answered the question nor ceased his suspicious scowling.

Logan winked. "To get him out of his barn. Why else? Meet me out back in fifteen minutes." Logan turned and walked across the room to Frank Barton's table. He and Barton eyed each other a moment while neither of them spoke. Ultimately Logan said: "Pert an' I rode out to your grandpappy's ranch this afternoon."

"Looking for me," said Barton, making a statement of it.

"Yeah. You'd never guess who we met out there . . . waiting for you."

Barton's gold-flecked wintry eyes gently widened. "Horton?"

"Yeah. Sedge and five of his boys. Good thing you never showed up."

Barton didn't speak. He picked up an empty shot glass and held it high enough to squint at. His regard of the little glass was both thoughtful and, Logan thought, a little cruel.

"Where did you go when you rode out, Frank?"

Still staring at the little glass Barton said: "Around. Got tired of just sitting. Rode around to get the lay of the land."

"Meet anyone?"

"Why?" countered the big cowboy. "Was someone else looking for me besides Horton?"

Logan wryly shook his head, his gaze turning flinty. "I'm asking," he murmured. "You're answering."

Barton returned to studying the glass. Eventually he said: "You know, Sheriff, you're a lot smarter than you look. Yes, I met someone."

Logan heaved a sigh. "Want to tell me about it."

"Not especially, Sheriff."

"All right. Then I'll go over to the livery barn and have a look at him myself. It was Forester, wasn't it?"

Barton raised his eyes and wordlessly nodded. He put down the glass and arose. "I'll go along with you."

"We got to pick up George," said Logan, turning away. "He's waiting for us out back."

XIV

Jack Forester was stiff as a plank and had two dark punctures in him, one over the heart, one directly above and between his eyes. He was wrapped in a dirty old length of wagon canvas and had been put carefully behind some loose hay Will Clampitt had stacked in a corner of his barn, down near the back alley entrance. Logan, down on one knee with a lamp, craned around to consider big Frank Barton solemnly, then Logan removed Forester's six-gun. He handed the lantern to George while he opened the gate and revolved the gun's black cylinder.

"Four shots," stated Barton quietly. "Two when he first saw me and the last two when I made my run at him. All four missed because the first pair were from too far away and because after the first two I zigzagged as I charged him."

Logan got back stiffly upright. George looked inquiringly at him. Logan nodded. "Four empty casings," he muttered. "Why'd you want to hide him, Barton?"

"That's obvious, isn't it, Sheriff? He didn't just happen to be sittin' out there, because he had no way of knowin' I was comin' along, which meant there had to be others with him . . . for all I knew Horton himself and all the rest of Horton's crew . . . so I waited until it was safe and brought him into town, hid him until I could get that nosy liveryman away from his barn, then rolled Forester into the canvas and chucked him back here. After that, I figured his friends'd be puzzled and wouldn't be concentratin' all their attention on me. That way, when they came, I'd have something close to a chance against them."

"I see. You figured some of them, maybe most of them, would be hunting Jack."

"Yes. So I went over to the Big Eagle and waited. But they never came. Until you and your deputy walked in, the saloon was as dead as . . . Forester is."

Logan said musingly: "There were some others with him. The way I've got it figured, if you showed up at the ranch, Sedge was going to salt you down. If you stayed around town, Forester was supposed to get you." Logan looked up. "What made you decide to go riding?"

"I already told you. I was bored, Sheriff, tired of sittin' in town."

"Just like that, no other reason?"

"No other reason. Just an urge I had."

Logan gazed down at Jack Forester and muttered under his breath. "I'll be damned. Old Man, it's maybe like you said. Folks don't depart right away. You keep looking after him and he just might make it, at that."

"What?" inquired George Henry, bending from the middle. "What'd you say, Tom?"

"Nothing. Go on back to your bar, George. Frank, you come along with me."

The three of them were leaving the barn by its front entrance when Will Clampitt came riding in stiffly hunched and holding an old-vintage rifle balanced across his lap. At sight of Frank Barton he shook his head and sniffled, clambered down, and stamped his feet. "It got dark on us," he stated. "Maybe, if I hadn't gone around to take a couple of friends along, we might've gotten a couple of 'em. You reckon they'll still be out there tomorrow?"

Barton said blandly: "Maybe. Why don't you try it about sunup again?"

Will nodded, sniffled again, and led his horse down into the barn where the hostler was just stepping forth from Clampitt's little cluttered office where there was a glowing iron stove. Logan and George Henry glanced at Barton. He met their looks with the same bland expression.

George headed on over to his saloon. Logan took Barton along to the jail house. As they were entering, Barton asked if he was being arrested.

Logan's answer was blunt. "Protected might be more like it. How long you figure it'll be, before Will or someone else finds Forester's body?"

The jail house was like an ice-coated cave. Logan lit a lamp with stiff fingers, then fired up his stove. He had nothing more to say until some of the coldness lost its sharp bite as the stove crackled. But even then he sat stiffly down at his desk without shrugging out of his sheepskin.

"You know," he told Barton conversationally, "maybe Clampitt's right. Maybe this confounded country is too cold for fellers our age. I've been through my share of blizzards before but one never got inside me like this one has."

Barton, wearing a long, blanket coat of rusty gray wool, sank down upon a little bench and faintly smiled as he studied the lawman. He didn't speak.

"Well," Logan finally said gruffly, "you settled with Forester. You've also, in your own way, settled with Henry Poole. But there's still a lot of us left, and you haven't hit the hard going yet."

"I told you," retorted Barton, "I'm ready."

"Yeah, you told me. But I can't keep you in here forever. Horton's going to. . . ."

The door flew open and Will Clampitt plunged headlong in out of the frigid night, his eyes wide and glassy. "Sheriff," he gasped, "Jack Forester's down at my barn . . . dead. He's rolled in canvas behind the hay with . . . with. . . ." Will's eyes, seeing Barton across the room watching him, slowly widened. He swallowed with obvious pain.

Barton finished it for Will: "With two bullet holes in him."

Clampitt felt for the back of a nearby chair and tumbled down upon it. "There weren't no damned elk," he whispered. "Barton, you just told me that. You snuck Forester in there."

"You're the undertaker, aren't you?" Barton asked. "You buried my grandfather, didn't you? Then why should burying Forester bother you? A dead man is a dead man, old or young, large or small."

Logan heaved around in his chair. He was tired and the stove heat was finally loosening his bunched-up muscles to remind him of it. "I know about Forester," he told the unsteady livery-man. "Go on back and take care of him. And, Will . . . this time, if you lie about what's in the pockets . . . you better make it real good because Sedge Horton's going to hit town about tomorrow sometime and ask a lot of questions."

Clampitt hauled himself back up to his feet. He hadn't stopped staring at Frank Barton. With another painful attempt at swallowing that made his Adam's apple pop vigorously up and down, Will fled back out into the darkness. Logan got up to close the door and said: "Well, by dawn everyone within shouting distance will know Forester's dead, how he died, and also who Will Clampitt's convinced did it. Maybe you'd better give me all the details, Frank."

"Sure, Sheriff. It happened about two miles northward along the stage road. There are some piñon trees up there. He was in among them with his horse tied to a low limb. I was ridin' parallel to the road off to the east. If I'd been closer, maybe I'd have seen his tracks."

Logan muttered: "Yeah. An' if you'd been closer, maybe he'd have gotten you, too."

Barton inclined his head. "Probably. Anyway, he fired his first round before I had any idea there was anyone besides me within miles of that spot. I heard the muzzle blast, swung around to see where it was comin' from, and started to jump off my horse. That's when he let off the second one. That time I saw the smoke, turned, drew my Forty-Five, and hooked the horse into a dead run straight at him."

"Probably rattled him, seein' you do that. A man doesn't expect to be charged when he's shooting from ambush. Go on."

"He got off the next two shots fairly swiftly. I crossed the road at the third shot and was within pistol range after the fourth shot. He jumped out and levered his carbine. I fired, and he staggered. The next time I fired he dropped his carbine and fell on his back. I was up beside him by then. Until that moment, though, I had no idea who he was." Barton spread his hands. "The rest of it you know. I brought him back tied across his saddle, hid him in the darkness behind town until I got rid of Clampitt, then hid him behind the hay."

"Why? Why did you put him there? Why didn't you just leave him out in the piñons?"

Barton's lips lifted in a cruel smile. "I wanted him found, Sheriff. I wanted Horton to know. I considered takin' him out to Horton's ranch and leavin' him there."

Logan pulled off his gloves, worked his right fingers, and, while he was clinically examining them, he said: "It's a damned good thing you didn't. You'd never have made it, not tonight. They were out after you." He put the bruised hand in his lap and gazed thoughtfully at Frank Barton. "They'll come tomorrow. Clampitt's tale will spread. Horton will be here probably about noon. I could lock you up pending an investigation. That's the usual routine where a killing's been done."

Barton stood up, shaking his head. "It wouldn't do any good. They'd haul me out of here."

"Not out of my jail," growled Logan, also arising. "It's never been done, and as long as I'm standing upright it'd be plumb fatal to anyone who tried it."

"All right, Sheriff, maybe they couldn't. But all they'd have to do is set one man to watchin' your jail house while the rest of them sat up at the saloon playin' cards until I walked out. The end would be the same."

"I reckon so. Still, I don't want any gun battle in Winchester Junction."

"Then I'll meet them out on the range."

Logan unbuttoned his coat, removed it, took off his hat, also, and vigorously scratched his hair. "You ride out on the plain and they'll surround you like wolves after a buffalo calf, and whittle you down to nothing."

"I'm not quite that dumb, Sheriff," said big Frank Barton, striding across to the door. "Full-blood or half-blood, Sheriff, an Indian's not easy to kill in that kind of a fight."

"Hell of a lot of consolation that'll be if they kill you even though you tip over some of them, Barton. No, you stay in town."

Barton lifted the latch and held it without opening the door while he stonily regarded Tom Logan. "Don't do me any favors," he said.

Logan screwed up his face. "I'm not doing you any, boy, but your grandpaw and I were pretty close. I owe him at least this much. By the way, Frank, you've made Henry Poole sweat, you've beat hell out of Toughy Hammond. You've hurt both those fellers the only way they can be hurt. What've you got planned for me?"

Barton hauled the door back. "Wait and see," he said, and went out into the night.

Logan had a long time ahead of him. It wasn't late when Barton left, but the heat of his office after the day-long cold brought him to a heavy drowsiness. He made some coffee and took a cup of it to the desk to sip while he did some recapitulating.

It wasn't hard to figure out why Barton was doing all this, and once he'd figured out the key, he knew exactly how he meant to exact his vengeance in each case. Henry Poole had been parted from his money. That would pain Henry as long as he lived. Henry could forget a lot of things, but never the loss of $100. Toughy Hammond had been humiliated before half the town. That was, as Logan had told Barton and Pert, the best and only way to make Hammond suffer. Now it was Sedge

Horton, and that, too, was beginning to be clear to Logan. Sedge had used the law to exact his vengeance, and he'd mocked the law by succeeding at his devious plan. Well, Frank Barton was also a devious planner. He was baiting Horton into a deadly breach of law, and Frank was going to use himself as the bait. He was going to make Horton try to kill him—perhaps, Logan thought, Barton would let Horton kill him—then Sedge would be outside the very law he'd made mockery of, and ironically that same law would then go after Horton.

The coffee began to get cold. Frost formed on Logan's office windows while he sat like stone, running all this through his mind. If, he reasoned, Frank Barton's revenge was pursuing these lines, it shouldn't be hard to figure out what Barton had in mind for Tom himself—or for George Henry who had been foreman of that hang-rope jury. For George there was only his saloon. Barton had demonstrated his scorn of that the night he'd flung Toughy Hammond through the window. He would destroy George's place. That left Tom. How would a devious, hating man get even with a peace officer who had performed his duty to incur the devious man's wrath? Logan got up, went to the stove, pushed in some wood, and stamped his feet to stir up sluggish circulation.

There were too many ways for him to be on guard against them all. Maybe with a gun, maybe with laughter, like jockeying Tom into some situation where he'd be ridiculed by his townsmen, his friends. Maybe in a fist fight over some minor infraction. No. Not like that. Barton had said he wouldn't break the law. Resisting Logan in the performance of his duty would be a felony, an act of lawlessness. Perhaps in some way Tom couldn't even think of. Perhaps he told himself wearily, Barton didn't mean to exact vengeance from Tom at all. He didn't believe that, though. Barton had upon several occasions now sat and gazed steadily at Tom. He was most Indian-like when he was quietly relaxed and totally silent. There was no way to say what he might be thinking. All a man could be certain of was that he was thinking.

Tom crossed to the stove, turned down the damper, and went over also to turn down the lamp. Afterward he groped his way through to his living quarters and left the door open so most of that lingering heat would come through. He shed his gun belt first, hung it upon the bedpost, then shucked his booted spurs, his hat, and sank down upon the bed's edge in the quiet stillness and gloom to search his mind for a feeling of guilt. It was there exactly as it had been since that day he'd sprung the trap door, but it wasn't the same kind of guilt an outlaw would feel. If anything, it was the guilt of blindly obeying, and, while that kind of guilt might trouble his sleep, it could never really bow his spirit for every man in every man's lifetime comes some time or another to the same position, and, although he can never entirely forget, nor even entirely forgive himself, he can come to live with it. Logan shed everything but his woolen underwear, slipped into bed, and heaved a loud sigh. Living was never easy. He wondered how it was, this night, with Old Man Barton.

XV

Pert came in after breakfast of the following day and told Tom he'd been talking to the hotel clerk, who had said that Frank Barton had placed his carbine behind the front door drapes at the hotel's roadside entrance. There was actually nothing odd about this under the circumstances. It was accepted practice among men in danger to locate weapons here and there so that, if they were maneuvered out of some central position, or if they fired their handgun dry, another weapon would be loaded and close at hand.

"He's expecting them," stated Tom from over at his stove.

"Care for some coffee?"

Pert had a cup. "You mean he's fixin' to face the whole Horton crew?" he demanded.

"I didn't ask him what his plans were."

"Well," retorted Pert, "you're not goin' to let them turn the town into a battleground, are you?"

Tom's eyes flashed with quick annoyance. "Drink your damned coffee," he said, "then we'll make one round together. As for Barton . . . leave it be until we see which way the wind's going to blow."

Pert drank the coffee, buttoned his coat while Tom got into his own sheepskin, and took down his hat, then the pair of them walked outside. It was early, the sun was up and dazzlingly bright to see, but it had very little real warmth. The air was utterly still. Northward, the mountains stood sharply cutting the new daylight, seemingly so close a man had only to thrust out his arm to touch them. There was a constant small popping where men and animals trudging across the roadway broke through the dry, brittle rind of new ice. A dog was excitedly barking, well up near the northernmost limits of town, some little distance away, but it sounded so sharp and close that Sheriff Logan made a face. It made his eardrums tingle, that high, piercing bark.

They started northward along the westward sidewalk. It was customary for at least one of them to make this routine inspection each morning. They didn't often do it together because it wasn't a two-man chore, but this morning they did.

At Clampitt's barn the place was as quiet as Logan had ever seen it. No one was in sight, the horses were eating, which indicated that at least Will had been there this morning, and, as Tom stepped in as far as the door to Will's office and peered in to see the stove popping, Pert said: "Look here, Sheriff. He's got a coffin fresh-made back here on sawhorses."

Logan closed the office door and looked. He didn't say anything about Forester, though. "He's around an' he'll be all right. Let's get along."

After leaving Clampitt's place, they continued their walk up as far as the northernmost ending of the sidewalk beyond which the open country began, crossed over to the east side, and strolled back southward again. It was their traditional route of patrol. Its time of day or night might vary but its route seldom did. When they came even with the Big Eagle, Pert pointed to the hitch rack. Five saddle horses were standing there.

"Sort of early in the day," murmured Pert.

Tom nodded, swung, and pushed on into the saloon. The room was warm and pleasantly redolent of masculine odors. At first, it seemed to the pair of lawmen that it had been their entrance that had brought on the silence, but one more look around showed that this was not only not at all true, but that those eight men up at the bar weren't even aware that Logan and his deputy had come in. Big Frank Barton was standing in the middle of the bar. Eighteen or twenty feet south of him, down where the bar curved inward toward the wall, Toughy Hammond was standing. Toughy's crushed hat was lying on the floor behind him, his hair was tousled, and there was no six-gun in his holster.

Frank Barton was methodically plugging the loads out of that .45 he carried with the carved walnut grips. Frank neither glanced around at the sound of the roadside storm doors opening and closing, nor even hesitated as he shucked out those heavy bullets. George Henry was farther along, up behind the northward bar where the rest of his early-morning customers were. George was watching Barton in total fascination. So were the other men ranged along the northward bar. It was quiet enough to hear a pin drop in the Big Eagle.

Pert started to push forward. Logan put out a stiff arm, blocking this movement. In a near whisper Tom said: "Stay back."

Barton finished with his pistol, closed the gate, spun the cylinder, flicked the gun around until he was holding it by the barrel, and put it down atop the bar. He looked at Toughy Hammond.

"All right, Hammond," he quietly said. "You don't want another crack at me with fists but you feel you've got to prove to your town you're my match. That's fine with me. There is one bullet in this pistol. I spun the cylinder so neither of us will know where it is." Barton gave the gun a hard push, sent it skittering down the bar to halt in front of Hammond. "Pick it up, cock it, take good aim at me, and pull the trigger. If nothing happens, push it back to me and I'll take my turn." Barton paused and grinned. "Sooner or later one of us will win."

Logan's brows dropped down into a black and disapproving scowl. This was not a gunfight; this was murder. He caught George Henry's look and George made a little tight negative headshake at him, warning Tom to keep back, to keep quiet. At Logan's side Pert was stiffening up to his full height. His expression reflected horror—and fascination. He'd seen his share of duels and had heard of a lot of novel ways for men to prove their courage, but this was one way he'd never heard of before—or seen.

Toughy Hammond's bruised face with its stitched lip looked less than human. The purple places stood out starkly against the fish-belly gray of Hammond's smooth cheeks. He looked for a long time at Barton's blue-black six-gun before gently reaching down and picking the weapon up. Everyone heard him cock the gun. When he steadied the muzzle straight up the bar, George Henry sucked back against the backbar shelves and the men across from him jumped as far away as they could get.

"Pray!" exclaimed Hammond in a thin, high voice. "Damn your lousy soul, Barton, pray!"

Toughy squeezed the trigger. It made a loud, flat click and the hammer fell upon an empty chamber of the cylinder. Barton had an empty shot glass in his left hand that he was holding up, looking at it the same way he'd held a similar glass the night before when Logan had spoken with him. Logan couldn't see Frank's face but he knew the cruel expression that would be there. Hammond put the gun down, hesitated for as long as it took to lick his lips, then gave the weapon a hard shove. It skidded noisily up as far as Frank Barton and stopped. Frank went on gazing at the shot glass in his left hand a moment, then he slowly picked up the gun, cocked it, held it tipped upward for a moment, and brought it down. He did not turn his head, did not once look at Toughy.

"The odds get smaller every time we do this," he softly said. "They were five to one when you tried. Now they're four to one. If you're alive five seconds from now and get another chance, they'll be three to one." He pulled the trigger, the same loud click resulted, and Tom Logan saw Hammond's shoulders convulse, then sag. There was sweat on Toughy's forehead and upper lip. His purple bruises stood out more darkly than ever from the ashen color of his face.

"Your turn," said Barton, put the gun down, and gave it a careless shove. As before, the weapon skidded down the bar and halted.

This time Toughy leaned there, staring at the gun for some seconds before he picked it up and cocked it. His tongue made another swift circuit of his lips as he lowered the weapon, steadying it upon Barton's head. Frank was calmly twisting the shot glass in his fingers, still not looking around. Tom Logan heard Pert's gusty breathing, which was the only sound.

Hammond squeezed the trigger and again the gun did not fire. For ten seconds Toughy held the gun aimed, his fingers and knuckles white from straining.

Barton said: "Come on, come on. We've each got one more shot. You got the first one an' you'll get the last one. That's more than fair, Hammond. This is my last shot. Push the gun up here."

Hammond's eyes jumped around the room. He saw Logan and Pert Whipple intently watching him, saw George Henry and the customers watching with frozen faces. He put the gun down with what faintly sounded like a sharp catch in his breath, gave it a hard push up the bar, and placed both his hands upon the bar's beveled edge.

As before, Frank Barton was slow in taking up the weapon, but, when he eventually did, he also put aside the little whiskey glass. "Three to one," he murmured, "two to one. Then big casino." He cocked the .45, raised it, and steadied his elbow on George's bar top. "You won't feel anything. Right between the eyes. You probably won't even hear anything. It's a good day to die, Hammond." He lowered the blue-black muzzle a fraction. Every man in a position to see could detect Barton's trigger finger tensing and curving around the little dagger-like, concave length of black steel that was a hair's breadth away from tripping the lifted hammer.

Hammond's eyes were fixed in glassy concentration upon that black muzzle. A small muscle in the lower part of his face jerked once and was still. Where he had a grip on the edge of the bar, his knuckles stood out from their straining. His body was slightly bowed backward from the middle as though to flinch away from a bullet. He made a low, little moan.

"All right," Barton told him. "All right, Hammond. You killed an old man. Let's see if you can die as well as he did."

Hammond broke. He had used up all his reserves of dwindling courage through the preceding moments of this deadly game. "Wait," he croaked. "Wait, Barton. I did it. I took Sedge's money to hold out for hangin'. I admit it. Don't pull that trigger!"

Logan could see Frank Barton's profile. The cruel look was there, deeply etched and unmistakable. "Well, hell, Hammond," the big cowboy said. "That doesn't let you off the hook. If anything, it puts you squarer on it. You took money to send an old man who'd never harmed you in your lousy life to his death in the dirtiest way a man can die."

"Listen," blurted Hammond, "I had to. Sedge owned a note of mine. He said, if I didn't hold out, he'd clean me lock, stock, and barrel. Listen, Barton, I had to. He give me back my note."

"And how much more?" Barton asked, still gazing at Hammond down the length of his pistol barrel.

"A thousand dollars more. I'll give it to you. I'll. . . ."

"A thousand dollars for a man's life?" asked Barton quietly. "Sheriff, what d'you think of that? Is that a fair price for the old man's life?"

Logan let his breath out slowly. He didn't answer or move. Frank Barton's tensed trigger finger was still curved tightly. Anything could make him give that trigger its last tug. Even a sharp indrawn breath could detonate the gun.

When Logan was silent, Barton said: "Toughy, what's your life worth?"

Toughy whispered: "Name it, Barton. Just name it."

Barton eased off his finger and let the barrel droop a little. "Get out of the country. Walk out of here, get on your horse just as you are, head south, and don't stop ridin' until this time tomorrow. Don't go near your ranch. Don't even look back. Is your life worth that?"

Hammond's head jerked up and down. His shoulders sagged and sweat dripped from his chin. "I'll do it," he said. "I give you my word."

Barton jerked his head. "Get out of my sight. There's the door. Get out of here."

Toughy Hammond let go of the bar and made an awkward turn; he staggered a little. He was facing Logan but gave no indication that he'd seen him. He didn't even bend over to retrieve his hat or gun. He started across the hushed room, reached the door, pushed against it with a little sob, and ran out of the barroom.

George Henry was the first man to move. He picked up a backbar bottle, plucked out the cork, and tipped back his head. As George's throat worked rhythmically to permit that fiery liquor to pass downward, Tom Logan unbuttoned his coat because it was suddenly very warm in the saloon, then started up to the bar. Pert came out of his trance-like stance and followed along.

Frank Barton turned, aimed off to the left, and pulled the trigger. Nothing happened. The hammer fell on an empty place in the cylinder. Frank raised the hammer again and looked at Logan. "You think I palmed that slug, don't you?" he asked, swung away, and once more pulled the trigger. This time the gun bucked and roared, making the ears of every man in the saloon ring.

"That one would have been his," Barton said, as he raised the weapon, opened its side gate, and plugged out the expended casing, turned back to the bar, and began feeding in the cartridges lying there. "Yellow, Sheriff. He was yellow clean through. He couldn't figure the odds. They were two to one in his favor but he was too scairt to figure that out."

The men around the room shuffled back up to the bar and pushed their empty glasses at George. He refilled them without a word being said, then he took the bottle on up and poured Barton's glass full, reached around for two more glasses, and also filled them. These last two he pushed at Tom and Pert. As he placed the bottle atop the bar, he gazed straight at Logan. "God damn," he whispered, and loudly cleared his throat bringing back the tone and depth to his voice. "Barton . . . you're an idiot. He'd have killed you."

Barton finished reloading, dropped the gun into his hip holster, and smiled. "But he didn't, George, he didn't. It takes a pretty good man to play cowboy roulette through to the finish. I never had him pegged for that good a man, and I've been studyin' tough men all my life. Mostly, if they're big, they're bullies. Nothing more. This proves my point."

Tom Logan and Pert drained their glasses and waited for the whiskey to untie the knots in their bellies.

XVI

Neither Tom nor Pert had noticed that Will Clampitt was among the men ranged along the bar until the liveryman's unmistakably nasal voice uttered a quavering curse and called for another refill of his glass. Instead of complying, George gave the bottle a shove, and sent it skidding down the bar. That bottle made the identical grating sound Barton's .45 had made when it had been slid back and forth between Toughy Hammond and Frank.

"You made your point," Logan finally told Barton. "But that's a lousy way to make it."

"Why, Sheriff? He was a big man in these parts. What I had in mind for him was to bust him down to size in front of his acquaintances."

"You did that the other night with your fists."

Barton lifted his glass, drained it dry, and set it down. "No, not really, Sheriff. All I proved to the town the other night was that Hammond could be fairly whipped in a dog fight. That could happen to any man. What I *wanted* to prove to the folks of Winchester Junction was that he was rotten clear through. I wanted you boys to hear him admit what he did to my grandfather. I wanted you all to see just how putrid he was through and through."

George said: "You proved it. But, Mister Barton, some of us never doubted that he was putrid through and through."

"Then why did you let him sit on your jury, George?" Barton inquired.

George's glance dropped. "We didn't let him sit on it, Mister Barton. Fifty names are written on pieces of paper and shoved into a hat. Twelve names are picked out an' read off. That's how the juries hereabouts are picked."

"Who picked out the names?"

George started to speak but Sheriff Logan broke in first. "Forget that," he said gruffly. "Frank, you've got your enemies singled out. Go ahead and do what you've got to do. What's the point in constantly adding to them?"

Barton turned. "Who are you protecting?" he asked.

Logan scowled. "No one I care a damn for," he growled. "I can tell you that. But you've got all the enemies you need."

Will Clampitt walked away from the bar but no one paid Will any heed. They never did. Clampitt opened the storm doors, passed outside, and closed them. That was the only sound for a while, except for men shifting their weight up the bar or replacing empty glasses atop the counter.

"It will come out," said Barton to Tom Logan. He cocked his head at the big Seth Thomas clock above the bar. "Nearly ten o'clock," he murmured. "How long does it take Horton to ride in from his ranch?"

Logan said nothing. Neither did Pert nor George Henry. A big, bearded man in a checkered woolen shirt shuffled over, picked up Hammond's crushed hat and gun, placed these objects atop the bar, and wordlessly turned to walk out of the saloon.

Logan eyed the hat and gun. "What'd you do," he growled at Barton, "catch him walking in?"

Barton didn't reply so George said: "He was sittin' by the

window an' saw Hammond ride up. He went over beside the door. When Toughy stepped inside, Barton caught him by the shoulder, swung him around, and yanked away Toughy's gun. In that little fracas Toughy's hat fell off."

Logan looked glum. "You think you'll be able to pull that on Sedge and his crew?" Logan shook his head. "Not a chance. Sedge hires hard men. He asks no questions an' pays top dollar. All you've accomplished this morning is to show up a yellow skunk for what he is, and put yourself squarely in front of a lot of guns that won't miss." Tom signaled for George to refill his glass. As he watched this being done, he told Barton about the green-pine coffin Will Clampitt was cobbling together over at his barn. "Maybe it's bein' made for Jack Forester," he mumbled, "but I'll give odds you'll wind up in it." He drank the straight shot and dashed away the quick sting of tears with the back of one hand. "Take my advice, for the last time it's being offered, Frank. Go get your horse and ride out."

Barton placed both elbows atop the bar and turned his head. He was entirely relaxed. The roadside door opened and several curious men came in. It was clear from their expressions that they'd heard what had happened and weren't entering to drink so much as to have a good look at Frank Barton.

Pert turned each time that door opened. Logan, too, raised his eyes, but Logan didn't turn, he simply looked ahead into George's backbar mirror to sight those new faces.

As though none of these interrupting little interludes were occurring, Frank Barton answered Logan's advice with a mild statement that was not in the least changed from similar earlier statements. "You know I can't ride out, Sheriff. Hell, I've only just got this thing goin' my way. Poole, Hammond, Forester. . . ."

Tom lifted his shoulders and resignedly dropped them. "Then you'd better take care of George and me right now, Frank, because after Sedge gets here, you won't ever get the chance again."

Barton's gold-flecked, wintry eyes got sardonic. "I've got that figured," he murmured. "Don't worry about it, Sheriff."

Will Clampitt came in out of the dazzling sunlight and halted with both hands behind him upon the storm doors as though he did not intend to stay. "Sheriff!" he called. "Barton. Sedge is comin'. I seen him out on the range from the back door of my place. He's comin' . . . and he's got a herd of men with him." Clampitt ducked back outside and didn't close the doors. George swore and went around the bar to rectify Will's oversight. He was about to slam both those heavy panels when Henry Poole appeared with an arm stiffly thrust out to stop the doors.

"Is Logan in there?" Poole asked.

They all heard that question and George's affirmative reply to it. Tom turned. So did the others ranged along the bar.

"Tell him," said Henry Poole swiftly, "that there are men approaching town from all four directions, George. Armed men riding up in little groups. It's being said around town that they belong to Horton, that they're members of his riding crews called in from the various cow camps. Tell Tom."

Henry flung around and went hastening southward back down in the direction of his general emporium. George finished closing the doors, swung around, and stared over at Logan without saying anything.

Tom said: "I heard him. All right, Pert, let's go."

"Whoa," murmured Frank Barton as the pair of lawmen moved. "They're not after you, Sheriff, they're after me."

"Not like this they aren't," Logan growled. "I think you're a damned fool, Frank Barton, but there'll be no murders committed in my town."

"How d'you aim to stop them, Sheriff?"

Logan walked as far as the door before answering that. "That is squarely up to Sedge. With talk, if that's how he wants it. With guns if he wants it that way. It'll be his choice." Logan turned his back on Barton, bent and whispered something to George. The swarthy barman listened with a gathering scowl, nodded, and walked away.

Barton let Logan and Pert Whipple leave before he went over to his corner table, picked up his sheepskin coat, shrugged into it under the carefully impassive stares of all the Big Eagle's other customers, then he, too, went out of the saloon by the front door.

Logan, midway between the Big Eagle Saloon and Winchester Junction's only hotel, stepped to the edge of the plank walk and looked up and down. Henry had been right. Pert pointed out the approaching horsemen from the south, and another band of them riding in from up along the northward stage road. "How'd he get them here so fast?" Pert murmured.

Logan's answer was gruff. "He's had the time. Sent for 'em the last day of the blizzard. The day he found out who Frank Barton was."

"All these men just to get Barton?"

Logan didn't reply. He was watching a new band of horse-men who had evidently entered town from the east, because they came around a southward corner where an intersecting back road merged with the main thoroughfare. The men were not close enough for Logan to determine whether any of them was familiar to him or not, but he thought, in the main, these out-of-towners would be strangers.

The southward group met the eastward band, paused to speak a little back and forth, holding their fidgeting mounts under a tight rein before resuming their onward way up toward George's saloon. The northward men halted up at the first westerly intersection.

"Waiting," purred Logan. "Sedge's went and planned this like an army general. They're to await his arrival before doing anything."

Pert, catching movement up the plank walk, turned fully. "Barton's up there," he quietly stated. "Standin' out front of the saloon big as life, a perfect target."

Logan wasn't interested. He stepped down into roadway slush and growled for Pert to come along. The pair of them headed on across, stepped up onto the opposite walkway in front of Will's barn, and went plunging straight on through. Will was standing just inside his office door, straining to see. As the lawmen trotted past, he squawked a quick question to which neither of them replied.

Out back, Tom Logan nearly collided with a scurrying figure of a gangling man clothed in rusty black. He snarled a curse and jumped aside. "What'n hell you trying to do, you old devil, get yourself killed? Get inside the barn. That's a good place for your kind. Get behind the manure pile!"

The gangling man winced from this lashing and turned his head so that Pert got a good look at his gray face. Pert grunted. "No place for preachers out here, Ezra. You better do like the sheriff says."

Ezra Benedict bobbed his head up and down and scuttled into Will Clampitt's barn.

Pert had a pretty good idea of what Logan was up to. To avoid an open war in his town, Tom was counting upon Sedge Horton's appearance to head it off. All those converging Horton ranch riders knew what they were here for, but since they'd ridden quietly in, it was obvious that they'd been ordered to do nothing until Sedge showed up. Logan meant to reach Horton before Horton reached town.

Pert and Tom went out through the back roadway until, where a head of dirty snow briefly barred their way and they paused to navigate a way around it, they caught sight of a party of bunched-up cowmen approaching from out of the western sunlight.

Logan pointed at the leader of those men. Horton was wearing a dark scarlet blanket coat that hung below his hips. On the right side the coat had been turned back and tucked under Sedge's gun belt. This, plus the way Horton had his hat brim tipped down low to shield his eyes from sun glare, left no doubt at all in Logan's mind about Sedge's intention.

Pert said: "I wish to hell he an' Barton would settle it out in the roadway man to man."

Logan made a harsh little laugh. "You're asking for miracles, boy. Why d'you think he's brought at least thirty men with him? Come along."

They cut around the snow heap, swung between two houses, and fetched up near a little smelly cow shed where a fawn-colored Jersey milk critter chewing her cud and standing utterly still in the good sunlight stolidly eyed them. Horton's party was about a half mile distant. Logan slowed his onward gait from this point. It wasn't far to the limits of town now. He and Pert walked along, sometimes hidden, sometimes out in the open where those riders could easily discern them. They were close to the farthest residence when Sedge Horton twisted in the saddle, said something to a pair of his riders, and squared up, facing onward again.

Logan hadn't missed that. He said from the corner of his mouth: "I wish you weren't in this, Pert, but it's too late now for that. Keep your eye on those two Sedge just spoke to. I'm guessing he told 'em to throw down on us, to neutralize us while the rest of them ride on in."

Pert reached down and lifted the little leather tie-down most lawmen and range riders used to keep their .45s from falling from their holsters. It was simply a small piece of oiled leather with a slit in one end of it that hooked over the hammer, holding the gun firmly in place. The other end of this small strap was stitched to the holster. Logan also loosened his tie-down. He now had a fair view of Sedge Horton and the men moving up behind him. They did not offer to veer away or attempt to avoid meeting the lawmen, who stopped well beyond the last building with the town at their backs and also with piles of shoveled snow around them, making of each peace officer a perfect target. Horton, with his reins in the left hand, dropped his right hand out of sight down his off side. Logan saw that and his jaw muscles rippled. He had no fear of Sedge Horton. He just had never really believed that he and Horton, despite their numerous differences in the past, would ever face one another like this.

Pert spoke, his voice sounding slightly higher and thinner than was customary: "Nine men behind him, Sheriff. Where's George?"

"Back there," mumbled Logan. Then he said: "I *hope* he's back there."

"I don't see anything."

Logan's retort was sharp. "Damn you, keep facing forward!"

Pert's face reddened but he straightened up, facing toward the oncoming riders. His lips grew thin and his eyes, already narrowed against the fiercely reflected sunlight off snow, turned coldly calculating.

That pair of horsemen Sedge had spoken to veered off to get between Horton and the lawmen. Logan was prepared for that. He turned, moved fifty feet to the right, and maintained his position facing the cowman. The pair of riders could not now shield Horton without cutting directly in front of him and stopping the entire party, so they looked inquiringly around.

Horton, staring hard ahead where Logan stood, wide-legged and resolute, made a deprecating gesture with one ungloved hand. The pair of cowboys turned back and returned to their places among the other riders.

Horton rode up to within ten feet of Logan before lifting his rein hand to halt his horse. Those two older men unwaveringly stared at one another.

XVII

Horton seemed to know what to say, but he kept silent, leaving the initiative to Tom Logan. Around the cowman his stony-faced riders edged up, flicking hard glances from the one lawman to the other one.

Tom said: "What do you want here, Sedge?" And Horton answered in the same cold tone of voice. "You know damned well what I want."

Logan nodded. "I do. But I had to ask. Now I've also got to tell you . . . not in my town."

"Get out of the way, Logan."

Tom did not move. "You're a damned fool if you think you can pull this off, Horton. And I've got a piece of news for you. You're under arrest for tampering with a jury. Toughy Hammond told Frank Barton in my hearing that you gave him a thousand dollars in cash and returned a note of his you had for bulldozing that jury into hanging Old Man Barton. That's a felony, Sedge."

Horton sat silently a moment, then put both hands atop his saddle horn and leaned down. Only his left hand was gloved, his right hand—the gun hand—was not. "How do you aim to prove that?" he asked, paused, then added: "Toughy is dead, Tom."

This jarred Logan, his rock-hard gaze wavered. "He was alive a short time ago. He had a showdown with Barton in George's saloon."

"That was a short time ago," said Horton coldly. "Now he's dead."

"How?" demanded Logan.

Sedge rocked back in his saddle, looking ironically downward. "He was cleaning his gun when we met on the trail. It accidentally went off and killed him. Unfortunate, but that's it. He rode out to tell me what Barton forced him to say."

"Some accident," muttered Logan. "I reckon there were no witnesses?"

"You reckon right. Not a single witness. That's too bad, isn't it?"

"Sedge, for God's sake get hold of yourself. You're putting everything on the line you've worked a lifetime to build up. Think, Sedge, think!"

Horton's bleak expression did not change. "I've thought, Logan. I've thought every day and every night since that dirty old devil killed my boy. What I'm puttin' on the line isn't worth a damn now. Do you understand that? My son was all I had in this lousy world. Why d'you think I built all this up? For him, Tom. And that rotten old devil shot him in the back." Horton's voice shook. "That dirty old devil killed my son!" Horton's nostrils flared. He closed his mouth and his jaws rippled. He spoke again, finally, very softly: "Now you better get out of the way, because I'm here to watch Frank Barton die. I've got thirty men to help me see to it that Barton dies, so you'd better get out of the way."

Horton lifted his rein hand to ride on. Logan did not make any move to get out of his way. Pert, eyeing the cowboys with Horton, was as pale as a ghost but unrelenting. Those range riders divided their attention between Logan and his deputy. One outcry, one fierce curse, and gun thunder was going to redden the day right here and perhaps empty some saddles. The odds were all with Horton, but none of those mounted men had any doubts at all about this implacable old lawman and his deputy getting in their licks, too, before they went down.

"Sedge," Logan said coldly, "this is your last chance. Get down off that horse and give me your guns."

It must have sounded as ridiculous to Horton for Logan to say that, standing practically alone as he was, as it sounded to Pert. Horton hesitated just a second longer, then started to move. Logan turned his head and called out: "Now!"

Over along the little roadways, among the houses and sheds and hen roosts over there, guns bristled. Sunlight struck along that array of armament, mostly Winchester saddle guns but interspersed also with old-fashioned long-barreled fowling pieces. There were also a few big-bored buffalo rifles, some Springfield Army carbines, and not a few shotguns.

Logan looked back, swallowed with prodigious relief, and looked forward. "Still want to make a battle of it?" he asked Horton, and the cattleman surprised him by saying that he did, and that furthermore, if those men over there so much as fired one shot, he'd personally give the signal to his men over in town literally to destroy the place.

Logan drifted his glance around. Horton's men were pale, but they showed no sign at all of being fearful despite the guns pointed their way. Logan shook his head. To despise a man you had also to scorn him. He'd thought he despised Sedge Horton but now he wasn't so sure. As wrong as Horton had been all through this affair, as contemptible, there he now sat looking like a conquering Hun, staring at those bristling rifles as though they were not loaded or zeroed in on his chest and face.

"Get down, the lot of you," Logan ordered. "Don't a man touch his gun . . . those fellers over there can mistake a low hand for a draw in this bright light."

"Who is that?" asked Horton, glaring.

"George Henry from the Big Eagle. When I heard your men

were converging on the place, I came out here to try an' talk you out of what you got in mind, while George rounded up enough guns to do it his way if my way failed."

"Where is Barton?" Horton demanded, still not dismounting.

Logan shrugged. He had an idea where Frank Barton was but couldn't be certain. "In town. Now get down out of that saddle."

"And if I don't, Tom?"

Logan started around the head of Horton's animal. Sedge's right hand started moving. On Horton's offside Pert said thinly—"Don't try it, Horton."—and Sedge swung his head at the unmistakable menace in Pert's voice. That was when Logan reached for him, caught hold of Horton's coat to drag him out of his saddle.

Behind Logan and shielded from Pert's sight by Sedge a swarthy range rider drew his gun, pointed it, and cocked it. Logan did not let go but he stopped moving everything but his head. He and the swarthy man traded glares.

"Leave him go," said the cowboy through thin lips. "Step back, lawman, or I'll bust your skull like a melon an' we'll get this fight past the talkin' stage."

A long way off someone in among the yonder buildings who could see what was happening gave a fluting high call of warning, followed by words of shouted explanation: "They've throwed down on the sheriff!"

Another man called out, this time in a deep-booming voice that carried easily even to the farthest man in Horton's party. "Logan. Let them ride in! Sheriff. This is Barton. I say let them ride on in. There isn't going to be any shootin' war, so just let them past."

Logan still did not relinquish his grip on Horton's coat, but neither did he finish his attempt to drag the larger man out of his saddle. The swarthy rider tipped his cocked gun at the sheriff. "You heard," he growled. "Leave go of Mister Horton. There ain't goin' to be no shootin' war." The swarthy man curled his lip sardonically at his own statement. He didn't believe it himself and was wolfishly smiling about it.

Other guns appeared. Pert was also covered. Sedge Horton reached down, caught his coat, and gave it a powerful wrench. The cloth was pulled clear of Logan's grip. Horton said: "Now go tell those fools with their guns if they start anything, Tom, that I've got another thirty men behind them in town, and the first one that starts anything is goin' to get it in the back."

Logan twisted to look over where George's armed cohorts were still holding their position. He wasn't thinking of Horton's threat; he was thinking of Barton's words. One thing Tom had learned lately, and that was simply that Frank Barton made no statement he hadn't thought out well in advance. If Barton said there'd be no shooting war, he had some good reason for making such a statement. The alternative to relying upon Barton's word was to give the order here and now for George's towns-men to open up, and that, he knew very well, would be the opener in the game that Sedge Horton was trying to deal all the cards in.

He decided, at last, to go along, at least for the time being, with whatever Frank Barton was trying to do. He stepped back around where Pert was standing, saw how gray his deputy's face was, and twisted to glance at Horton. "All right, Sedge, you ride on in. Just one word of warning."

"Save it," growled Horton, starting to move.

"No, I'm not going to save it," snarled Logan. "Just remember, the roadway is wide, there are armed townsmen on both sides of it. One drawn gun among your riders and I'll start the war for you."

Horton didn't even look back as he went past. Some of his men dropped stony glances at Logan and Pert, but none of them said anything. Logan turned, jerked his head at Pert, and started back the way he'd come. He was red-faced and prickly with anger. He was also a little confused and doubtful.

There was scarcely a sound as Horton's party walked their horses toward the houses. Armed men exposed themselves here and there to watch. Mostly they leaned upon their rifles and were entirely silent. A little feisty mongrel dog darted out and excitedly barked as the horsemen rode past. No one paid him the slightest attention. George Henry stepped forth to meet Logan as the lawmen came walking along.

George said flintily: "What'n hell's Barton up to?"

Logan didn't answer that; he paused and looked around among the nearest men. "Where is he, George? Sounded like he was over here with you."

"Around front somewhere, at least it sounded like he shouted from around there. Come on."

The three of them turned to push on. Several townsmen came at them with questions. Logan said the same thing to all of them: "Get under cover, get inside the stores and houses, an' keep close watch. If I fire, open up on them. Keep them out in the roadway. Whatever happens, keep them out of the buildings. Pass that along."

George had his scatter-gun in one hand and a belted six-shooter around his middle. He led the way back among the sheds and houses until they came to the alleyway behind Clampitt's barn. There, instead of following the logical route to the front roadway by passing up through Will's barn, he turned abruptly and passed southward to a little dog-trot between two buildings and squeezed his way on through until, where the plank walk lay, he paused to look left and right before stepping out into plain view. Logan came next and Deputy Whipple was the last man to step forth.

Up in front of George's saloon Horton's riders were mostly

sitting their saddles, looking and waiting. A few of them, less bold and contemptuous or perhaps just more prudent and experienced, were on foot with their saddle horses swung across to protect their upper bodies, should the firing start. Otherwise, though, both the roadway and plank walk were empty. Winchester Junction had ducked for cover.

Logan looked for Barton and failed to find him. As he looked, though, he saw the townsmen filtering back into town. Gun muzzles began to appear here and there from windows and doorways. Generally these were on the west side of the main thoroughfare. On the east side there were a few weapons but not many. At Henry Poole's store, for example, two old Springfield Army rifles showed, but in the stores on either side of Poole's emporium, the buildings were closed, barred, and evidently hastily abandoned.

Sedge Horton turned the far corner with his stony-faced riders, saw his waiting men down by the saloon, and rode on toward them. There wasn't a sound except the steady *clop, clop, clop*, of horses moving through roadway mud. George and Pert turned as though to hike northward, but Logan growled at them. "Stay put. Let's see what Sedge does. It's his play now."

Horton passed down to where the balance of his men were, and halted. A burly man wearing a small-brimmed hat got down and walked over beside Horton to lift his head and say something. Horton listened, then turned to look around. He couldn't help but see the guns jutting from the buildings, but he gave no sign that this threat bothered him in the slightest. He seemed to Logan to be coming to some kind of a decision. That massive man beside Horton's left side waited as though he expected an answer from Sedge. It came finally, as Horton leaned from the saddle. Logan, standing between his deputy and his friend, felt that he'd quite lost all the initiative now and was nothing more than simply another spectator. This rankled.

And yet, wherever Frank Barton was right now, Tom decided, against his better judgment, to let him make his play. After all, this was not Logan's fight. It wasn't even the town's fight, and, if Horton and Barton kept it like that, Logan was perfectly willing to go along. But what he'd said about no one turning his town into a battlefield he had adamantly meant. Obviously, since Barton was only one man, he couldn't make a battleground out of Winchester Junction, so in that direction Logan had only to keep a sharp watch on Sedge Horton and Sedge's gun-handy range crew.

Horton straightened up from his conference with the scarred and burly man beside his horse. He looked out and around, then called out in a ringing voice: "Barton! Come on out! You wanted to fight this out with your hands, well, come on out and try it now!"

"Ahhh," groaned George Henry, staring hard at the massive man beside Sedge's left boot. "Now I recognize him. That there feller with the battered face an' the small-brimmed hat, that's Honey Jim Fitzhugh. I saw him fight once down in Denver against Big Jim Corbett. He's said to be the best fighter in the land, after Gentleman Jim himself. Now I see what Horton's up to."

Logan, who knew of Honey Jim Fitzhugh's awesome reputation by word of mouth, looked with curiosity up the roadway. Horton had indeed reacted to his own whipping and the whipping of Toughy Hammond in his typical manner. He was doing now precisely what he'd done to get Old Man Barton hanged; he was maneuvering another man toward his doom by using wealth and power to hire other men for the killing. Tom started walking northward to look over those other men up there with Horton. He knew that Sedge wouldn't have ended his planning with just Honey Jim. There would also be other hirelings—other specialists—among Horton's crew. When he was nearing the doorway of Will's barn, he saw what he was seeking. A wispy, dark-attired man sitting slightly apart from Horton's other riders. The Carlsbad Kid, one of the most notorious gunmen in the West. If Honey Jim couldn't finish off Barton, that gunfighter would.

XVIII

From off on Horton's left, over at the storm doors leading into George Henry's saloon, a big man stepped out and said quietly: "You don't have to yell, Horton. Here I am."

Logan heard Pert mutter something beside him. He saw Will Clampitt walk out of his barn runway with a rifle in his hands. Only George Henry said anything distinguishable, and it wasn't repeatable.

Horton's men swung as Barton shrugged out of his sheepskin coat, draped it across a railing, and started forward saying coolly—"Hello, Jim."—to Horton's hired fighter.

Fitzhugh's scarred brows rolled down as he sought recognition, then, when Barton was weaving through Horton's watching horsemen, Honey Jim's face cleared and broke into a big wolfish smile. "Be damned," he thickly roared. "So it's Barton now, is it? I had no idea it'd be you, Frank. I'll be bloody well damned, I will."

Barton stopped ten feet off and kept smiling straight at the professional fighter. "It's been a long time, Jim. How much is this scum payin' you?"

Fitzhugh's smile wavered. He made a little apologetic gesture. "It's been a bad year," he said. "Nothin' personal, mind. He's give me five hunnert to rub your face in the mud, Frank. Y'know how it is."

Barton chuckled and stepped on out past Sedge Horton, past his riders into the ankle-deep mud of the roadway. As he turned back, he looked up. "What you don't have the guts for yourself,

Horton, this is the next best way, isn't it?"

Horton glared a moment, then turned on Honey Jim Fitzhugh. "Beat him to death," he said quietly, "and there'll be another thousand for you."

Fitzhugh removed his little hat, his coat, and his vest. He studied Frank Barton from beneath puffy brows as he rolled up his sleeves. He muttered something under his breath and started ponderously forward through the cloying mud. Logan, scarcely breathing, got the impression that mud was hampering the big man's movements.

Will Clampitt moaned. "He's big as a bear, Sheriff. He's as big as Barton an' look at his face. He's been fightin' all his life. This'll be murder."

Tom grunted: "Wait an' see."

Frank stood there, waiting. He had his fists balled but had not raised his arms. He was still softly smiling at Honey Jim as the other large man stalked forward. Fitzhugh pawed with his left to make Frank move. All Frank did was roll his head left and right to avoid contact. Fitzhugh lowered his head, raised his shoulder to protect his face, and made a slippery little rush. Barton swayed clear of a sizzling right. Fitzhugh swore and shook one leg to get the clinging mud off his foot. Barton swung, caught Fitzhugh across his guard, and jarred him with a heart strike. Honey Jim's teeth showed in a small grimace, half of pain, half of acknowledgment. He began his bear-like advance again.

"Lord," whispered Pert to George Henry. "Nothin' short of a bullet can stop him."

George, chewing savagely on his nether lip, growled: "Shut up!"

Sedge Horton and his range riders were straining forward in their saddles. Along both sides of the roadway gun muzzles drooped where the sentinel townsmen forgot their vigils to concentrate on this battle of titans. The only sound was an occasional squeak of leather, and the sloshing of big feet shuffling through that ankle-deep roadway mud.

Barton did not give ground in the face of Honey Jim's advance. His lips were faintly tilted at their outer corners in that same half-friendly, half-mocking smile. But the moment Fitzhugh slogged up into range, Barton launched himself ahead. He blocked a hard right and slammed Fitzhugh in the middle; he swung away sideways to let a violent left swoosh past, swung back, and cracked a right against Fitzhugh's jaw. He ducked down and rolled both shoulders in behind two blasting blows to Honey Jim's middle. Then he sprang away backward and watched Fitzhugh shake his head, lose his grin, and begin that slippery advance again. They all heard Barton say: "Jim, you're out of your element."

Honey Jim growled a deep answer: "It's this damned mud."

Logan looked over where the Carlsbad Kid was sitting his horse apart from Horton's other riders. The notorious gunman was scornfully regarding the two large men, his thin lips lifted in obvious contempt.

Fitzhugh got close, halted, tried a feint, and, when Barton did not open up, Honey Jim crouched, swung his body to the left, and, when Barton turned to be clear, Honey Jim whirled with a blasting right that sank deeply into Frank Barton's middle. Frank gave ground and gasped. Instantly Fitzhugh was after him. They slipped and slithered, one back-pedaling, one rushing. Logan groaned and clenched his fists. Sedge Horton leaned stiffly forward awaiting the certain kill. But Barton was better at this slippery footing and kept away until his mind cleared. Finally Honey Jim stopped, his barrel chest heaving from exertion, glared at Frank, wagged his head, and started ahead again. He was angry at himself, evidently, and at the mud, for permitting Barton to get away.

Frank circled, first to the left, then to the right. The watching men did not all understand this, but Barton was simply keeping his adversary off balance. Fitzhugh constantly had to shift stance, had to slip repeatedly in the oily underfooting. When he slipped backward eventually, Frank went after him. This time Frank caught Honey Jim over the eye, down along the cheek, and, when Jim rolled his head, he made a miscalculation that brought his rolling head flush into contact with a blasting right fist. Honey Jim fell to his knees and hung there, trying to clear his head by shaking it.

Barton stepped back, dropped his hands, and gazed up at Horton. "You're next," he said, then watched Fitzhugh get back upright. But after that it was all Frank Barton's battle. Fitzhugh instinctively protected himself, but he was now on the defensive. Frank shook him badly with a jarring left. He made Jim stagger drunkenly with a right. He broke past Fitzhugh's guard with a series of punches, and he finally downed the other big man with a rolling blow that cracked like a pistol shot off Honey Jim's exposed jaw. Fitzhugh went down and floundered in the cold mud trying vainly to get back up.

Barton stepped over, leaned, and placed a hand atop Jim's head, gave a push, and Fitzhugh fell flat and weakly threshed. "Stay down," Barton said. "Stay down, Jim. You gave it your best. Don't get up again."

It is doubtful whether or not Honey Jim heard those words or understood them. Even from where Logan was standing, he could see the glazed, unfocusing way Fitzhugh's eyes were aimlessly rolling.

Barton straightened up, facing Sedge Horton and his stony-faced riders. "Get down off that horse," he said quietly to Horton. "I said you were next an' I meant it. Get down!"

Horton, watching in fascination as Honey Jim floundered out there in the mud, slowly brought his gaze up to Barton. He started to turn, to speak. Tom Logan, anticipating what Horton meant to say, went for his gun. Back a good twenty feet and apart from the others, that wiry gunfighter in his rusty black attire was also moving. Without any warning gunfire exploded beside Logan, making him jump and rip out a startled curse.

George Henry's six-gun smoked. On Logan's far side Will Clampitt's long-barreled rifle bucked and roared. Over across the way, from the emporium, another rifle exploded. Logan didn't get off a shot. The Carlsbad Kid went off his horse as though an invisible hand had caught him from behind. His six-gun roared and a solitary bullet went skyward.

Logan roared out: "Hold it! Hold it!" As Sedge Horton's range men began to drop from their saddles and go for their guns, looking wildly in all directions. "Hold it, damn you! Hold it!"

Logan's oaths and orders filled the roiled air. Men obeyed in spite of themselves. Even those over in front of the Big Eagle with their guns drawn and cocked did not now fire. Gun muzzles bore directly on them from both sides of the roadway. One shot would have resulted in a massacre; the cowboys seemed to grasp this at once. They would fight, obviously, but ringed round as they now were with riflemen who hadn't wasted the time during Barton's fight with Honey Jim Fitzhugh, and emboldened by the example of other townsmen, both sides of the roadway now showed an overwhelming superiority of firepower, as additional townsmen joined this impending battle.

"Sedge," Logan snarled. "Get down off that horse!" Horton did not move. He had his right hand curled around his holstered .45. He tilted back his head and glared. He was not yet whipped, but he was stopped. "I said get down off that horse!"

Horton's shoulders jerked a little, his face paled. Logan raised his six-gun, stepped to the edge of the plank walk, and aimed. "For the last time, Sedge. Get down!"

Frank Barton stepped away from Fitzhugh, walked over, and reached. That was when Horton went for his weapon, and that was much too late. Barton's huge arms gave a mighty wrench. Horton was nearly lifted from his saddle. His right hand was frantically swinging to club downward. Logan dared not fire; neither did any of the others on both sides. Those two big men were locked together.

Barton swung his head and took the brunt of that gun barrel on the shoulder. They all saw his mouth open in a grimace of agony. He swung Horton around and released him. He swung his right fist, caught Horton flush in the face, and blood sprayed. Horton dropped his gun and raised both hands. Barton hit him again, forced aside Horton's hands, held him with his left and beat him with his right. Horton sagged, his face smashed. Barton kept on beating him until Horton's senseless weight was too much, then Barton let him go. Horton fell in the mud, making gagging sounds, his breathing loud and bubbly.

Logan started on across. From among the stores and houses other men also came out and started across toward Horton's men, leaderless now and no longer so full of fight. Tom put up his gun and blackly scowled at the cowboys. "Throw your weapons behind you on the sidewalk," he growled. "Carbines, too. One funny move and we'll bury the lot of you. Move!"

The riders began to obey, slowly at first, then with more rapidity as townsmen poked at them with rifles and carbines, and even shotguns.

Logan stepped over where the gunfighter lay. He bent, looked closely, straightened up, and looked back down the plank walk where Preacher Benedict and Henry Poole were standing, Benedict looking gray and denunciatory, Henry looking crestfallen as he fumblingly re-loaded his old Springfield rifle. "Hey, Henry," called Logan bleakly. "Good shooting. You an' Will an' George did yourself proud. You were watching this one when most of us weren't. Good shooting, Henry. I got to change my opinion of you."

"He," pronounced Preacher Benedict, "broke divine law. There will be fire and brimstone forever after. The Lord has spoken!"

Logan regarded Benedict coldly a moment, then he said: "Ezra, pack up, saddle up, and be out of this town by sundown. If you aren't, I'm going to . . . to wale the tar out of you. As for the Lord speakin' . . . that was you, not the Lord. It was the Lord that saved these men and this town from ruin. Not your Lord, but *our* Lord. Now get out of my sight!"

Several townsmen were dragging Sedge Horton over to the plank walk. Logan saw this and said: "Pert! Take him over to the jail house and lock him up. I'll file enough charges against him to keep him out of circulation for the next twenty years!"

Pert moved over where the men were dragging Horton, to take charge. He had been helping Fitzhugh to his feet, along with Frank Barton, who was still steadying the vanquished fighter. Fitzhugh was using a sodden handkerchief to push mud off his face. He was mumbling to Barton all the while and Barton was smiling. Not that little cruel smile Logan had come to know so well, but a genuine smile. It was a pleasant, boyish look and lifted Logan's spirits a little, so when he faced around where George and Will and others were still guarding the Horton ranch men, he didn't even sound mean as he said: "Herd 'em down to the jail house, boys. We'll hold court tomorrow, maybe. Check 'em over for hide-out weapons, and tell Pert I said to squeeze 'em all into the cells somehow. I'll be along later."

Barton guided Fitzhugh over to the plank walk where awed townsmen stepped back to give those two large men plenty of room. George, starting off with the cowboys, looked back, saw Logan heading over for the same plank walk, and turned back, holstering his six-gun as he did so, and hanging his backbar riot gun in the crook of one arm. George arrived upon the yonder sidewalk the same time Logan did, and, before the lawman could speak, George said to Barton: "Fetch your friend inside where it's warm an' the drinks'll be on the house."

Logan turned as Barton and Fitzhugh also turned. The three of them stamped off mud on their way into George's bar. Will Clampitt trailed along. Farther back, Henry Poole, leaning upon his re-loaded Springfield rifle, looked wistful. Will glanced back, saw how Henry was standing, lifted one arm, and waved for Poole to come along. Henry straightened up, turned, handed his rifle to Preacher Benedict, and hastened forward.

The Big Eagle was crowded, so crowded in fact that Barton took Fitzhugh to his far corner table and called for a basin and some towels. Tom Logan also went along to that table and sat down, uninvited but nevertheless resolute about it. When the materials were brought for Honey Jim to clean up, Logan leaned across and touched Frank Barton's arm. He was not smiling. "All right," he said. "You've settled with Hammond, with Forester, with Horton, with this whole damned town. Now . . . how about George and me?"

Barton smiled at Logan. "Henry did himself proud. You and George . . . you boys risked your hides to help me break Horton. A man couldn't ask any more than that, could he?"

"It was simply my duty," muttered Logan, leaning back.

"All right," agreed Barton. "It was your duty. That other thing was your duty, too. All I wanted to prove to myself was that you'd do your duty one way the same as you'd done it the other way. But George . . . that wasn't *his* duty, Tom. He had no call to draw a gun against that hired killer of Horton's, did he?"

"Well, but George doesn't believe in Horton's kind of ridin' roughshod any more than I do, any more'n Will Clampitt or the rest of Winchester Junction does. That's all."

"That's all I wanted to prove, Tom. To you, and to myself. I didn't have in mind fightin' your whole town. Like you once said, the old man wouldn't have approved of that."

Logan continued to sit there until the warmth began reaching through his coat and turning him loose and relaxed. Then he got up without another word and walked out of the noisy saloon where men were loudly talking, clinking glasses, and stamping their cold feet upon George Henry's sawdust floor. He walked outside where the sun was turning a little red as afternoon advanced down across the land. He gazed up a while at Old Man Barton's beloved Teton Mountains, raised a hand in a little salute, and muttered: "All right, old-timer, you've stayed around long enough to set things to rights. Good bye, and good luck." Then he went trudging on down in the direction of his jail house.

ABOUT THE AUTHOR

Lauran Paine who, under his own name and various pseudonyms has written over a thousand books, was born in Duluth, Minnesota. His family moved to California when he was at a young age and his apprenticeship as a Western writer came about through the years he spent in the livestock trade, rodeos, and even motion pictures where he served as an extra because of his expert horsemanship in several films starring movie cowboy Johnny Mack Brown. In the late 1930s, Paine trapped wild horses in northern Arizona and even, for a time, worked as a professional farrier. Paine came to know the Old West through the eyes of many who had been born in the previous century, and he learned that Western life had been very different from the way it was portrayed on the screen. "I knew men who had killed other men," he later recalled. "But they were the exceptions. Prior to and during the Depression, people were just too busy eking out an existence to indulge in Saturday-night brawls." He served in the U.S. Navy in the Second World War and began writing for Western pulp magazines following his discharge. It is interesting to note that all of his earliest novels (written under his own name and the pseudonym Mark Carrel) were published in the British market and he soon had as strong a following in that country as in the United States. Paine's Western fiction is characterized by strong plots, authenticity, an apparently effortless ability to construct situation and character, and a preference for building his stories upon a solid foundation of historical fact. *Adobe Empire* (1956), one of his best novels, is a fictionalized account of the last twenty years in the life of trader William Bent and, in an off-trail way, has a melancholy, bittersweet texture that is not easily forgotten. In later novels like *Cache Cañon* (Five Star Westerns, 1998) and *Halfmoon Ranch* (Five Star Westerns, 2007), he showed that the special magic and power of his stories and characters had only matured along with his basic themes of changing times, changing attitudes, learning from experience, respecting Nature, and the yearning for a simpler, more moderate way of life. His next Five Star Western will be *Man Behind the Gun*.